SILENT THUNDER

BY

Ephraim Weisstein

Registration Number: TXu 2-401-047

For Ellen on our 50th

Prelude

In 2054, worldwide temperatures had risen by two point-five degrees breaking through the one point-five barrier that scientists had warned if breached would lead to catastrophic results. And that was indeed the case.

Heatwaves and droughts had cut agricultural productivity in some regions, while rain and unexpected frosts did the same in others. Flooding and other weather extremes continually assaulted vital infrastructure and severely slowed supply lines. All of this meant that food costs were soaring.

Mass migration spiraled out of control; from poor to wealthy countries and from regions ravaged by the climate to those better protected. In America, one state even closed its border to those without special clearance.

Meanwhile, health-care systems were teetering in the face of more frequent epidemics and an uptick in chronic conditions like asthma related to climate and air quality. The breaking point was the onset of a relatively new condition that made people unable to speak. Researchers spent untold time and dollars trying to determine why as the world's angst grew exponentially.

The result of these slowly compounding catastrophes was a declining economy and all of the tensions resulting from that. Working and middle-class people blamed each other, the growth of the non-speaking population, and people on the other side of the political aisle for the state of affairs. In the U.S. it seemed like hostility could erupt at any moment and dwarf the uprisings of 2020. Anyone could be the catalyst, including a twenty-year-old woman in New York City.

Part I

Gathering Clouds

1

How Did We Get Here?

Pia turned 21 in her new home, Camp Tranquility. It was not by her choosing.

Everything changed on December eighteen 2056 when the President issued his executive dictate, ordering all non-speakers above the age of 17 to report for processing. Before that and her dad's suicide 11 months earlier, Pia would have described her family as her dad Henry (or Dr. Johnston to his patients), her mom Delores, aka "The Rock," and her little brother, Taylor as complicated but loving.

Before things fell apart, Pia lived with this conflicted but loving bunch in a medium-sized brownstone four blocks from Canal Street on the Lower East Side of New York. The smell of the East River often traveled to her bedroom where she could see the Chrysler Building if she rotated her head ninety degrees while extending it as far out her window as biology would allow. She especially loved to do that when it was snowing, especially if Chrysler's lights were nearly invisible because then the storm was rocking. She could feel her jet-black hair rise and fall with the wind.

By most standards, Pia had been living large, sucking up the city's grittiness by day and cocooning with her family at night. Life hadn't been perfect, but it was warm and predictable. Any worries that she carried about her family felt small compared to the support she felt from them and the wonder of growing up and discovering life in the whirlwind of New York.

The seeds of her current predicaments, her dad's death, her exile to Camp Tranquility, and her inability to see or even communicate with her mom and Taylor took root when Pia was a toddler. Her parents had always been open with her and later Taylor what had transpired during those difficult years. They did so with the hope that a fact-based explanation would help their kids withstand the slow percolating fear that they must have felt in school, with their friends, everywhere.

Pia incorporated their explanations with what she inferred. The Johnstons were a typical, solid, middle-class family. Her dad's psychology practice took care of that. Having Pia, their first child, must have been exhilarating. But those early parenting years were undoubtedly clouded by the slowly unfolding worldwide phenomena: children's failure to learn language, or FLL as it started being labeled.

At first, there were scattered reports of children between two and three who should be speaking in sentences yet remained mute. The local newspapers and online gossip feeds picked up what sounded like a juicy human-interest story. *Oh, those poor parents,* people empathized, all the while counting their blessings that whatever the source of this phenomenon their kids weren't affected.

But as the numbers grew exponentially the worldwide communications net caught up with reality on the ground and the story finally exploded on the major networks and papers. The facts were all the same. These toddlers were not uttering a sound, but why? No one knew, and everyone speculated. These children appeared physically intact in every way. Without identifying a cause, doctors and scientists couldn't begin to find a cure. They were at a loss, so the career opportunists and politicians rushed to fill the void. Far-right wingnuts offered their reasoned explanations. It was a result of the breakdown of traditional family values and the loss of godliness. Lefties blamed the poisoning of the environment.

Sociologists speculated that it was somehow tied to society's obsession with technology at the expense of authentic human communication.

At first, many people ignored the chatter as the usual media hype. Pia's parents tried to also, but it must have become increasingly difficult as they anxiously watched her turn three without having yet uttered a sound. By the time she was four, they were in a state of shock.

Pia's parents took her to see every imaginable specialist in those early years. With her dad's professional standing and her mom's doggedness, the Johnstons had the will and means to leave no stone unturned. But eventually, having pursued every alternative explanation they had to face the facts. Their wonderful daughter had drawn the dreaded evolutionary card. They were left with but one option, to prepare for life with a daughter who would never speak and might grow up the target of abuse. The upside was that they weren't going through it alone, and eventually, Pia's lack of speech started seeming less like a disability and more like just another facet of her personality.

The government sponsored a Full Life Integration Program in an attempt to ensure that these children would grow to become productive citizens. Non-speakers were taught the ability to sign as their primary language.

But despite Full Life Integration and other efforts by the United States and other governments, first cracks and then craters began to appear between those who thought non-speakers were just like anyone else and therefore deserved the same rights and opportunities, and those who thought they should be isolated or, in extreme cases, eradicated. It didn't help that by the end of 2053, the first hints of a worldwide economic downturn were flashing yellow signs. Long-term investments in innovation and development began to dry up as speculators looked for safe havens to park their money such as government bonds and money markets. Capital likes as much certainty as possible and the future was looking like it held anything but. The receding economy was but one indicator that the world was on edge. Americans and the citizens of the world hoped for the best while preparing for the worst.

With the shift in government policy away from treating non- speakers as a social service issue, the authorities began classifying and labeling muteness. Agencies referred to people like Pia as part of Gen 1.0. By 2054, they were joined by Gen 2.0 and less than three years later 3.0. Gen 2.0s signed much less, and nearly all 3.0s adopted advanced forms of something that came to be called Language of the Streets, or LOTS for short.

The first "hospitality" camps were opened with great fanfare in 2053, one month after the presidential order. President Miller described the camps with euphemistic language that made it sound like he was opening a cultural exchange program. There were hundreds of such camps scattered across America, although the exact number remained classified as the government slowly tightened its control over communication.

2

Opposites Attract

Pia was introduced to life at Camp Tranquility on a freezing January 2055 morning. The tall, pencil-thin guard led her to bunk 18, which was one of 30, all of which were painted military green. He pointed to the door and left.

Pia prided herself on being able to get along with most people. With no explanation as to what to do next, she ambled over to two of her new bunkmates and started to sign. "Hello, my name is Pia!"

She waited for a response, but it became clear that none was forthcoming. Pia sat down on her cot and wondered what to do next. Was anyone else new, or was she the only one who had no idea what she should do? Pia looked around at the faces of her 14 new bunkmates before she wandered over to another person and began to sign. She felt a hand around her neck and was violently whirled around. Standing an inch from her face was one of the two women to whom she had just tried to introduce herself.

"Listen you little bitch," her antagonist slowly and mockingly signed, "I don't know which spoiled life you came from, but this is not it. If you want to sign go find some other sellouts, but here, we don't use the master's language except toward kiss-asses like you. Learn how to communicate without playing Hellen Keller, or stay the hell away from us."

Without thinking Pia started to sign again to seek clarification when she was knocked to the floor by her short but muscular antagonist. At five feet ten and rail-like115 pounds, Pia didn't have time to taste the blood in her mouth before the now red- faced woman was on top punching her in the face over and over again. Pia tried to cover up by pulling her hands over her face.

But suddenly her attacker was hurtling through the air. The woman, who, moments ago, Pia had tried to sign with before her nemesis had whirled her around, was kicking the shit out of her attacker. Pia was in a state of shock watching the scene unfold while oozing blood from her mouth and nose. What was happening? Pia sought refuge on her cot and pulled the blanket over her face to stanch the flow of blood and to escape the mayhem. The noise from her attacker being beaten continued for another minute. Then Pia heard shuffling feet and opened her eyes to see a medium-sized woman with a buzz cut and piercing black eyes, who had just saved her from further damage peering down.

"Come with me," signed the woman. "It is breakfast and then work."

There was no further explanation as her savior walked out of the building and Pia scrambled to catch up. She caught up with the woman, but it was clear that she would provide no more information. So, Pia simply walked behind and followed her into a large building, found a seat, and ate her first meal at Tranquility.

Over the next several weeks Pia did her best to learn about Tranquility, most importantly, how to stay safe. Her facial wounds healed quickly but Pia remained tense and vigilant within the cabin. Her attacker left her alone for now but there was no guarantee as to what might happen if they were isolated together. So, Pia observed and kept her head low. She soon learned that Charlene, her rescuer on that fateful first day, was a leader within her cabin and perhaps across all of Tranquility. She gleaned from carefully observing exchanges among cabin mates that Charlene was part of Silent Thunder America or STAM. It was some type of resistance group, but that was the extent of her knowledge.

Since the incident, Charlene had communicated with Pia on a few occasions, mainly regarding how to stay out of trouble, either with other camp mates or guards. Pia studied Charlene to try and decipher the mystery of her protector. But other than her appearance short, muscular, and attractive with closely cut brown hair with large greenish eyes -- Pia had yet to get a full read as to what made Charlene tick.

"Pia, in order to survive in here you must quickly, like starting now, improve your non-signing skills. It's up to you. I can't help you unless you step up."

While Charlene was a Gen 1 non-speaker like Pia, she and other founders of STAM played a role in propagating an emergent method of communicating, Language of the Streets, or LOTS. It consisted of facial expressions, lip-smacking to generate sounds, lip reading, and strategic gesturing. For many, LOTS represented resistance to the efforts of the government to teach, some would say force, non-speakers to learn to sign and in other ways blend in. More importantly, LOTS had the potential to build community according to Charlene. Its mixing of communication modes and displays of emotions encouraged people to be present for each other in ways that signing and verbal communication did not. Pia was skeptical but wanted to believe. She would observe it for herself.

Two weeks after Pia first arrived everyone was asleep in their bunks when there was a loud bang at the door and guards rushed in.

“Get the fuck up and get your asses against the wall,” one of the guards shouted. “We know that there are weapons here so tell us where they are and we can save time and pain.”

Pia held her breath all the while staring at the guard shouting instructions. She didn’t know his name or anything about him but she sensed that he was evil. His huge black pupils seemed to project a bottomless pit.

“Okay, you all want to play games well that’s fine with me. It’s been a slow night anyway. Guards, turn the place over.”

With that, the uniformed men noisily pushed over mattresses, hit their large Billy clubs against everything that they saw, and dropkicked prisoners’ personal possessions. Apparently, they wanted to maximize destruction as much as find anything. One of the guards kicked a ceramic bowl that exploded, revealing a small fork.

“Well, well, what do we have here?” said the menacing guard. “I believe that you ladies know the rules, and this, my friends is clearly contraband. Whose is it?”

Time stood still.

“No volunteers?” He asked as he slowly walked the line of the 15 cabin mates pressed against the wall.

“Last chance ladies,” but before he even finished the last syllable, he swung his club violently across the side of Charlene’s head producing a loud thud as she fell to the floor.

The man calmly hovered over the fallen body glowering while Charlene attempted to roll away.

“Vinaceous, where are you going? Given that you think of yourself as the leader, I am going to assume that this fork is either yours or you know whose it is.” As he spoke the sadistic figure held his leg in position to kick Charlene in the head again.

Pia stepped forward and raised her hand. Her stomach turned and she exerted every ounce of strength not to pee her pants.

The menacing figure withdrew his leg and wheeled toward Pia. She had never been so terrified in her life, more so than even the day the police took her away and brought her to Tranquility.

“Who the fuck is this,” the guard asked one of his men. “Sergeant Totali, this is Pia Johnston, a new camp mate.”

Totali slowly approached Pia, who could no longer keep it together as urine flowed down her leg and gathered around her sneakers. He was an unremarkable-looking man of average height and weight with those large bottomless eyes. He radiated danger.

“Jesus Christ, we’ve got a bed wetter here men,” Totali taunted.

His crew laughed with a shallowness that revealed more fear of him than the sharing of a joke. Then Totali inched so close to Pia’s face that she could smell his coffee breath.

“So, this contraband is yours Ms. Pia? And you understand that the consequence of owning contraband is quite severe?”

Pia’s hands shook as she tried to sign yes it was hers but that she did not understand the rules. “I am sorry,” she added, her shaking so extreme that Totali looked away in disgust and told one of the guards to take her to isolation.

“Well, Charlene, I guess I owe you an apology,” sneered Totali. “I hope that your head doesn’t hurt too much. I suggest that you ask one of your STAM maggots to stitch you up because unfortunately our medical facility is shut for the night. Good night girls.”

With that, Totali exited the building.

Pia was pushed into a small windowless room in the back of what she thought might be the administration building, judging by the cubicles and computers upon first entering. She had no idea how long she would be locked up, but Pia was actually relieved. Her one wish was that she would never have to face Totali again. In that moment remaining locked in that room and having to sleep on the floor was greatly preferable to being in his presence.

She soon fell asleep having expended a vast amount of adrenaline that left her exhausted. Before long, she thrashed on the floor in the midst of a nightmare that included being chased by a fire-breathing dragon. No matter how fast she ran or where she hid the dragon remained in hot pursuit. Pia realized that there was no escape and snapped awake in a hot sweat.

As she shook the remnants of the nightmare from her head Pia began to question what she had done. What had possessed her to sacrifice herself for someone she barely knew? Was it an act of bravery? She certainly did not consider herself a coward, but she didn't fashion herself as some kind of action hero either. But perhaps her motive was in character. Pia was once again trying to please everyone and smooth things over. She had been grateful to Charlene for saving her and couldn't let her go down.

Pia continued her soul searching for two long days in solitary until she was suddenly returned to her cabin after dinner. She walked to her bunk and lay down. It was the first time in days that she had not been standing or lying on the cold ground. Charlene came over and gave her a hug. Pia had survived Totali and perhaps made a friend, or at least earned some respect.

In the weeks that followed, Charlene explained the nuances and complexities behind the daily grind at Tranquility.

"Pia, you got to understand that the guards are not all the same," Charlene explained, gradually incorporating some LOTS in with her sign language so that Pia would learn. "We actually work with some, buy them off. But a few are fucking crazy, almost as much as that son of a bitch Totali. They just look for reasons to brutalize us. Some of the most vicious are hardcore members of Speakers First. But even a few from that group can be persuaded with a few one-hundred-dollar bills to smuggle in food, drugs, and in rare cases, weapons."

Charlene went on to explain that a few of the guards sympathized with the non-speakers for one reason or another. There was even a rumor that someone close to the top of the Tranquility hierarchy was helping.

"But you need to be careful," Charlene signed, "some guards who we buy can quickly become unbought."

"I don't understand," signed Pia, "unbought?"

"Yeah, unbought! This place is a cesspool of fear and greed. You probably didn't even hear about what happened last week. One of my friends was beaten unconscious by the same guard who had recently smuggled in a crowbar for us. Who knows why, but my guess is that the guard got scared that Totali was on to him and wanted to convince the administration that he was not the source of the smuggling operation."

One month after Pia was released from solitary, Charlene motioned for Pia to follow her as dinner was ending. So, Pia followed until they came to a relatively isolated place near the north wall of the prison. Charlene looked around to make sure that they were alone and began to sign. "Pia, I have been watching and keeping tabs on you to see how you are fitting in. How do you think it's going?"

Pia paused wondering whether there was a correct answer. "Okay I guess," she answered after seeing that Charlene was impatient with her delayed response.

"Pia, I really like you, but I worry about how you are adapting. It's not that you are doing anything wrong but I don't think that you always see what is going on right in front of your face."

Pia was taken aback. Instead of signing she used her rudimentary version of LOTS to ask Charlene to clarify. Charlene smiled, and Pia, interpreting it as laughter at her attempt to learn the new language, turned away. Charlene reached across her shoulder and gently turned her back face to face.

"Listen, Pia, you are a good person. I know that much about you. In fact, I trust you more than some of my comrades because even if you do the wrong thing, it won't be out of spite or jealousy. So, what I am about to tell you is for your protection. Even though every prisoner is a non-speaker, you cannot think of everyone as a potential friend or ally. Like anyplace, people in Tranquility, non- speakers or guards, have agendas. So sometimes what appears to be happening is not. This place is infested with collaborators. Most are minor like those wanting to get their hands on more food from the store. They will provide small information to the guards. Generally, these small-timers don't know much and don't want to. They just want to survive in here a little more comfortably."

Charlene was about to continue when Pia gave her an incredulous stare.

"You mean to tell me," Pia began signing, "that more than a few non-speakers in here cooperate with the guards for a few snacks?"

Charlene sighed.

"Of course, what did you expect? Why are you so surprised?"

Pia looked down but again Charlene reached across to her new friend and raised her face upward to meet eyes. "Pia this is what I meant by you being a little naïve. You need to toughen up to the reality in here or you won't make it. But there is only so much that I can do. Some inmates come here already hardened by life. For whatever reason, you aren't."

"That's bullshit," Pia signed back. "Do you think losing your father and being yanked from your family is nothing?"

"That's not what I am saying. Your life has been hard, but you aren't. I haven't even told you most of it. Totali and his few trusted acolytes depend on real intel from a few serious collaborators. If you talk to the wrong person your life might be in danger. Anyway, I told you this not to scare you, but to encourage you to use your time to learn how to survive. I don't want to lose you, not on my watch."

As Charlene communicated those last words, Pia noticed a slight tic that began at the bottom corner of her friend's mouth and worked its way up her cheek. Had Pia seen that before? She couldn't remember. What was behind it? Was Charlene less confident and omnipotent than she appeared?

Pia left the conversation confused. But the more that she thought about her peers selling out for a few snacks, the angrier she became. So much so that she began fantasizing about choking them. Charlene had told her about two non-speakers who were removed in shackles before she arrived at Tranquility based on direct intelligence given to the top camp administrator. No one knew for sure what happened to these two, but rumors abounded.

In truth, Pia was angry with everyone. She could tell herself that the politicians, the government, or the police put her here, but they felt distant and abstract. Instead, she began to focus on individuals. Pia started dividing the camp into good and bad guys. Black and white with no grays sustained her fury. She hated the bad guys, some more than others. Sometimes, someone surprised her, and she'd move them out of the good guy camp. But transferring out of the bad guy's camp and into the good one was a higher bar.

Charlene came from a very different background than Pia. She grew up in the rural Finger Lakes region of update New York. Her father was the fire chief of five small communities, and her mom worked as a school administrative assistant. Charlene's politics were informed by her rural, somewhat isolated upbringing and were difficult for Pia to fully understand. She identified as a secessionist, meaning that she believed that non-speakers must move to separate themselves from speaking society.

The next day, Charlene invited Pia to join her, LJ, and two other bunkmates at the lunch pavilion. Pia could only guess as to the reason and hoped that it signaled that Charlene was trusting her more.

"It will be so liberating not to have to explain to speakers what we are doing and why," LJ communicated using LOTS. "They will have their society and we will have ours."

"That's right, LJ" Charlene responded. "But there is a lot of work to do to determine how we are going to pull this off. Having these kinds of theoretical discussions is one thing, but determining where and how we will seize our own land is another."

Pia was about to ask a question about the practicality of secession but thought better of it. Holding back did not change her basic feeling that the only way to get to a better place was through building a united America – speakers and non-speakers a like around principles of decency. Despite these and likely other differences with Charlene, Pia shared hope that a better life was possible and perhaps, she was discovering, the willingness to take risks to achieve it.

3

Pia the Enigma

Charlene

Who is Pia? If you had asked me after her first day beat down, I would have said someone who is too weak to survive, even in a moderate prison-like Tranquility. While her face has a slightly androgynous almost surly look, she projects fragility. But then she stepped forward to take the hit for all of us. To say that her spontaneous act of courage caught all of us by surprise would be a massive understatement. Even Totali, the master of the dark arts, it seemed was taken aback.

Now my assessment of Pia is that she is genuine and guileless. Tranquility could use more of that. I mean, in some ways, I like her more than some of my comrades. I have been trying to unravel her mystery. Is she straight-up humble or is she just insecure?

I don't know how to interpret her fascination with my background as a working-class girl from upstate New York who turned "militant" -- her term, not mine. It could make me mad if I interpreted her interest as patronizing, but I don't. No, she really wants to understand what makes me tick. But I don't want to get too close because I might start feeling overly responsible for her, even protective. I know that most of the inmates are harmless, and the guards are lazy idiots who will leave you alone unless you do something stupid. But that's the problem: Pia might not even know the difference. Perhaps I am not giving her enough credit, though. I do sense in her more than decency. I think there's an intuitiveness that might save her.

The bigger question is how much should I share with her? I can probably placate Pia with empty descriptions of growing up in the Finger Lakes as the gay daughter of the local fire chief.

But I don't really want to do that to her or me. As it stands, Pia doesn't know much of anything about me. About how hard life was on the outside before I was sent to Tranquility.

Since I was about 10, I dreamed of changing my reality. Life with my mom and dad was safe but suffocating. I was an only child, and it seemed a smart decision by my parents who perhaps had me only because it was expected. My muteness only added to their discomfort as parents. Mom and Dad enthusiastically embraced government services to integrate non-speakers such as myself. They pushed me whole-heartedly into learning how to sign. They ignored my aversion to making myself fit in with speakers the same way they ignored my emerging gayness, and it made for a toxic brew. By twelve, I was in full rebel mode. One thing led to another and before long I was sent packing to live with my Aunt Carol in Syracuse.

I was pissed at first, but the change may have saved me. Carol was kooky in a wonderful way. She was the first straight speaker I knew who welcomed me unconditionally. Her acceptance gave me the freedom that I needed not to have to act so tough. Carol helped me begin to see the world in shades. Being a speaker didn't mean that someone was an asshole. Slowly, I began to deepen my worldview. My self-appointed kickass persona was not necessary, and even more importantly, was holding me back.

My world expanded over the next five years. I stayed with my aunt through middle and high school, and she served as my sounding board, as it were. I communicated occasionally with Mom and Dad, but it remained tense and pro forma. I cannot even tell whether I even loved them, as horrible as it might sound.

I found love elsewhere, though. There was Aunt Carol, and then I found romantic love with several classmates. LJ, an activist who is locked up here with me in an adjacent cabin, may be my greatest love so far. LJ is the person with whom I have most been able to be myself. We have shared so much. I'm talking about the kind of stupid shit and fears that you can only share with the few you trust absolutely. *LJ, do you think people like me? LJ, would I be a sellout if I quit fighting and just worked on getting out of here? If we get out, what do you think about opening a hardware store in rural Maine?*

I don't know. I get the sense that maybe in time I can share more of myself with Pia. First, I need to trust her. Her taking the blame with Totali gave her a lot of credit in my bank. I watch her from afar here and there. Sometimes I notice her watching me. In the six months that we've been thrown together, Pia has never mentioned any sexual relationships. Is she gay? I don't think so. Asexual? It just seems strange that someone who seems so interested in me and my background seems Totalily indifferent to my sexuality. But big surprise, right? Pia the enigma wrapped in a puzzle. LJ told me the other day that I should stay away from Pia. Do-gooders, as LJ labeled her, cause trouble. She went as far as to label her a self-hating non-speaker, which seems a bit extreme to me. But I don't want to make my partner uncomfortable, so perhaps I should at least consider her warnings.

4

The Nightmare

Since childhood, Pia had a sense of impending doom. As a kid, she sat by the window of her brownstone fantasizing about looming disasters. Many of them focused on Taylor but she was an equal opportunity worrier. Was Dad, okay? What about Mom? Did she carry too much of a load on her shoulders? Why was she so negative? Was Mom too hard on Dad? Was Dad too busy with work to take care of Mom's needs? Did Taylor carry too heavy a burden being the younger brother to a non-speaking sister?

Her role in the family was to smooth things over. When Mom blew up at Dad, Pia worried and searched for ways to make the conflict go away. She would cajole Mom into feeling better or check to see if Dad was alright. Some memories scarred her so much that she could still play out every word in her head. Years ago, her dad had casually announced that he might be a few days late joining the family for a New England vacation.

"What Henry? Are you goddamn kidding me? Again?" Delores had spit out the words with such anger that the words hung in the air like a fist. Pia felt her body move involuntarily into the middle of the fray. But before she could intercede her mom slammed the dishwasher shut and ran to her bedroom, where she stayed for the next 12 hours. When Delores emerged the next day, she was wearing sunglasses. For two days, she wore those same shades to highlight that she had been crying.

Fast forward to Pia's current dilemma as an inmate at Tranquility, where despite her own predicament, she found lots of time to worry about Taylor and even more about her mom. A fighter by nature, Delores had left no stone unturned in trying to get Pia released. Often that meant handing out leaflets, calling radio and TV stations hoping for some response, or raising money while working in the face of growing opposition. But Pia worried that Delores would take things further and put herself in harm's way. She couldn't shake the fear that her mother's activism would end badly.

Pia read her mom's letters, which always accentuated the positive. She searched between the lines for clues as to what her mom might really be thinking. After six months imprisoned, Pia worried that her mother harbored doubts as to whether her daughter would ever be free.

Creeping hopelessness was Pia's enemy, but it was the relentless fear for the safety of her mother and Taylor that occupied her mind at night and her gut by day. Delores wrote about how Pia's now-thirteen-year-old brother was growing into a little man, but it didn't fool Pia. What must it be like for a thirteen-year-old to have to explain to his friends and others why his sisters are in jail?

Late in the afternoon, just before Pia's second work assignment was ending, she was summoned to the main administration building and handed a phone. Puzzled and alarmed Pia heard her mother's words.

"Hi, honey, I am okay."

Hours earlier during rush hour, Delores had been standing on Fifth Avenue and 34th Street doing a live interview with CNN about her work to free her daughter.

"What message do you have for the American people" asked her interviewer.

Delores took a moment to compose her face and smooth her hair. Her green eyes, unblemished skin, blond hair, and slender figure gave Delores the look of a movie star on a good day.

"My message is simple: my daughter and all non-speaking daughters and sons pose no danger to anyone. Please call your congress people, senators, and the president, and tell them to free our children!"

"Hey Delores," someone had shouted in the background. She'd instinctively turned toward the voice and saw a large, tattooed man wearing the now-recognizable black Speakers First hat. Before she had been able to react the man reached down, picked up a can, and threw a gallon of red paint on her. Oil-based. Delores screamed as the thick product slowly dripped down her face. She wanted to call Pia and share the story before Pia saw or heard it and had a chance to worry.

"Grab him," the CNN interviewer had shouted, but no one moved. Delores, recovering from her shock, leaped at the man but stumbled and ended up crumpled at his feet. She had tried to hold on to his foot hoping that someone would intervene and grab him.

"Fuck you, Delores," the man had yelled as he shook her loose from his left leg. Then, yelling the slogan, "Mutes will not replace us," he quickly melted away into the crowd.

Her attacker must have painstakingly investigated the type of paint that you can't wash off. Paramedics and eventually two of NYPD's finest arrived and took her to the hospital, where they cleaned her up with a chemical mixture. Pia was glad to hear from her mom, but the story only made sense of isolation and impotence to protect her family's growth.

While the attack on Delores was stunning, Pia heard from radio news reports of hundreds of acts of hate and violence on the outside during her now-eight months of captivity. Most had been small but there were also nine reported assassination attempts against those advocating for reintegrating non-speakers into society. Two succeeded.

So now, faced with increased danger for her and other families of non-speakers, Pia had to take a step that didn't come naturally and join the resistance. She knew that others would think of it as a baby step, but she started accepting as reasonable ideas that she would have rejected only weeks ago. And while she would never call herself a militant, she began to agree more and more with the camp radicals who said that if you were on the outside, you were either helping with the resistance or tacitly collaborating. She did not and could not imagine ever becoming a secessionist like Charlene, yet her sharpening world view was opening new possibilities.

Pia tried engaging Charlene in discussions about the future, if for no other reason than to help hone her own view of the world. Secession where and how she wanted to know. Pia tried to pry practical long-term solutions out of Charlene. But her friend would simply smile and tell Pia to observe and remain open to new possibilities

"Let's keep talking," Charlene would say. "What you see as radical and impractical now may change in a matter of months, if not weeks."

Each night Pia, Charlene, and her thirteen other bunkmates listened to the slow cook of America's fear crackling over the airwaves. Scattered yet powerful news helped provide a sense of what was going on. There was a brief story about a protest by non- speakers and speaking allies in Topeka that was met with eggs and bottles by counter-protesters. In other news, the vice president attended a ribbon-cutting ceremony in San Francisco to publicize the opening of yet another "cultural exchange" camp. On the international front, the G7 world leaders met to coordinate emergency plans to contain any efforts at coordination between protest movements.

The backdrop for all of this was emerging reports about American scientific and military studies that modeled the future course of the non-speaker phenomena. Sources described the projections as "troubling" for speaking society. The most likely scenario was for geometric increases in the percentage of non- speakers over time. The current understanding was that less than .04 of the population comprised non-speakers. Despite the growing antagonism toward this group by right-wingers, the relatively minuscule numbers of non-speakers had thus far dampened panic. But if the number of non-speakers was growing faster than projected, the fringe who wanted them locked away would grow, as would secessionist movements like STAM. Then, the powers that be might feel compelled to heighten their response or risk escalating civil unrest.

Inside Tranquility, Pia heard tidbits of such speculation from the outside while she navigated the daily dullness intertwined with occasional drama and an unrelenting sense of anxiety. She so missed her old life. Her new one began every morning at seven sharp, with the national anthem. Inmates were lined up so that guards could take attendance to make sure that no one had escaped, and to hammer home who was in control. Those late or deemed unprepared by guards forfeited cooperative points, the currency by which inmates acquired daily rewards such as Pepsis or energy bars at the commissary. The latter was conveniently located in the middle of the camp next to one of five-armed watch towers. From their perch, guards could scan the 30 drab green bunks that contained the roughly 450 prisoners.

After the lineup, it was off to morning assignments. Pia worked on the laundry detail. During her first days, she was introduced to every imaginable stain. Many appeared innocuous, and Pia's inmate trainer, Shirley, was typically more than willing to offer up explanations, some amusing others straight-up disgusting.

"Look at these frigging sloppy eaters or bed-wetters," she would say.

But her laundry mentor was more laconic a week into Pia's training when the pair opened a new pile of sheets to see globs of blood that seemed to tell a tale of something far more diabolical than someone's menstrual cycle. Shirley and Pia elected not to speculate as to its cause, at least out loud, but Pia's fears turned to the shadowy figure of Totali or some inmate bully.

Lunch was served promptly at noon, which was good for Pia because she was not much of a breakfast eater. By twelve, she was famished. Lunch was typically the highlight of camp life during daylight. The food wasn't bad, and it was the one time when the guards seemed to relax. Inmates formed a long line where the grub was generously ladled out by their peers. Once served, inmates would scurry to find a table with their friends. Theoretically saving spots wasn't allowed but anyone with any clout did it openly.

The mess hall was surprisingly small so the 450 huddled together in close quarters. On good days it felt like a low-cost sleep- away camp. Lunch could be a time to laugh and forget, even if just for five minutes. The guards were often the subject of hilarity, whether it was the expanding girth of one or the piercing body odor of another; anything to distract and amuse. There was one uncomfortable aspect, though: Charlene and LJ nearly always sat away from the group, holding hands and laughing. This made it precarious for Pia when decide where to sit. She was mostly in good standing with her bunkmates, but her original tormentor still blamed Pia for the beat down administered by Charlene.

Despite the upsides of lunch, the hardness of life at Tranquility sometimes played out. While all the inmates were non- speakers, there was still plenty of intramural tension just below the surface ready to explode. Two weeks ago, the kitchen turned out such a foul-smelling mac and cheese that everyone recognized it as some type of punishment. While some inmates pushed the food to the side and others gagged, several guards snickered among themselves. Then Totali walked in and asked what was wrong while doing a hybrid snarl-smile. He then ordered all the guards out of the building for a "staff meeting."

"Who the fuck snitched and got us this shit food and Totali to boot?" LJ communicated using LOTS, despite the fact that as many as half the inmates were not fluent in it. Pia slumped back into her seat not understanding what was happening. Then Charlene and several of her STAM comrades stood up and looked around menacingly. The comrade standing next to Charlene slowly walked the room and stopped by a woman Pia didn't recognize.

"Anything you want to tell us, Loretta? LJ saw you talking to Sergeant Frank for a real long time yesterday?" Suddenly Loretta was swinging by her ponytail. Higher and higher she rose all the while frantically kicking her legs to try and break free.

Before Loretta would experience further pain, the door flew open and

Totali stood there mockingly.

"Okay, your little inmate meeting is over. I hope that you were able to resolve whatever differences you may have had. Eat up, girls. This yummy mac and cheese won't last forever."

All inmates changed jobs in the afternoon. Whether it was intended to break the monotony or to stop individuals from spending too much time together and possibly plotting, no one knew. Most liked to switch, especially if their morning assignment was building maintenance, a euphemism for cleaning shit in the bathrooms.

At six the whistle blew to end the day. The inmates headed off to wash up before the dinner bell. Just eighteen months ago, Pia's biggest decision had been whether to eat dinner with Dad, Mom, and Taylor or to go out with her friends. Chinatown was just a stone's throw from her old brownstone, so her buds often suggested it as a cheap destination meal. Now, her choices were eating the lousy camp dinner or squandering daily and weekly allowance on snacks from the camp store. Few from the outside would call it a store as it consisted of a small cramped indoor area no more than five by five where the inmates sailed through and ordered what they could afford from the backroom storage closet. Nothing was displayed and many products ran out before the store closed for the day. It was particularly tough on inclement days as dozens stood out in the cold, rain, and snow before making it to the indoor counter.

The guards usually became more uptight beginning at dinner and the tension ratcheted up until the lights were shut off at ten. It was common knowledge that all camp staff attended a security briefing around four every afternoon. Inmates speculated that administrators, led by Totali, leaned on the guards during these meetings to suppress STAM. The result was often intimidation or beatings of the inmates regardless of one's innocence or guilt. Justice was typically less important than meeting Totali's quota for action.

One night, the loud shouts from guards and objects falling jolted everyone awake in Pia's cabin. Piercing screams sounded as if they came from right outside the door. Pia got up and approached the sound, but Charlene frantically signaled to her to get back in bed. The next day speculation ricocheted around the dining hall during breakfast that a camp mate named Matt Chase had been hauled away. No one had seen him since.

So, vigilance remained the motto. Charlene's cabin had someone assigned to guard duty each night. Rumors circulated that another raid was coming. But no one knew of anything specific. The usual greasing of palms had not produced much in the way of intelligence. The inmates of Tranquility carried on, not with hope but with resolve. Some like Pia believed that justice, whatever that meant, would eventually prevail. That's what she had to hold onto. It would have to do.

5

You Say You Want an Evolution

Pia spent some of her alone time at Tranquility pondering the reason for muteness. Did it even matter? She doubted it, but at least the wondering sucked up time. Her dad used to share his perspective and [illegible] about all of this and more. He told her that over time humans had changed their behavior in order to survive. For example, early man relied on hunting wooly mammoths for food, but when the wooly mammoth died out, mankind took up hunting other animals and learned to farm. Those were conscious behaviors.

Then there were the involuntary changes that Darwin studied. Humans and every other species underwent random genetic changes all the time. Some of those were bad, such as the development of Tay-Sachs disease, but others conferred advantages and made the individuals with those mutations better able to survive.

So, what was going on? Were humans simply unwitting participants in the next chapter of nature's work? Pia speculated that there were likely voluntary and involuntary forces at play. Being mute was obviously a genetic mutation. But nobody knew whether it conveyed any genetic advantage. As her dad would say, it was too soon to tell. Perhaps it would become clear over the course of a few generations.

Recently, there has been increased speculation that the genetic part might be a response to an over-reliance on social media. With emoji's replacing verbalized emotion, people texting each other from the same room, and the general dumbing down of discourse, some argued that there was less need for spoken language, so the ability was simply disappearing.

As to the voluntary, non-speakers were making choices such as whether to use traditional sign language or adapt through languages like LOTS. Some speakers consciously paid attention to non-verbal forms of communication and incorporated them into their lives, often to demonstrate support for non-speakers. Others did not, including those who rallied around opposition to non- verbal communication the same way that the MAGA crowd had with Spanish-speakers. Groups like Speakers First and some everyday-speaking citizens increasingly took umbrage at being urged to learn to read signs and to make other accommodations for non-speakers. With economic uncertainty looming, this divide was likely to deepen.

Everyone had a story about how the emergence of non- speakers had impacted them. For Pia, the reality of her status seemed to hit home when she turned nine and was in third grade. Pia had been notably bummed out that year, feeling lonely and tired of being different. Her Dad sat her down and said that yes, of course, she was different, but it was a good thing. Pia remembered just staring back at him blankly. He must have seen the dazed look on her face, so he simply handed her two articles that he conveniently had at his side.

"Pia, please put these away for now in a safe place," he had said. "In a few years, when you have more questions, you should read them."

Pia forgot all about the articles, but soon after her father's suicide, she stumbled upon one of them. It was from the Smithsonian Institution's Human Origins Program. It basically said the same thing that Charlene would tell her: non-speakers were evolutionary pioneers, like it or not.

When she could find time in Tranquility's library, Pia accelerated her investigations. She began reading about Indigenous cultures, trying to better understand other forms of language and communication. The first stuff that Pia read was pretty obvious: a lot of North American Indigenous peoples traditionally had no written language. But why? The common-sense explanation provided was that they didn't need to. And what could that tell her about a potential future society without spoken language?

It turned out that text beyond the cuneiform systems used to share information about hunting and gathering first arose in tandem with religion and commerce, and so it was immediately a symbol of power. The people who could read and write held the key to the word of God and records of who owed whom what goods and services.

Maybe, then, what some feared from the non-speakers was that their lack of spoken language signaled a lack of respect for their authority and contempt for how they measured wealth. In rejecting both religion and their form of commerce they were essentially telling the man that they would not be cogs in their machine. But it's not as if non-speakers as a whole, or even the movement, was offering up a revolutionary new economic system. Maybe just the hint of rejecting these systems made some individuals feel rejected too.

But there was more to it than that. Some of the non-speakers were not only incapable of oral communication, but they rejected language itself. After all, they seemed to suggest, that if the purpose of language was fundamentally just to facilitate transactions, who needed it? In fact, weren't people better off relying on more sensory and elemental forms of communication? Just as trees and plants communicated the presence of food or the risk of an encroaching danger through scents and chemical emissions, people could communicate real human emotions like love and hate without relying on words in any form. Their grimacing or smiling faces, tensed or relaxed bodies, hair on arms standing up and alert or resting peacefully against the skin, a touch that was tender or fierce, the pheromones and auras and vibrations humans emitted—all of those physiological changes probably signaled more about how people were feeling than language ever could. So, shouldn't humans embrace what nature was teaching daily rather than trying to dominate it with bullshit ideas dressed up in words? Would the growing swaths of society who refused to learn or use signs because they considered it an attack on America and traditional society be a blip on the historical screen or have a long-term impact?

Further confusing Pia was that big evolutionary changes typically play out over centuries, not decades. Yet this form of muteness seems to have sprung up basically overnight.

Rather than comforting Pia, the more she thought about genetics and interaction with human behavior the more worried she became. Her mind was in overdrive. She remembered the earlier days when an international white supremacist movement, the Defenders, started using the tactics and style of rhetoric now adopted by groups like Speakers First. A novelty back then, their numbers had grown exponentially over the decade. For every non- speaking militant there seemed to be five Speakers Firsters, some of whom were members of armed militias. Had people done more to stop the conspiracy militias back then perhaps Pia and others wouldn't be locked up four decades later.

But Pia could find little solace in her replaying of history and evolutionary social theory. Her question was where was it all going, and how might it end? She didn't see much light at the end of the tunnel, nor did many of her fellow inmates. Discussions about the future often escalated into anger or simply changing the topic, but the rage was constant and burned bright despite the underlying despair.

Pia felt her eyes closing so she shut off the mini-flashlight that she had bought off another inmate through Tranquility's well- established black market. She slept deeply and dreamlessly. But sometime later that night, she re-lived the horror of that fateful December afternoon.

It's warm, real warm for winter and I feel good. I'm in my favorite store. I hear a loud sound and look at the other people to see what is happening.

Their faces are twisted into fearful snarls. I am scared and now I remember this nightmare. But it's real.

I try waking up but can't. The police are marching down Canal Street toward the river. I try to run but my feet are cemented to the ground. Finally, I shake myself free. I am running. Help me someone screams. I pick up an old woman. People are racing beside me and some are falling. We run together like animals fleeing a fire and then we hear the bullhorn "per order of the President of the United States everyone is to get off the streets.

President Miller has declared martial law. I repeat, everyone must immediately get off the streets."

"Mom, dad, where are you? Where is Taylor? I can't find them in my dream.

Now we are sitting in front of the TV together starring at those words, those fucking words.

All Non- Speakers Must Register with Local Authorities by this Time Tomorrow or Face Fines and/or Imprisonment

6

Visiting Day

"Good afternoon," Totali sneered. "As most of you know, there is an election coming in November and therefore it is time for meat-and-greets. The president wants some nice photos of his team kissing babies and talking to mutes."

"In just a few moments, I am going to re-introduce you to my second in command, Sergeant Kenney," the jeering voice continued. "As you know, the sergeant is a reasonable man. But let me be clear, do not mistake the Sergeant's milder manner for an opportunity to pull a stunt. Any attempts to communicate to outsiders other than approved camp messaging will be severely punished. Sergeant, it's all yours."

"Thank you, Chief Administrator Totali."

Pia had seen Sergeant Kenney once or twice before, but this would be the first time she had heard directly from him. Word in the camp was that he was as nice a guy as could be expected under these circumstances. Some had commented in the past that he resembled Malcom X with his reddish complexion and freckles. Pia eagerly awaited his words.

"First of all, I want to acknowledge your cooperation over the past month. Tranquility has had zero reported incidents of disciplinary violations in

September, a notable record that you should all be proud of. It is one of the reasons that President Miller's Health and Human Services Secretary Jenna Rudolph will be visiting next week with a Congressional delegation. With the Presidential Election less than four weeks away, the Miller administration wants to highlight its work to defuse national tensions and progressive camps like Tranquility are part of their message."

Pia looked around to see reactions and found Charlene's face, which remained blank.

"Needless to say," continued Kenney, "we expect each of you to stick to established schedules and to speak only when and if you are directly asked a question. Chief Totali made it clear, and I want to underscore, that we are counting on each of you not to say anything controversial that might embarrass us and cause kickback. Does anyone have any questions?"

Pia again looked around. She saw a mixture of annoyed rolling eyes and boredom.

7

Lonely at the Top

Sergeant Kenney

What a strange journey it's been. I finally "made it." I did the career ladder thing only to find a shit sandwich at the top rung. In fairness to me, how could anyone have imagined that becoming a criminal justice major in college would place me in the middle of a national meltdown? Totali is the only one who really knows my complete situation. That, unfortunately, gives him quite a bit of leverage over me. To this point, it's been implied, not stated, that he could ruin me in ways beyond a simple firing.

When Tommy was born three years ago, he was living proof that an interracial couple from Totalily different backgrounds could make it. We had endured. Somehow, it never occurred to either of us that he might be a non-speaker. Not that it changes our love for him one iota, but it certainly complicates things—the biggest being my career. Tommy's situation has the potential to make things tough. To add just a bit more heat to my life, Mandy has been a progressive white activist since I met her in college 20 years ago.

Even before we suspected anything might be amiss with Tommy, Mandy was already out there advocating for the rights of non-speakers. Most recently, that included organizing to shut down the camps. She has tried to do all of this as discretely as possible so that she doesn't compromise my career. Nevertheless, every time the chief opens his door my heart skips a beat, expecting him to tell me to meet him in his office with an HR rep. Not that I wouldn't welcome getting out of this hellhole named Tranquility.

I met Mandy during my first month at Stony Brook University. I decided at the last moment to go to a homecoming mixer at which she walked right up to me and introduced herself.

Mandy called herself a townie, but I quickly learned she was smart as could be and suffered no fools.

I wasn't exactly smooth in those days, and she quickly de- weaponized my embarrassing attempts to share big ideas garnered from my first two months of academia. My impressive vocabulary landed like a waterlogged thesaurus. Long story short I fell in love with her right then and there and everything in my life began to change for the better. But it took time for me to share my secrets and nightmares.

I grew up in suburban Westchester County, just north of New York City. My sister Tiffany and I were luckier than many in that we had solidly middle-class parents paying the bills and keeping us safe. But our family had a secret: Tiffany was fighting lifelong depression. Her struggle should not have been a Totali shock. I had my own issues with anxiety. Who knows what our parents were feeling as one of the few Black families in this largely white community? Tiffany slowly but steadily started finding her way to whatever high was available. I reluctantly served as a go-between, because my best friend Martin was her dealer of choice. He was discrete, enterprising, and offered top-shelf stuff. I didn't necessarily approve of Martin's business, but I went along with it. In a sense, that was my story—go along to get along.

Why didn't I confront Martin or at least say something, anything? I've asked myself that question hundreds of times. What I came up with is sad but true: I was too insecure and frankly weak to tell my best friend and sister to stop. I didn't think they'd listen, and I wasn't prepared to cut either of them off if they didn't. So, while I knew what they were doing was dangerous, I held my tongue. But the price for my cowardice came due when they found my sister's body under an Interstate 95 bridge on New Year's morning.

The repercussions were quick. A price would be paid for shocking and embarrassing our peaceful suburban hamlet. For Martin, it meant three to five for manslaughter and drug trafficking. For me, it was off to boarding school and far away from the scene of the crime. My parents would soon follow to complete our exile. At that point, with Tiffany dead and our family an embarrassment to the community, I think the three of us welcomed the opportunity to leave what now felt more like a sentence than home.

Life at Higher Visions Boarding school in rural Colorado would have been worse had I actually been emotionally present. But I wasn't. Not even close. I was lost deep inside myself going through the motions of school and the daily grind. My only ambition was to be left alone. The last thing that I wanted was to talk about who I had been before Higher Visions. I cooperated but never really participated. I was liked but not known.

My view of myself began to change when I met Dr. Jordan. He had just been hired to replace an English teacher who was so boring that it seemed like he had died years earlier but never received the memo. Doc was the polar opposite. With passion and energy, he introduced me to ideas about redemption and fortitude. I don't know where Doc got his ideas, but they seemed to be some mix of religion, grit, and common sense.

As a joke, I started telling Doc that he had founded a new movement, Jordani's. I wasn't entirely fooling, because to me it seemed that Doc's brew was simple yet powerful: always try to do the right thing and have fun doing it. By fun, Doc didn't mean partying. He meant living life with a passion for your community and yourself.

"This," he said, "is the only salvation for an American society founded on slavery and the continued oppression of so many groups including women, immigrants, LGBT, *etcetera*."

Doc emphasized the word etcetera in his own distinctive style to indicate that he wasn't talking about some alphabet soup of oppression. He truly believed that it didn't matter if you were gay, black, a woman, Latino, or something else. What mattered was that everyone deserved respect unless they surrendered it. Under that definition, if you were a victim of the American meat grinder, it was your responsibility to do or say something. Take a stand.

When I graduated two years later from Higher Visions, I felt more in touch with who I was and wanted to become. I was psyched to get accepted by Stony Brook. To me, it symbolized my progress and growth. Despite Doc's cautionary note about choosing criminal justice as my major, I convinced myself that I could apply Jordani's in this or any field. I might have even naively thought that I could change things from within. But truth be told, it was probably a foolhardy attempt to make up for my guilt about my sister.

And then I met Mandy.

I immediately felt her strength and sensed that she might balance me out. I spent the first few minutes focused almost entirely on her lips moving as she spoke. They seemed average as was her overall appearance but somehow mesmerized me. At first, I was confused by her political and personal ideology, but I soon realized that we were on the same side. While her brand might look different, her basic beliefs and core integrity squared with Jordani's. Most importantly, Mandy was grounded in understanding that life was complex.

I wasn't necessarily the greatest student, but I damn well had more authentic life experiences than some of my peers and professors. I challenged them when I thought they were talking shit. I slowly felt more self-assured, and at some point, realized that I had lost a few boulders from my back. The weight of my sister's death and my own culpability in it was lessening, although I knew the latter would always be with me. I wanted it to remind me of the price of cowardice.

I graduated four years later and entered a special internship program with the New York State Prisons system. One thing led to the other, and by 40, I was ascending to the top with a progressive reputation for fighting corruption and punishment for punishment's sake.

But simultaneously, I felt the walls of America slowly tightening around me. The progress that America had made over the past forty years seemed to be stalled or going in reverse. Rumors were flying around the internet amplified with every retweet. The shit was primed to explode. It wasn't just the divide between speakers and non-speakers, but growing international hysteria about the ravages of climate change. The steady flow of populations from poor countries to wealthier ones accelerated with rising coast lines and drying interiors. Some of the anti-immigrant rhetoric was being used against people trying to relocate within their own countries, including here. The most extreme example was Idaho passed laws making it harder for people fleeing the heat of the southwest to cross its border and establish residency.

Still, when young Tommy was born, Mandy and I were as happy as we'd ever been, despite the national tension. Somehow, the growing panic seemed far away. Neither Mandy nor I gave it too much thought. By the time we realized Tommy was a non- speaker, Mandy had gained more prominence within the progressive movement. She was someone as willing to do the hard and often arduous work as she was to give a speech. For a while, we felt like we had the tools to navigate life with two growing careers and support for our non-speaking son within a loving and accepting community.

We lived in Queens close to the Nassau County border in an area with decent schools and a large multicultural community. We were happy and felt safe. As I think back to those days, I wonder how we could have been so blinkered to the times of strife we were about to enter.

Perhaps the fickle finger of fate was having fun with me. It seems quite a coincidence that my next career assignment was this highly prestigious move within New York State's criminal justice system. I, Sergeant Kenny, would be named the most prominent of the young Turks to help with the humanitarian dilemma of opening Tranquility. It was an offer that they said I couldn't refuse.

8

Things Fall Apart More

"Welcome to CNN's breaking news. My name is Sean Wise, the host of CNN's Money in America series. At this hour on October 15, 2055, the stock market is in free fall, with the Dow down more than 2,000 points, and other indicators such as the S&P in similar decline. Emergency breaks have kicked in, meaning that trading was automatically suspended for the day. But futures markets are indicating tomorrow might be even bleaker. To help our viewers make sense of all of this, we have Dr. Lawrence Pettigrew from Harvard University as our special guest. Dr. Pettigrew, please help our viewers understand what is happening, why, and what they might do to protect their money?"

"The quick answer, Sean, is that markets have lost confidence in the American and international economies. As to the why, the stock market cratering is likely due to a combination of factors beginning with the decades-long impact of climate change. As you know it has sent the world into a slow but steady productivity slide which combined with rising prices has created a toxic brew. Now add the instability created as the world grapples with the non-speaker phenomena and it seems to be the straw that is breaking the camel's back. As conflicts have broken out over the treatment of non-speakers, we've seen strikes, protests, and people on both sides stockpiling goods. Meanwhile, the latest numbers on consumer confidence have plummeted. Not surprisingly in such an economic environment, capital investments are way down as people seek safe places to park their money."

"What, in your opinion, can the Miller administration do?

And how can individual citizens protect what they have?"

"Well, Sean, first and foremost we need to acknowledge that these are unprecedented times. There is little or no criteria that I know of to gauge where this is all going. Remember that the rationale for removing non-speakers from the general population was to reduce societal conflict. As I am sure you recall, a few short years ago, the Miller administration doubled down on its policy to integrate ever-growing numbers of non-speakers. This strategy eventually cratered, as resentment from some citizens grew because they felt they were being forced to accept a lifestyle they found unnatural. We were on the brink of civil war. As a result, the Miller administration was forced to turn on a dime and begin to segregate non-speakers. Ironically, those efforts to insulate the economy now appear to be doing the opposite."

"Okay, so what is your advice to President Miller, who I don't need to remind you, is but a few weeks away from Election Day?"

"I am not trying to be clever here when I say that if I were the president, I would be looking for real estate outside of the White House."

9

Dogs & Ponies

Pia was on edge, as were most inmates and guards. It was the day that HHS Secretary Jenna Rudolph and a congressional delegation would be visiting Tranquility just two weeks before the election. So much had changed in the 21 days since Totali had announced the impending visit. Initially, the Miller administration had intended it to be part of a well-orchestrated victory lap to highlight its handling of the non-speaker crisis. But the economic meltdown had imploded that narrative. Canceling the visit would be worse, so the stage was set for a visit that no one wanted, with the exception of Totali. He saw it as a potential career booster.

Pia and her bunkmates reported to breakfast at their normal time. She was seated with a group of inmates she barely knew. In his wisdom, Totali had ordered Sergeant Kenney to mix up who sat with whom to reduce familiarity among the inmates. Totali reasoned that if the residents were too comfortable, they might feel emboldened to complain to reporters.

Less than five minutes into a joyless breakfast, the doors opened and the delegation entered, followed by the press and photographers. Secretary Rudolph was smiling so intensely that it looked to Pia as if her mouth might permanently freeze in place. The dignitaries slowly made their way toward the designated meet- and-greet front tables and began shaking hands with inmates and guards. But after a minute or two, some of the press broke ranks and walked toward other tables at the back of the dining hall.

One reporter approached the table at which Pia and twenty others were sitting.

"Ladies and gentlemen of the press, please do not approach any of the non-designated tables and clients," shouted Sergeant Kenney. "Please return to the front of the dining room and rejoin the secretary and congressional delegation."

Secretary Rudolph and the delegation looked confused by the breakdown in the protocol but did their best to ignore it as they continued to shake hands at the official tables.

Totali, who had been explaining to Rudolph all that he had accomplished at Tranquility, looked annoyed as he advanced toward Kenney.

"What the fuck are you doing Kenney? Get this shit under control. Now!"

Sergeant Kenney again tried to get the press back to the greeting line, but only a few complied.

At Pia's table, the reporter introduced herself. "Hi there, my name is Nancy Rucker from the *New York Times*. What is your name and how long have you been in Tranquility?"

Pia held her breath and nervously looked around. Out of the corner of her eye, she saw Kenney advancing, followed closely by a fire-breathing Totali.

The inmate hesitated for a moment and then signed to Rucker's interpreter that her name was Chantelle and that she was sent to Tranquility just last week.

"And how has your time been here? What is it like for you and your peers?"

Chantelle interpreted the moment as her opportunity and signed "Please help me. I don't want to stay here. I want to get out."

Sergeant Kenney, having finally made his way over, said "Please stop, now!"

But seeing a possible story, the reporter ignored his entreaty and began to ask for a follow-up. Totali rushed past the Sergeant grabbed Rucker by the arm and pulled her away. Other reporters saw the scuffle and moved toward the table. Pia and others edged away.

"Let go of me," screamed Rucker.

Totali held on to Rucker and yelled to the guards to end breakfast and send the inmates to their work assignments.

The guards, intimidated by Totali's anger, began pushing inmates to the doors. At the northern exit, a guard pushed so forcefully that two inmates stumbled over each other and were soon on the ground. The guard, either unaware or unconcerned, continued to push the inmates out, creating a mini stampede over the fallen pair. Cameras snapped, and reporters pointed excitedly to shots that they wanted their photographer colleagues to capture for the unfolding story. It was sheer chaos.

Luckily, Pia was being ushered out the east door and was untouched physically by the action. She watched as the secretary, delegation, and reporters were evacuated, and Totali, now free from Rucker, screamed at Sergeant Kenney. As the mayhem ended, the two stampeded inmates lay on the ground motionless. Pia's last visual was of Kenney, free of Totali, kneeling by the inmates' sides as he checked for signs of life.

10

The New Boss

Sergeant Kenney

"Sergeant Kenney, take a seat." So began a new phase of my relationship with Chief Totali, one that I feared was doomed to end badly for me.

"Kenney, you and I have had our differences in the past, and for that, I apologize. I realize now, with a fresh perspective, that the fiasco with the secretary's visit was not your fault. It was mine. You know the expression: if you want a job done well do it yourself. Anyway, thankfully for both of us, things have worked out. With that pansy President Miller about to be gone, you and I can finally get down to business. I am sure that you agree that Tranquility needs more discipline. I have been speaking with high-level administrators in our penal system and they assure me that we now have a freer hand. The soon-to-be incoming Sanchez administration is making it clear that it wants to tighten things up. There are likely to be a whole host of policy changes coming down the line, and I am sure that both of us want to be on the right side for our careers. And you, with the challenges presented by your son Tommy, will certainly need both money and influence to help him."

I stared straight ahead barely blinking at Totali. I knew that he was looking for a reaction, and I would give him none.

"Anyway Sergeant, we have a serious security threat, and its name is Charlene Vicnacious and her not-so-merry band of mute commies. I have it from confidential sources that they are seeking weapons from the outside. Apparently, she doesn't trust that you and I will keep everyone safe. Beginning as soon as our little chat ends, you will be in charge of a task force made up of our best and brightest. Your task is to prepare for a raid that will put an end to Vicnacious and her acolytes once and for all. What questions do you have?"

"Chief, with all due respect, when you say 'put an end to these inmates,' you don't mean to kill them, do you?" I watched as Totali's expression slowly morphed from performative and sunny to black without pretense.

"Sergeant, did you hear what I said to you moments ago about your career? If not, let me spell it out for you. There is going to be a new sheriff in town living in a big white house on Pennsylvania Avenue. I, for one, intend to be on the right side of history. I look at my time at Tranquility as just one step in my career. I strongly suggest that you do the same. Think about your poor son and the care that he will need. And your wife, what's her name, Mandy? It wouldn't be easy for her to get a job if her past activism were to get publicized widely. This is all to say that the times have changed and that you need to get fully behind the program. That's all, Sergeant. Good day to you."

I pride myself on being inscrutable, especially with those that I don't trust. Totali would certainly be on that list. Yet I left shaken and worried that he had smelled my fear. That would make a man of Totali's make-up all the more dangerous to deal with.

11

All the Breaking Pre-Election News

"Hi there to our viewers. I am Vicki Hightower reporting from CNN headquarters in Atlanta. Well, folks, it is not an exaggeration to say that we are a nation on edge as we head into the last weekend before the Presidential election."

The anchorwoman looked coiffed and caffeinated as she continued.

"It is an understatement to say that the past ten days have not gone according to plan, especially for President Miller. First, we had the Wall Street crash. Just yesterday, the Bureau of Labor Statistics reported that first-time unemployment claims skyrocketed by an astounding 875,000, leading most economists to say that the

U.S. is on the brink of a significant recession. So clearly tensions are high as we approach Election Day. CNN has reporters fanned out across our great nation to check the mood. Peter Klinger, what do you have for us?"

The screen split to reveal a windswept reporter in one box, while Vicki's face froze in a mask of concentration in the other.

"Thanks, Vicki. I am standing in a park northwest of the UN as a huge crowd continues to gather. It is organized by Mothers for Sanity, M4S for short, a group that is led by parents with children confined under the Miller administration's recent policy. I have spoken to the police who told me that they are concerned that a smaller but militant group of counter-protesters might clash with M4S. Anyway, we are on top of this story and will check in as events unfold."

"Thank you, Peter! Let's go to Washington D.C., where Sovacki Sumunera is standing outside of the U.S. Capitol Building. Sovacki, what's going on there?"

Peter's face was replaced by Sovacki's, grave with concern.

"I am following the story about last week's incident at Camp Tranquility. While details are still sketchy, the *New York Times* has reported that one of its reporters was assaulted by a prison official. We are hoping to get members of the Congressional delegation who were part of that visit on camera to learn more about what actually happened."

"Thanks, Sovacki, good stuff! Next, we have Johnny James on the campaign trail with President Miller who is about to—hang on for a second. I am hearing from the studio that we need to go back to Peter King in New York for breaking news."

This time, Peter filled the whole screen, police cars' flashing lights racing behind him.

"This is CNN breaking news. Hi, Peter Klinger again, and chaos has broken out in a park close to UN Headquarters. We are trying to determine exactly what is going on. For the past two minutes, we have seen squadrons of police rushing toward the northwest corner of the park, and we can hear sirens from what sounds like ambulances and first responders. Hold on. Let me try to get a police person on camera. Officer, officer, please tell our viewers what is going on?"

The officer averted his face from the camera as he said, "Move back sir. Move back onto the sidewalk."

"Okay officer, but what is happening?" Peter persisted.

"We have reports of multiple gun shots but move back now," the cop said, placing a hand on Peter's shoulder while still refusing to look directly at the camera. "I am not going to ask again."

"Okay, folks you just heard it," Peter maintained his calm. "We have reports of gunshots fired. I am going to try to make my way back around to the part of the park where the police appear to be headed. Stick with me".

"Peter, this is Vicki Hightower back at CNN headquarters. We are going to follow your movements, but please stay safe. I am going to bring cut over to our security expert, Breana Maters, the former police chief of the District of Columbia, to tell us what she makes of this news."

"Thanks, Vicki," said the short-haired woman. "Well, from all signs, there appears to have been a serious incident just based on the movement of police and first responders. One can only hope that it is not as bad as it sounds."

"Breana, what should we be looking for?" Vicki paused to check her monitor and then held up a finger and said, "hold on a minute. We are going back to Peter Klinger."

"Vicki, I am here with someone who says that she witnessed the incident," Peter said. "Ma'am, what did you see?"

"It was horrible, that's all I can say," screeched an older woman whose shoulder-length hair was blowing straight back behind her. "I am getting the fuck out of here. I can't believe it."

"Ma'am, I can see that you are upset, and our viewers at home are too because no one can tell us or them what happened. You'd be a real hero today if you could please tell our viewers exactly what you saw."

The woman clenched her jaw, appearing to steel herself to tell the story.

"I was standing by the fountain in the park with my friend when I saw a group of five or six men dressed in military fatigues or something rush toward a group of moms who were handing out leaflets and speaking through bull horns. My friend and I were scared by how they looked so we moved away in the opposite direction, and then I heard *pop, pop, pop* followed by screams. I am sorry, I need to leave."

"Ma'am please can you—" Peter stopped talking and turned his head to the left. The woman took the opportunity to scuttle off, and Peter continued. "Wait a minute, Vicki, I see Tamara Johnson from M4S about to speak to a group of reporters. Let me make my way over there."

"Please everyone from the press, stop shouting questions at me and I will tell you what we know," said the tall blonde standing in front of a few dozen women. "Members of our group were peacefully protesting minutes ago when they were attacked without provocation by a group of terrorists. We don't know for sure, but I will bet that they are associated with Speakers First. There have been several serious injuries, and those wounded are being transferred to Lenox Hill Hospital's trauma unit. I would be remiss not to mention that this is the type of violence that we have been warned about. To date, the local and national authorities, including President Miller, have done too little to protect law-abiding citizens from these extremists. That's all for now, we will be issuing a press release after we learn more."

Peter looked at the camera and said "It looks like that's all we'll get for now."

"Thanks, Peter," Vicki said, her face once again filling the screen. "Please stay safe. We'll check back in with you later. CNN is now learning from police that at least four individuals have been transferred to Lenox Hill and that one has been pronounced dead on the scene. While police have not released any names, our reporters have learned from witnesses the identities of two, Denise Jenkins and Delores Johnston. Stay right here with CNN as there will be more to follow with this explosive story."

12

Shock Waves

After hearing the CNN story, Pia went into deep shock. All she could recall was an arm around her shoulder and someone urging her to move. Then she noticed people scurrying about like manic cartoon characters. Where were they all going? Wasn't that Charlene? Why was she running toward Pia? What was she doing, and why did she seem so upset?

Just as Pia was trying to figure it out, a camp guard tackled Charlene, who rolled on the ground. Pia could see the anger and determination on her friend's face. The guard tried to reach for his Taser, but Charlene was quick and punched him in the face. She was instantaneously smothered by several more guards who were swinging Billy clubs wildly in all directions, hitting each other as often as the inmates. Pia tried to orient herself but couldn't shake the cloud that had enveloped her mind. Several other camp mates rushed the scrum. The pile expanded with dozens of inmates squaring off against the guards.

Pia stood staring, unable to take her eyes off the chaos while struggling to understand its context. She only realized that she landed on the ground at some point because people fighting were moving crazily, upside-down, and sideways. She wanted it to all go away. She closed her eyes.

The very next thing that she remembered was waking up in the infirmary. Pia smelled smoke and gas and tried to imagine what was going on beyond her bed. Then she began to remember. Those horrible minutes rushed back to Pia, and she felt nauseous. Had it been real? She tried telling herself no that everything had just been a terrifying dream but her gut told her the awful truth. Her mother was dead.

13

All-Day Coverage Continues

“This is Peter Klinger. Welcome back to our all-day coverage of the rebellion at Tranquility. For those just tuning in, let me briefly catch you up on the events that began yesterday afternoon and have not only continued today but spread to at least five other facilities across the country.

Peter was comfortably seated behind a desk this time, his voice hitting that perfect reporter balance between somber and chipper, as he continued.

“Here’s what we know. The shooting of four members of M4S and one death outside the UN seems to be the likely cause for a riot at Camp Tranquility. It was triggered by the false report that Ms. Delores Johnston had been killed during the attack. In fact, she survived but is in serious condition at Lenox Hill Hospital. According to our reports, Ms. Johnston’s daughter is an inmate at Camp Tranquility, but we are not certain of her involvement in the riots.

“We have an official version of events given to us by the assistant chief at Tranquility, Sergeant Kenney. His superior, Chief Joseph Totali, and other camp officials have been said to be too busy to speak with us directly. Camp officials have reported no deaths but approximately sixty injured occupants and staff. We need to inform our viewers that CNN reporters have seen several of what look like body bags leaving the facility, but we have been unable to confirm their contents. From our vantage point, we can see numerous buildings on fire and at least part of the north wall damaged. Several National Guard units have been deployed although we have yet to get an official estimate.

“Additionally, we have reports from our affiliates across the nation that at least five other facilities are currently in some state of conflict. Sit-down strikes and similar protests appear to be spreading across the country. It is not clear whether the other conflicts and protests have any direct connection to Tranquility, some of the experts with whom we have consulted speculate that Tranquility was simply the spark that set afire longstanding grievances.

“We believe that the president will address the nation later today, although no time or details have been set. Okay, I am told that we are ready to go to our reporters in Washington D.C., Oakland, California, and other locations. Let’s start with Katy Gonzalez, who is standing outside of the White House. Katy, what can you tell us?”

A young brunette in the famous White House Rose Garden appeared onscreen.

“Thanks, Peter. We just learned that the president will indeed address the nation at approximately three o’clock Eastern Time today. We have received a brief press release from the office of outgoing President Miller which reads as follows:

'Our entire country is saddened and shocked about the occurrences that began yesterday at Camp Tranquility, which as many of you know is a model for how to reintegrate non-speakers back into mainstream society. While all of the details are not yet known, what is clear is that several agitators within Tranquility staged an unprovoked attack upon guards who were comforting the daughter of Delores Johnston. Needless to say, I deplore all forms of violence, including those outside of the UN yesterday. I call on peace-loving Americans, wherever you are, to reject violence and to help authorities bring an end to these tragic events.'

So that's the written statement. Thus far our attempts to get more information from the White House including the number of deaths and injuries, how many facilities around the country are impacted, and the number of National Guard units either deployed or planning to be remain unanswered. Peter, back to you."

"Thanks, Katy. I understand that Vicki Hightower is standing outside the main gate of Tranquility with Sergeant Kenney."

Outside of Tranquility, Vicki looked small and cold next to Sergeant Kenney.

"Thank you, Sergeant, for taking the time to talk. I'm sure that you have your hands full. First of off, we have received numerous reports of deaths at Tranquility; what can you tell us?"

"Well Vicki, thanks for having me. Let me make it clear that I am speaking on behalf of Head Camp Administrator Joseph Totali in expressing our sadness and frankly shock at what has occurred. As I'm sure your viewers know by now, our staff were attacked in an unprovoked manner by perhaps a dozen camp residents. We are doing everything to restore order and expect to have the camp under complete control by nightfall. As of now, I am sorry to announce that at least eleven people have died. This includes ten camp residents and one staff member. Additionally, sixty-three people have been injured, many seriously, with at least forty-five transferred to outside facilities for medical help. We are treating at least one of the rioters at our infirmary, as she has been identified as one of the organizers of the riot and is too dangerous to transfer outside of Tranquility. I'm sorry that I can't answer any of your questions at this time. As I'm sure that you appreciate, we need all hands-on deck. Thank you."

14

Pia, the Morning After

Pia guessed that one day had passed since she last woke up in the infirmary, although she seemed to have lost most of her sense of time. She heard strange sounds, different from the usual daily diet of monotone commands and low-level chatter. Her memory of the events that put her here was slowly returning. The main thing was that her mother had not been killed as reported. She was alive.

Pia couldn't get out of her hospital bed to see what was going on, but she still smelled smoke in the air and heard the squeal of truck tires. She looked over in the direction of the camp psychologist. Their eyes met, and she began signing to ask what was happening. He looked away and acted as if he didn't see her. Pia tried waving her arms in the air to make him look at her, but they barely moved. Pia wondered if they had drugged her, or perhaps she was just numb from injuries. She checked her body, and everything seemed intact.

Pia wondered if the camp had been liberated. Had the gates fallen? Had sense returned to the land? Or was it the opposite? Soldiers were pouring in to hurt Pia and her peers. Trucks were razing buildings with inmates cowering inside. The more that she thought about the possible scenarios, the greater her will became to stand up and walk to that window. But she couldn't. Her body refused to respond. Pia tried again to get the attention of someone, anyone, to ask if anyone had been seriously hurt or even killed. Were her friends, okay?

Pia tried to stop the vicious feedback loop in her head by reminding herself that her mother was alive. She remembered the discussion that morning with the social worker, and her relief upon learning that her mom would be okay.

But as the shadows moved on the wall indicating that it was late afternoon, Pia grew sad. Hours passed meant more time that she wasn't released to be with her family. Was it possible that she would never see her mom again? She struggled to stop herself from sinking too deep into her mind's dark place, a location that Pia had occupied more often since that day on Canal Street that heralded her forthcoming detainment. How had everything gotten like this? What was going to happen to Taylor? First her dad, now Delores, and her lying there not able to talk to her little brother, hold his hand, and assure him that she wouldn't abandon him. Taylor has been through so much and he's just a kid. *Stop*, she told herself. Pia did not want to cry anymore. Not today.

She tried to focus on positive thoughts. What would she do when she got out, whenever that might be? First of all, she'd get the three of them the hell out of New York. No more living at ground zero of this war. No sir. Taylor, Delores and she would head for the hills. Perhaps they'd settle in rural Pennsylvania. Maybe she'd join the Amish. Delores had lots of talents and Taylor had a creative mind, so how about opening some type of crafts store?

The vision of that simple bucolic life was so cool and chill.

But in the next instance, Pia's mind returned to its dark place. How could she be so selfish? Would she abandon her friends here? *Stop it*, Pia told herself again. She had to be practical. She could barely help herself, so how could she help anyone here? Then she wondered if she was being weak, thinking that way. What would Charlene say?

Just then, the two infirmary doors blasted open, and a hospital bed sped past Pia. She turned her head to see but was too slow to catch much at all.

Pia's helplessness increased her frustration, and she was thus moved to get someone's attention. She tapped weakly on the side of her bed, but no one responded. Pia thought that one of the nurses was looking at her, so she signed to ask for a cup of water. Again, nothing. Had she become invisible in addition to being mute?

Pia turned her attention back to the gurney. Whoever lay in it must be in tough shape, she thought. The victim's head and upper body looked like a mummy fully covered with gauze. Why the fuck did they have the poor soul in leg irons? It sure didn't look likely that this patient was going to get out of bed anytime soon. Pia thought back to the melee and tried to inventory those she saw fighting with the guards. She vividly remembered Charlene, but Pia had seen her being walked away; she couldn't have been this badly hurt.

So, who was it? She tried to think about what TV detectives would do, if for no other reason than to keep her mind occupied. First, check for anything that the perp was wearing to make a positive ID, but there was nothing. Next step, she tried to establish the mummy's sex and decided it was definitely a woman based on the body shape and the unlikeliness that it was a guard. Admittedly, she didn't have much. She watched intently to see if the subject made any motions to try and communicate with the outside world.

As if reading her thoughts, the mystery neighbor began limply trying to sign. Finally, someone could actually see her. Pia lifted and tilted her head to get a better view of Jane Doe and signed, "Who are you?"

"It's me, Charlene. Pia, please help me."

15

The Price is Right

Everyone has a price and a breaking point too. Charlene told Pia the story of how she ended up lying next to her. How her friend summoned the strength to communicate was something Pia found inexplicable. Over one full day, Charlene gave as much information as she could about the events leading up to them lying together in the infirmary. Charlene stopped narrating during the infrequent medical visits and the constant security checks. These also offered her time to rest. Signing was exhausting in her condition.

Charlene described the network of resisters at Tranquility. "I am the leader at Tranquility with cadres spread across many of the bunks. I didn't want to tell you, not because I don't trust you, but because the wrong Tranquility staff might stop at nothing to get you to talk. It was for your safety."

Charlene went on to say that the group in Pia's cabin consisted of nine people, more than half its occupants. All members had been at Tranquility for a minimum of six months, which was the unwritten observation period to evaluate whether someone could be trusted. When a newbie arrived, they were to be observed for at least three months before any initial determination was made about their worthiness for recruitment. If the new arrival passed the initial observation, the camp network launched a more intensive observation and background check using its internal and external go-betweens. While there is no specified period of time for this second phase, it typically lasts at least another three months and often more. Charlene said that this was necessary because mistakes can have awful consequences.

The process appeared to be working well, not only for Charlene's group but throughout Tranquility. Individual groups paid off the necessary administrators and guards. That's how Charlene learned that the stampede that landed them both here was a raid planned by Sergeant Kenney at Totali's command. The STAM group had planned an uprising in response. The timing of it all, with Pia's mom being shot, was purely coincidence. Most of the staff who helped the resisters profited handsomely from sharing that sort of information, Charlene explained. But among those who were bought only some could be consistently trusted. The rule was to only use the shaky guards if you knew that they had some critical information that no one else did. But those staff would sell you out without hesitation if a better deal came along or if they needed to cover their tracks.

Charlene's closest friend in her affinity group was LJ. Pia had seen the two of them together often, but she didn't know their history. They were tight on the outside, first as activists and then as lovers. Charlene considered LJ her best friend in the world and one of the few people she could tell anything. As she signed more of her story, the puzzle as to what made Charlene run started to make more sense. Yes, she was strong, but she was also fragile in her own way. It might sound obvious, but that vulnerability was a surprise to Pia. Charlene had loved LJ deeply; maybe still did despite the news that she had been a paid informant for Totali.

"I still can't process that LJ sold us out," Charlene said with surprising composure. Pia guessed that it was just a cover for the shock her friend felt. "To make it worse, I was the cliché of the last to know. I only found out when Totali told me everything before he kicked my ass into here. He was sure to give me enough detail to make me know it was true."

LJ had been one of the most reliable members of STAM inside Tranquility, often urging others on while and stepping forward at critical junctures to help the group reach a consensus. Just two days before Pia's mom was shot, the group was stuck after months of debate about whether to proceed with a deal to smuggle in defensive weapons. Was it too risky? But what if they didn't, and the guards decided to again administer frontier justice as they had months earlier with several former inmates?

LJ helped resolve the stalemate.

"Hey comrades, it's riskier not doing anything than us sitting on our asses hoping that the guards won't brutalize us."

No one, especially Charlene would have suspected that LJ was working hand in glove with Totali, and by extension, Kenney, to flush out Charlene and the militants. After another lengthy debate, the group had agreed that the transfer of primitive knives and hand-held tools would be made and where they would be hidden to avoid being uncovered during another surprise raid.

Totali's trap was set. But less than two hours before the shipment was set to arrive, LJ grew concerned that the group had learned that it was all a setup and might know that she was at the center of it. Unable to use her usual electronic communications protocol immediately she decided to take the unusual step of leaving her post to sneak a note to Totali, calling the whole thing off. He and his team now Totalied more than fifty staff and agents inside and out waiting for the scheduled transaction. They were like hungry dogs straining on their leashes to feed.

The entire group had been in their bunks for afternoon break preparing for the transaction when Charlene heard a commotion and saw guards manhandling Pia. Charlene must have wondered what the hell was going on and whether somehow it had anything to do with the action that was planned to go down. What she could not have known was that thirty seconds before Pia had learned from another inmate about the shooting near the UN and that her mother was one of the two injured and perhaps dead. Pia had stumbled from her work assignment out into the yard and guards had sprung into action in order to avert a scene.

Charlene's loyalty toward Pia blurred her logic, and she ran outside with an iron cooking plate. She was followed closely by at least six other members who collectively leaped into the developing scrum just outside their bunk. Unfortunately for the group, Totali's team which had just been told to stand down was serendipitously still in position to strike. They would feed after all.

The rest of Pia already knew, except for the brutality that followed once the authorities got their hands on Charlene and the rest of her group. Totali demonstrated great patience in executing his plan, including transferring Charlene to an infirmary bed next to Pia. They knew that Charlene would likely tell Pia at least some of this and that other inmates would eventually learn as well. He was saying not to fuck with him, the same words that he had whispered in Charlene's ear just before he beat her into her current state.

"Pia, there is something that I don't want to tell you but need to. I had a sister, Chandra, and you remind me of her. She was a good person, and even though we were very different, we were close. Chandra was a speaker and she would stick up for me even though I told her that I didn't need her protection. I mean shit, if anyone needed protecting it was her because that bitch was too fuckin nice." With those words, Charlene's body shook with emotion as she unsuccessfully tried to shut down her grief.

"I'm so sorry," signed Pia. "Don't be sorry, be smart, Pia." "I don't understand Charlene"

"My sister was murdered, ok? I don't know why or by whom. The fucking incompetent cops never solved it. But to this day I can't help but believe that it had something to do with me. I can't put it all together but I just know. If I hadn't been so stubborn and hard and not gone out of my way to challenge all of the assholes in town who picked on me, my sister would still be alive. And fuck Pia, you remind me of her."

Pia looked away as Charlene muttered these final words. She had never felt such emotion and pain from her friend and she wanted to give her space.

16

Conference on Non-Speaker Metrics

"Welcome! My name is Dr. Sydney Moncrief, and I am here representing the United States. I would like to share greetings from President-Elect Sanchez, and to thank President Miller for his support," the man boomed from his podium.

"As you know, this is the first gathering of scientists and mathematicians from around the globe dedicated to estimating the projected growth in the population of non-speakers. Before jumping in, I would like to thank the city of Geneva for hosting this event. For the record, this gathering is academic and not political. As such, everything discussed today should be within the boundaries of scientific inquiry.

"The number that I would like us to begin with is nine percent, the approximate percentage of human babies born today who will grow to be non-speakers. Our initial calculations indicate that there will be approximately 720,000,000 non-speakers around the world by 2057. While this number may sound relatively small the scientific evidence indicates that the rate of growth has doubled since 2053, and it continues to escalate.

"So, while only an estimate, there is reason to believe that within five years, by 2062, the number will be eighteen percent, or 1,440,000,000. Should this trend continue, as appears likely, the majority of children born in the twenty-second century will be non- speakers. While difficult to ascertain with complete certainty, we believe that the numbers show that non-speakers will be the majority of the world's population in the latter part of this century, calculating births and deaths. The impact will likely be enormous.

"As I noted earlier, our charge today is not to discuss the social and political impact of this but to provide the world with the best estimates possible. Therefore, in a few minutes, I am going to ask that you choose which of the 10 work groups you would like to attend. We will gather in approximately five hours to review the highlights of your discussions and product. Have a fruitful day, dear colleagues."

Nearly seven hours later, the ten work groups were ready to report back. Fatigue ran high, as did anticipation for cocktails and play following the conference. Those who had already mentally checked out might have missed two interesting points. First, there was a strong minority opinion that the algorithm used to calculate the expansion of non-speakers would not accurately capture the evolutionary explosion. According to the minority report, the tipping point for when non-speakers would become the majority would be around 2080, not the end of the century.

The second point came from the group reporting on communication among non-speakers. There was an emerging trend away from the sign and toward a new communication system that emphasized a mixture of facial expressions, lip-smacking, body movements, and other non-signing techniques. Referred to as LOTS, it had not been widely reported or studied as it began mainly within fringe radical elements of non-speakers. The group strongly suggested closely following and studying this trend in order to better understand its emergence. The group noted that this hybrid model appeared to encourage, or even require, a high degree of collaboration between and among non-speakers. As to why it was emerging or as to its significance, the group wouldn't speculate.

17

Trying to Make Sense

Pia had finally been able to visit her mom. As she stood there in the ICU, staring at the woman she had always called The Rock, she considered the possibility that none of this was real. Perhaps she was still lying in her infirmary bed drugged up and dreaming.

The doctors had told Pia that there was no way of knowing when or if her mom would regain consciousness. But still, she was alive. Truth be told, Pia might accept a bargain with the devil to freeze time so that she could stay by her mother's side forever. At least then she would be safe. Pia's family of three would be out of harm's way. Knowing her family was safe, Pia could adapt to life anywhere, even in a hospital.

In her fantasy, Pia would keep Taylor under her wing and somehow the authorities would forget about her. She'd become a tiny footnote in the tale of Tranquility. Taylor was now fourteen, still too young to handle possibly losing his mother so soon after his dad. Was there ever a right age for that? While at the hospital she could protect Taylor, be by her mom's side, and pretend that she would never again be a prisoner.

Taylor walked up to Pia and gave her a strong nudge. She jumped and just like that the fantasy was broken.

“Hey, Ty, how are you doing? You, okay?” she signed “Sure, Pia, what could be wrong?”

“Come on, little man, you know what I mean.”

“Yes, I’m doing okay, but we don’t know whether mom will ever get better, or how long it will be before they come take you away again. So that’s not so great.”

“I know, but let me work on it,” Pia signed. “Believe me, I don’t want to go back either. With mom facing a long recovery maybe they won’t make me go back.”

“Sure, if you say so.”

Seeing her brother’s skeptical expression Pia tried to change the subject. “Ty, did you hear that the cops announced an ‘all out’ dragnet to identify and capture the monsters who shot mom?”

“Do you believe them?”

“Well, no, not really but maybe pressure will force them to arrest someone. After all, these Speaker First crazies have been hiding in plain sight all along. I saw a picture that witnesses helped police sketch artists put together. It had a lot of detail so who knows? But you’re probably right about the cops. I would hardly have known that the sketches even existed if I only watched the news. But mom’s group has been great and circulated these on the social media platforms, at least those that the government hasn't shut down."

"Pia, can I ask you something?" "Of course, anything, what is it?"

"I don't understand why you don't seem angry. Look what they did to us."

"Ty, of course, I am angry. Why would you say that?" "I don't know. Let's just drop it."

"No, we can talk about it. What do you mean?"

"I don't know. You always seem so calm. Even back when mom and dad were fighting, when they picked on you at school, always. I don't understand how you do it, because I can't. Everything sucks!"

Pia started to answer Taylor, but she realized that it wouldn't do any good. Instead, she looked away and tried to recapture the calmness that her brother was so confused by. She returned to the place where she and Taylor could sit suspended in time feeling strangely relaxed for the first time in six months. In this place of refuge, she might completely forget why she was here at the hospital and fight off the horror of flooding back.

Pia looked back at Taylor and saw that he wasn't waiting for an answer. Perhaps he realized that none was possible. Pia reminded herself that she was let out on temporary humanitarian leave, the terms of which had not been explained. She had no idea how long—or short—it might be. Despite her asking repeatedly, she had never been given much information, let alone an answer. Pia knew in her heart that she needed to prepare Taylor for the possibility that she would be returned. She just couldn't do it now with her mom in this state.

She worried that Taylor was growing away from her. It seemed impossible. He and Pia had always been so closely connected. When he was younger Taylor loved Pia's signing, gesturing, and other ways of communicating. Non-speakers often complained about the lack of understanding by straight society, especially about the increasingly complicated communication system. This existed within mixed families like the Johnstons and at times she could sense it from her mom and dad, but never from her Ty. From the time that he was old enough to understand the sign, Taylor had been able to decipher Pia's thoughts and moods easily. Despite the playfulness between them, Pia constantly worried about him. Was he growing up normal, whatever that meant? Taylor was always a bit of a homebody. He had friends, but they seemed like him: introverted and geeky. Pia remembered the night about one year before Dad killed himself when Taylor snuck into her bedroom and begged to sleep next to her. She'd asked him what was wrong, and he said everything. At the time she interpreted it as an overstimulated worry response. But why hadn't she dug into what he meant?

After her father's suicide Pia was flooded with memories and questions. Top of the list was why Taylor had often expressed worries about their father. What was it Ty saw that she didn't? Pia was troubled by remembering how she repeatedly assured him not to worry because they were a strong family.

It was just in the past few days that Pia began coming to grips with not understanding her Dad's fragility in the way that Taylor did. When she found her brother more than once sitting by the window waiting for Dad to walk home from the train station she had asked why. He told her it was because he knew that one day dad wouldn't come home. Pia had tried dissuading him from such thoughts, even laughing at it. Now she couldn't help but feel foolish.

Pia redirected her thoughts back to her status as a temporary release and what she might do to make it permanent. There had been no explanation from her Tranquility monitor, only instructions not to leave the city. So, her hope was just that, hope. She would try to stay calm and present, to maintain some level of big-picture perspective.

She found herself analyzing recent history and current events as if she could think herself out of her current predicament. She thought about Generation 1.0 and how her peers assertively— too assertively, according to some—organized early on. The narrative being spun in the media was that she and her peers did so well that people organized against them. The not-too-subtle implication was that non-speakers brought it on themselves.

Non-speakers adopted a different set of rules to define themselves, but she reasoned that they really had no other choice. Whatever the cause for the non-speaking "condition" they were who they were. No one had asked to be this way. Non-speaking wasn't an ideology. So, they could either feel like second-class citizens or be proud of this identity. The latter was certainly a better option in Pia's mind than buying into society labeling non-speakers as deficient and to be pitied, or worse, feared and hated.

To the extent that Pia could stand to think about it, she found it interesting that people hated so much the non-speakers who were proud of their identities. The truth was, from Pia's perspective, that up until recently, the movement of non-speakers hardly had a clearly articulated vision, much less a set of demands. While not exactly analogous, one might say that her peers were flying their flag. Gen Z gave themselves an ID with tattoos, and Boomers had their hairstyles, once upon a time. Still, Pia, always looking for compromise, couldn't help but question what her generation might have done differently.

It was true that over time many of her generation of non- speakers did increasingly put a stake in the ground against the out- of-control materialism and selfishness of America. At first, Pia hadn't thought of that as a political stance so much as a reaction to the way they were being treated by society. Do they say we're a drain? Well, then, let's show them what it looks like when our numbers opt out of the economy they value over our humanity. Generation 1.0 had grown up in the shadow of a series of pandemics. You would have thought that Americans were being asked to die on the beaches of Normandy when implored to get vaccinated in order to protect themselves and others. Meanwhile, they were more obsessed than ever with glitzy advertising and social media. To Pia and her peers, that's who America was.

All of this began rolling up to a principle for non-speakers growing movement. Why stigmatize them for not speaking when speaking society was not saying anything of value? If legitimate discussion about saving the planet from climate change was drowned out by the Flat Earth Society, why waste the energy it took to speak? Just do your thing, speaking America, and leave non-speakers alone. Was that why Pia and her peers couldn't speak? Who knew? Some hypothesized that the condition was nature's response to generations of language becoming a less and less authentic tool.

But still, she wondered how things got to their current state and why speakers were so afraid of non-speakers. Every time she thought that she understood, Pia realized that she hadn't a clue. She could give you the tried-and-true narrative that non-speakers threatened straight America's whole delusional story about itself. But that seemed far too simplistic. There was something else that had been percolating for decades. It felt and smelled like fear, but of what? Was it simply differences of a tribal nature? Still, she couldn't really fathom how a group of mutes would scare anyone.

18

Going Home

Pia was ecstatic on the December day her mom was being sent home. It felt like a miracle. Time had stood still in the seven weeks since Delores was shot. In one sense, Pia had welcomed that as she was still free. But the most important thing was that her mom was well enough to leave the hospital.

The Rock was not only tough but also lucky as hell. The two shots that hit Delores missed most of her vital organs. There had been considerable liver damage that her surgeons repaired, but her spleen was destroyed and the remains removed. Pia and Taylor sat outside Doctor Foz's office waiting for the pre-release meeting to review their mom's home care plan. After a brief and fidgety wait, the door opened, and the doctor waved them in.

"Well, it's the big day," said Foz. "How are you both feeling?"

Taylor looked at Pia to see if she was going to jump in.

When she hesitated, Taylor asked the big question on his mind.

"Doctor, you said last week that it might take up to one year for Mom to fully heal. Does that mean that eventually she will be the same?"

Foz looked at Pia, hoping that she would answer the question. He had previously explained to both on several occasions. Pia took the hint, turned toward Taylor, and began signing.

"Ty, remember that the doctors told us that while mom will fully recover that doesn't mean that she will ever be exactly the same."

"How do you know Pia? And how do they know? Mom is tough. Maybe she will get back to one-hundred percent. Nobody really knows for sure!"

Foz jumped in and said, "Let's not speculate now on the future but focus instead on today and this week, okay? Let me review the details of the release plan to make sure the three of us are on the same page. Your mother will sleep in your living room in a hospital bed for at least the first month. For the first week or so, it would be good for the two of you to alternate sleeping close to her on the couch, in order to keep an eye on her. I expect it will take some time for her to regain her balance, so one of you will need to monitor her nighttime visits to the bathroom. Any questions thus far?

"Okay, now let's talk about the tricky part: your mom's emotional recovery. I know that you have both met with the hospital's social work staff to discuss other aspects of the release plan. One of the issues that I'd like to check is that you are both feeling capable of helping manage your mother's doctor's visits, long-term psychological counseling, and filling and refilling prescription drugs. Are you both feeling okay with that?" The pair nodded. "Fantastic! I know that your medical insurance will cover most expenses, but the part-time home nursing help will get cut off at three months. A few weeks before it expires, someone from the social work staff will contact you to make sure that you are both ready to fully take over.

"Well then, I have another patient in a few minutes, but I do want to ask you both one last time, and I promise that it will be the last: Do you have any further questions?"

Taylor looked down at the ground. He had wanted the meeting to have ended minutes ago. Pia signed thank you to the doctor, trying to deflect from Taylor's rudeness. They both stoodup and left. The doctors had warned the siblings several times over the past weeks that progress would be slow and not to expect full recovery.

The overall damage was too severe to realistically expect a return to exactly who Delores was. Despite her toughness, hospital psychologists and social workers said that their mother had yet to come to grips with what happened and might never fully do so. When her friends visited one could see the faraway look that came to her face anytime they said something about that horrible day.

With the meeting over, Pia and Taylor made final preparations to leave. They spoke to hospital security and NYPD about the route that they would take out of the back of the hospital. Since the shooting, there has been a daily vigil in front of the hospital. Most had been supporters praying for Delores's recovery. A few had been advocating for her death and eternal damnation. The tabloids, of course, had been in a feeding frenzy: "SHOOTING SURVIVOR TO GO HOME: THE UNTOLD STORY BEHIND THE WHAT

HAPPENED." "WHY DELORES JOHNSTON CAME TO HATE AMERICA."

After a week or two the crowds had thinned, but word had leaked that Delores might be released any day now, so reporters, demonstrators, supporters, and curiosity seekers had returned in droves. NYPD was in no mood for extracurricular activities. The mayor made it abundantly clear that he expected the Johnston's move back home to be without incident and the message had flowed downstream to the lowest street cop.

At two in the afternoon, the back door opened, and an entourage of NYPD blue escorted the family into a black hatchback provided by the hospital. The crowd of nearly a hundred people in front of the hospital was unaware of the escape plan. The police had contained them within temporary barriers. Little was left to chance. In the back of the hospital, Pia helped her mom with her seat belt and waved goodbye to a few of the hospital staff. It was time. The driver looked at Pia, who nodded yes and he slowly turned out of the hospital parking lot into a long connecting back road.

Coming full circle around to the front, the car came to a red light where the family was able to gaze at the crowd across the street in front of the hospital. Pia looked at the crowd and then at her mom. Delores seemed not to notice the scene. Taylor lowered the passenger window to get a better look and was immediately told by the driver to raise it back up. He either didn't hear or chose not to.

“Raise the window, buddy, or I will.”

Taylor remained transfixed by the scene. Pia started to frantically gesture for Taylor to close it when she heard muttering coming from Delores.

“Mom, are you okay?” Taylor quickly closed the window. Delores continued to stare at it and through to the gathering on the street. Her muttering got louder.

“Mom, what’s the matter?”

The driver stepped on the gas trying to get away from whatever it was that was agitating Delores, who had escalated to a scream. Taylor started crying while helping Pia calm their mom.

And so, it went for the nearly 25-minute drive back to their apartment on the Lower East Side. Something in the crowd had caught their mom’s eye. Whether it signaled a step forward or back in her recovery, Pia could not tell. But the sound of Delores’s scream stuck deep inside Pia’s psyche.

19

New Year, Same Problems

The curtain for 2057 rose tethered to heavy bags of national angst. The shooting two months earlier had stunned the progressive movement. It, combined with increasing signs that the American and international economies were teetering, formed a toxic brew of fear.

To top it off, President Sanchez would be inaugurated on January twenty-first, and transition in a time of crisis only added to the general unease. Pia followed the events from a psychological distance as she was singularly focused on helping her mom recover and parenting Taylor. Still, she was struck as the initial paralysis of the movement following the shooting evolved into anger and then resolve. Progressives became determined to send a clear message to the Sanchez administration that despite its tough rhetoric about cracking down on non-speaker radicalism, they would not stand down. The movement would demand security for non-speakers, their families, and allies, something that the Miller administration promised but never delivered.

A broad coalition of progressive forces including M4S had announced a major event in Washington D.C. on April 1 culminating in a march to the White House. Federal authorities were on high alert, as they'd announced a series of steps to counter what they've called a dangerous escalation in threats and actions. To provide more security for the inauguration and through the planned April demonstration, the outgoing Miller administration mobilized the National Guard from five surrounding states.

While Pia found taking care of her mom and Taylor a welcome distraction from the rattle of discontent, she found it difficult to get Tranquility out of her mind. Pia repeatedly asked her liaison for information about her status but heard little. She was left to conclude that either the authorities didn't know their next move or just wouldn't say. The one nugget from her handler that only made Pia worry more was when she said the decision was somewhat in Pia's hands. Translation: play nice with the press, do not make waves, be a good girl, and she might be able to stay below the camp's radar out here. Sprinkled in was her liaison's cynical concern with how much Taylor needed her and how worried everyone was for his future.

As far as Pia's assessment of Taylor, he seemed okay but a bit distant. Yesterday out of the blue he asked her about Tranquility. "What happened there the day mom was shot? You never talked about it."

"Well, what would you like to know?"

"Like, everything, but start with how you found out and what you did."

Pia told her brother everything that she could remember about that awful day. She mentioned Charlene in passing.

"Who is Charlene? How do you know her?" He saw his sister starting to tear up and he dropped his default mask of teenage indifference and got closer to Pia placing his arm on her shoulder.

"Ty, Charlene is my friend and I think that she may be dead.

The guards may have killed her."

"What do you mean killed her? They can just do that?" "You don't understand what it's like inside that place, Ty.

They have Totali control of you. Mostly the guards left us alone, but if they think that you are a troublemaker, look out."

"Was Charlene a troublemaker?"

"No," Pia answered decisively. "Charlene was fighting for all of us. I don't agree with her on a lot of things, but she is a good person. She tried to protect me. I think that you'd like her. She comes off as super tough, but underneath, she's got a big heart and is scared like the rest of us. She tries to hide it but every once and a while you can see her vulnerability."

"Pia, I am sure that she's alive. Have you tried to find out about her? Is there any way that I can help?"

Pia looked at Taylor and smiled, feeling the pure connection that she had to him before tragedy intruded. She thought back to the last time that she saw Charlene lying nearly helpless in the hospital bed. Pia shook from the image. While she knew that it was naïve, Pia could not help but wonder how people could be so brutal to one another. It made her want to turn away from society.

Even when she tried to substitute that awful violence with images of beauty, queasiness lurked at the edges, along with something else that gnawed at Pia's psyche. It was guilt. No matter how many times she told herself that she was an innocent spectator as the news broke about Delores, Pia felt bad that she was safe, at least temporarily. Those who rushed to her side were either dead, severely injured, or locked away for God knows how long. She knew intellectually that it was not her fault. But somehow that explanation seemed to track with Charlene's audit of Pia: authentic but naïve.

20

The Crash

Pia felt energy rising from the street below her apartment. She got up from her seat on the couch opposite her mom and peered out the window. Nothing was immediately obvious, other than people seemed to be moving faster than normal. Toward the end of her street, a line was rapidly growing outside the Bank of America, and there was some pushing and shoving as people jostled for position.

Instinctively her thoughts turned to Taylor, but then she remembered that it was a teacher professional training day so no school and he would be safe in his bedroom, likely still sleeping. Pia switched on the TV to see if there was any news to explain what was happening.

"This is CNN reporter Peter Klinger here with breaking news. An economic collapse seems to be ricocheting across global markets. As news of this unprecedented event has begun to hit, we have reports of panic runs on banks and financial institutions around the country. For an explanation of what is happening, why, and the possible ramifications we have with us our financial commentator, Sean Wise."

"Thanks, Peter," said another talking head behind a different desk. "As our viewers are well aware, the stock market has been in bear territory for quite some time, and the overall U.S. economy has been in a technical recession since before the election. But what we are seeing today in international markets is something of a much larger magnitude. Governments in at least nine countries have temporarily closed their banks to prevent devastating runs. Futures markets are indicating that the U.S. stock market could be at the beginning of a historic plunge.

"As to why this is happening now and with such ferocity is open to speculation. What we do know is that the international economy has been flashing red for quite some time. Where this is headed is impossible to say. But all signs point to the economic situation only darkening over the next several months, if not longer. Fasten your seat belts folks!"

Part 2

Eruption

21

Alone Again

Pia prepared to sit out the 2057 Independence Day celebration Totali had announced. She was not feeling in a party mood given that she was back in Tranquility, separated from her mom and Taylor. Her nightmare about being sent back to the camp was at least somewhat balanced by Delores's recovery, which had gone better over the past year than she had anticipated. Ironically, it had given the authorities the green light to send her back.

As of late, Pia had begun journaling to help her manage the despair and to chronicle her life, should it end unexpectedly. If that were to happen, she hoped that someone might find it and use it for some undetermined good.

Pia began by capturing as much as she remembered about her childhood. The Johnstons must have done a great job insulating Pia because she remembered life as normal until it crashed and burned around age eight. To that point, she had felt like a typical kid despite being part of the non-speaker minority. But starting in grade three, it became clear to her that she would no longer be an average kid.

Almost overnight, the school became ground zero for a conflict that Pia didn't understand. Her mom and dad sheltered her from the worst, but some spilled over. Parents at Pia's elementary school began angrily complaining about Pia and the two other non- speakers in her class. In her journal, Pia vividly recalled Ms. Yang, her teacher, as a kind and steady voice trying to guide the class through the turmoil. Ms. Yang's motto remained etched into Pia's memory: be empathetic, courageous, and always kind to each other. Ms. Yang told the class that differences were often treated hostilely by society, but that in her class respect for every individual was non-negotiable.

The event that shook eight-year-old Pia was a protest right outside of her school led by parents. They chanted about removing non-speakers from regular classes; some were tame while others were downright mean. The one that she would never forget was "save America, remove non-speakers." It scared her in a way that she had not felt before. Her mom whisked her away while teachers formed a human barrier to keep the protesters away. But the damage had been done. Whatever childhood innocence she wanted to hang onto vanished with the angry chants.

The next chapter in Pia's life began with the police marching down Canal Street followed by the Presidential Order. It shattered whatever illusions she had left about being safe. Despite all that had transpired to that point, she still hung on to the belief that the overwhelming majority of people would ultimately do the right thing. But they didn't, at least not enough of them. American democracy did not hold. Instead, people gave into their own fears and selfishness and our institutions proved no stronger than the humans who ran them.

The third was her father's suicide. It shattered Pia's last protective layer, her family. She now felt completely vulnerable to the savagery of the world.

The final chapter began and ended with Delores's shooting. It was the final break from any hope that life in America would return to some form of normalcy. Things were too far gone to ever go back. So, Pia began embracing what was left, becoming increasingly committed to forging a new future that she hoped would be better than the past. Much of her resolve was based on a lack of alternatives. She desperately wanted to save what was left of her family and believed that activism was the only way forward.

Her only ideology to that point, if one can call it that, was decency. Be a good human. She now understood that wasn't enough, but she still wasn't sure how to act out the realization.

During the many months that Pia was home with Taylor and her mom, she held onto the hope that her days at Tranquility were over. Pia took her prison liaison at her word to get small and be invisible to the outside world, which was easier said than done. The press continued to milk the Delores shooting saga for all it was worth. She could not control what others said about her and her family. They were non-consenting actors in an out-of-control play.

Still, the months passed and Delores slowly regained some of her strength. She never spoke to Pia about her psychological pain, but it was obvious. Meanwhile, Taylor seemed distant and moody. In Pia's eleventh month at home, the visits from nurses and social workers assigned by the government increased dramatically. In retrospect, she should have been suspicious. Sure enough, one gloomy day her liaison arrived along with a stranger from New York State's penal system. They told Pia that her mom had been deemed strong enough to take care of Taylor without outside intervention. Therefore, her humanitarian leave was immediately rescinded. Pia was given five minutes to pack. Taylor was at school, so she did not even get to say goodbye.

Pia was back in detention before lunch. A new interagency task force had established several levels of detainment, and Tranquility was deemed to be a minimum-risk facility. Pia was rated a three on a scale of one to five, meaning that she was considered the highest risk possible within Tranquility, which didn't hold fours and fives. She theorized that her high-risk rating was only because the authorities feared the symbolism as the daughter of Delores, now a wounded living icon. Charlene had been sent to a different prison as a level five. The authorities had succeeded in having the courts declare Pia's friend an imminent threat. But at least she was alive, which Pia had only learned upon her return to Tranquility.

Within weeks of her return, hints began circulating that something big was about to happen. The buzz was about an international conference coming up in Jakarta, Indonesia. It was named "Vision 2060: Building a Sustainable Future." People at Tranquility had lots of opinions as to its significance and, of course, conspiracy theories. The prevailing one was that the conference was window dressing for a further crackdown against non-speakers. The more militant inmates warned anyone who would listen that the clampdown would be more sophisticated, involving a new level of propaganda. Totali announced that the event would be carried live within the camp, which only heightened feelings of anxiety and dread.

The next day the guards herded Pia and the other inmates in their seats by 1:55 p.m., five minutes before the international simulcast was set to start. Reportedly, more than 100 countries around the world will be participating. Pia wished that she could treat today as a brief respite from the numbing tedium of camp life, but she couldn't. Her stomach hurt and her mouth burned like acid as she awaited the big countdown to show time. And then the clock struck two and the big screen came to life.

"Hello around the world to literally billions of global citizens from 111 countries," came a voice from thousands of miles away. "I am President Zhao, speaking to you from the People's Republic of China. The past eighteen years have been trying. If we are to survive, let alone thrive, it will be together, not in competition with each other. That is why the leaders of the Vision 2060 coalition made up of Indonesia, the United States, the European Union, Brazil, and the PRC, supported by the United Nations General Assembly, are simultaneously addressing you today. In a few minutes, you will hear separately from the leaders of your own countries or blocks. Your leaders feel that it is abundantly important that every citizen of the world understand the threat posed by the two existential crises facing our planet: global warming and disunity among and between the speaking and non-speaking citizens of the world. That is why today you will be asked to make sacrifices to ensure our future survival and prosperity.

"While some may think of coordinated worldwide action as somehow scary, let me assure you that what will discuss today is anything but. Rather, our collective action is to ensure that no nation or group of nations uses the crisis as an excuse to seek an unfair competitive advantage. With a spirit of cooperation, we will not only survive together but thrive. With that, I want to wish each of you a great day of conferring with your leaders and I look forward to addressing you at the conclusion of today's historic event in exactly ninety minutes. Thank you. Now, we begin the hard work. We will resume in five minutes with national and regional sessions."

Totali broke the spell by rising from his seat and leering menacingly at the assemblage.

"Dear residents of Tranquility, thank you for your attention thus far," he said smugly. Barely able to contain a smile, he urged everyone to listen carefully. "What the President is about to say will have a major impact on your lives. Seize the opportunity." He slinked off, and familiar faces appeared on the screen.

"Hello, Americans. This is President Patricia Sanchez addressing you from the Oval Office. As President Zhao mentioned in his opening remarks, this is a truly historic day. What I am about to speak with you about is the culmination of fourteen months of international and domestic discussion involving thousands of the most knowledgeable experts and patriots from around the world.

"In the United States, I have spoken with the titans of industry, science, medicine, religion, philosophy, and economics, along with every day citizens like your selves. It is no exaggeration to say that my consultations and those of your government have reached into every facet of American society and the [illegible]

"I would like to repeat the word *community,* because without your complete support, America and the world will fail, and that will mean catastrophe for all of us. By community, I refer to the thousands of grassroots institutions and organizations that everyday Americans rely on. Let me take a minute to name just a few that I and your government have consulted: the NAACP, La Raza, the American Red Cross, the Knights of Columbus, the Jewish Interfaith Task Force, the United Way, the Cooperative Circle, The Big Picture, Forum Force, Meaningful Connections, Next Door Nation, and United We Stand. Please take a few minutes after the conclusion of today's conference to examine all of the names of organizations that have made today a truly historic event.

"In a moment I am going to turn you over to Vice President Wei, who will share with you some vital information. But first, I do want to thank you in advance for your full support. It will be vital in putting America at the forefront of the Vision 2060 international movement. As you know, it has and will always be that America's greatness is a direct result of the courage and selflessness of our citizens. Generations of Americans have risen to the challenge going back to events like the American Revolution, World War II, the Apollo Missions, and the invention of the internet. And, *we* will do it again, beginning *today*.

"In closing, I want to applaud and second the words and sentiment expressed by President Zhao. The world stands as one today. At the same time the specifics that I am about to announce represent America's own strategy for contributing to the international vision. At the conclusion of this historic event, I have ordered all branches of government to begin taking concrete steps to fully implement the main pillar of Building an American Future, the reintegration of non-speakers into the American mainstream as part of revitalizing our economy. I will now turn you over to Dr. Wei, who will help explain the specifics. She has assembled an incredible panel that will explain the high-level aspects of Building an American Future and answer a handful of preselected questions.

Thank you, President Sanchez. I want to quickly turn it over to the experts on this interactive panel as you have been patient listening to several speeches. Let me begin by framing the key challenge for our panelists. President Sanchez has tied America's future economic expansion to reintegrating as many non-speakers as possible into the mainstream of society. What do you believe should be the criteria for doing so? And if I may be slightly provocative, what metrics might you use for determining which non-speakers are simply too dangerous to re-integrate at this time? Let me start with Dr. Ezra Cooper from the Rand Corporation. Dr. the stage is yours."

22

Separate and Not Equal

Following the Visions 2060 event, life slowed at Tranquility. The summer heat combined with the crash of staff adrenaline following the high-stakes conference resulted in a few quiet weeks. That all ended with a shocking announcement from Totali. Camp Tranquility would be dramatically reducing the number of inmates in the coming weeks. That was it for information from the chief. It was classic Totali: keep them guessing to provoke anxiety.

Pia did her best to gather information. The problem was that it mostly consisted of conjecture, conspiracy theories, and false information planted by Totali and his guards. During Pia's first tour of Tranquility, Charlene and her comrades were usually able to gather reliable information for the right price. This was no longer the case. Totali's control over Tranquility was now complete. In addition to getting rid of Charlene and her comrades, he had transferred a handful of guards believed to be less than loyal.

Pia did hold one card. During her time in the infirmary after the prison rebellion and before she was granted her temporary release, Sergeant Kenney had come by to see how she was doing. It had surprised Pia because she and the sergeant had but the briefest of communication prior to those three terrible days.

She hoped to be able to pull Kenney aside during one of his tours of work details. But she would have to be lucky and careful. It was rumored that Totali had the sergeant on a short leash, so any discussion would have to be out of sight of Totali's many sets of eyes. Despite the risk, she had to try, as the unknown was slowly eating away at her. Night times were particularly hard with images of her dead father, wounded mother, and angry Taylor dancing across her mind as she tried to fall asleep.

Finally, opportunity knocked. Pia was finishing changing fluorescent bulbs when Kenney came ambling through the door. Her workmate was off on another assignment, so Pia was alone and pounced. Kenney had nodded at her as he entered but was about to exit as quickly as he came in when Pia clapped to get his attention.

"Pia, do you need something?" asked Kenney.

She began slowly signing asking for information about the changes Totali had announced.

"Pia, I can't tell you anything more than the chief told everyone," he said with a sigh. "You know that."

"Sergeant, please! You were so kind when my mom was shot, and now I am scared. What are they going to do with us, with me? I want to go home to be with my family."

"Pia, if I could help you, I would, but I can't. There is a new president and policies are changing. Exactly how I don't know. I can say that beginning next week your status and that of others will become clearer. Try to stay positive and don't make waves. This is a dangerous time for everyone." With that Kenney was out the door before Pia could ask any more questions.

A week later, Pia was told by a guard that she would be interviewed by a government official the very next day. She began signing to ask what the interview would be about, but all that she got back was a menacing expression, so she dropped it. After another restless night interview day arrived, but interview for what?

At the appointed hour, Pia was taken to the main administration building and locked in a small room. A few minutes later, a man entered and identified himself as Agent Evans from the Federal Bureau of Investigation. He was accompanied by a young woman whom Pia assumed would translate.

"Let's get started, Pia. I have fifty other inmates to interview today. I am going to record this session. First off, please confirm that your name is Pia Johnston and that you are twenty-two years old."

"That is correct, Mr. Evans," signed Pia. "But why am I here? What is going on?"

"I'll get to that in a moment, but first what can you tell me about Ms. Charlene Vicnacious?"

"I don't understand. What does Charlene have to do with this? I haven't seen her since I was released after my mom was shot."

"Ms. Johnston, let me assure you that the more you cooperate the more likely you will be to see your mother and brother again."

"I told you, I haven't seen or heard from Charlene in months."

"Okay, but what about before that? You shared a bunk with her. Do you know that she is considered a terrorist by the FBI? If you knowingly hide information about her, you can be charged too."

"I told you; I don't know a thing other than she helped me when I first arrived."

"She helped you? Helped how? "

"She was worried about me. She thought that I was too, too—" Pia hesitated.

"Too what?"

"Too soft," Pia signed.

"That is all well and good, Ms. Johnston, but you must know more about her and her terrorist friends. I mean, they infested Tranquility. What did Charlene and her comrades talk about?"

"I don't know, I wasn't one of them. I mean, I liked Charlene, but I didn't share her beliefs."

"So, you knew that she was a radical? What did she say or do that made you think that?"

"Nothing in particular. Everyone knew."

"Listen, Pia, I am trying to help you, but this is not going well. You either cooperate or you can forget about seeing your family again."

Pia looked away not wanting her interrogator to see that she was upset. When she turned back to face him, she wore a new expression: determination.

"I have told you what I know," she signed. "It is the truth. If that is not sufficient, then I don't know what else I can do. I desperately want to get out of here and be with my family. I am no threat to anyone. Please let me go."

"Unfortunately, Ms. Johnston, we can't do that. As you probably know by now, Tranquility will be converted to a max facility and everyone else will be transferred to the West. Of course, a few will be released back into society. But not you. We will release only those who are completely beyond suspicion, and you aren't in that category".

"So, Agent Evans, you never intended to release me no matter what I told you, right?"

"Thank you, Ms. Johnston, this interview is officially over."

Pia later learned that she would be sent to one of the most remote destinations on the U.S. mainland, the Wind River Indian Reservation. She felt depressed and hopeless. The following Saturday morning at five o'clock sharp, she would be placed on a train operated by the United States Penal System along with 199 other inmates. Two days later, she would arrive at the Wind River Indian Reservation in remote Wyoming.

Pia couldn't jettison the growing feeling that she would never see Taylor and her mom again. Despite occasional access to TV and radio, Pia and the [illegible] other inmates were being loaded on trains, or where they were going. Did speaker citizens know what was going on? Was there any remaining resistance, or had it been completely silenced?

Feeling alone and hopeless was not conducive to Pia thinking creatively about options. So, what was left was complying and getting on the train. She briefly fantasized about going on a hunger strike or perhaps lighting herself on fire to garner maximum attention. But would anyone see it? No, it would be a performance without any audience.

Instead, when they came for her, she would simply climb aboard the train to nowhere. Vision 2060 was now coming into view. President Sanchez's plan would be to dump tens of thousands of non-speakers across the most inhospitable parts of the Western United States in the hope that they would never be heard from again. How diabolically clever; to double down on screwing Native peoples by using their land to make non-speakers disappear. At least that was Pia's conclusion.

Ever since Pia learned her fate it had been even more difficult to sleep, but never more so than this night, her last at Tranquility. It was three in the morning, and time had come to a halt as she waited to hear the word that it was time to leave. She wondered if this is what it would feel like to sit in a cell awaiting execution, or if that was a little dramatic. But for Pia, it really was hard to imagine her life continuing in any real sense thousands of miles away on remote lands separated from her family. She might as well be sent to die.

Her self-pity was eventually broken by the words, “Wake up and move to the van to which you have been assigned.”

Pia was as prepared as she was going to be.

“Take nothing but the suitcase and belongings that we have approved and screened. Any attempt to do otherwise will result in immediate punishment. Are there any questions?”

Before anyone could possibly formulate one, Pia and the other 199 were hustled off onto one of the twenty-numbered vans lined up at the camp gate. In less than ten minutes, they were on the move. Pia felt nauseous, but she didn’t want to give the guards the pleasure of seeing her retch.

The drive to the train station took less than thirty minutes, and the 200 were methodically transferred from van to train. How impeccably efficient her captors were, thought Pia. They had left nothing to chance. She daydreamed about running for the hills. Would they shoot or just shackle her to the seat?

She thought about Charlene. There had been rampant rumors about life in level five camps for those the authorities considered the most dangerous.

Compared to those horror stories, life at Tranquility had been brutal only in its isolation and lack of hope.

Pia told herself that she was ready, sufficiently numb for the journey. But once they pushed her down into her seat on the train, she lost it. Tears streamed down her cheeks accompanied by a silent scream. *Mom, please help me! Don't let them take me away*. Eventually, she caught her breath and looked around to see if anyone had seen her meltdown. She hoped not but just then a hand from behind patted her on the shoulder. Pia turned to see a face that she recognized from the Tranquility mess hall but whose name she didn't know. Pia felt embarrassed and continued to look away, but the person passed over a tissue. Pia turned to thank the person not wanting to appear rude, and Desiree Johnson Lawrence introduced herself.

"I know this sucks," signed Desiree, with a warm smile. "But you are not in this alone. We will all need to take care of each other. When we get to Wind River let's talk."

Desiree switched to LOTS for that last part, piquing Pia's curiosity as to what she wanted to talk about.

Pia looked around at the mix of expressions on the faces of her fellow inmates. She saw loss and hopelessness but also looks of resolve. She again wished that she could be tougher, not to fight, but simply to not suffer. Pia thought that she had hit rock bottom days ago, but right now, she felt as empty and alone as she had only once before when she learned that her father had killed himself. Pia searched for her mother in her memory as a way to comfort herself. She found the perfect one, taking the D train with Delores to shop for presents on the eve of her eighth birthday. She transported herself into her carefree child's thought process as her eyes slowly closed.

What fun! Mom and I are going shopping for my birthday gifts. These are going to be real ones—not the baby things I used to get. Next week I turn eight, and in five weeks I start third grade. That means I get to read real books in school! I liked my teachers last year and hope my new one is good. The work might get harder, and only Tiffany and I are non-speakers. But everyone at my school is nice, so it should work out.

Soon we will get on the subway which is so cool. I love when the train leaves the station and everything goes black inside the tunnel. When baby Taylor is with us, I make him laugh by opening and closing my eyes as it gets lighter and darker in the train. And those screechy train wheels! Like chalk on my teacher's board.

My mom tells me to ignore the few meanies we see. The last time the three of us went out she had to yell at a group of teenagers. I didn't understand it, but my mom told them shame on you after they seemed to be making fun of me. The oldest one was wearing a shirt with a picture of the old guy with yellow hair who my dad told me had been president a long time ago. When we get to the toy store uptown, it's going to be so cool. Mom will let me get two big birthday gifts. I'm going to spend lots of time looking around because once I decide, that's it for this year.

I wish Dad could come but he's busy working. Mom works too, but not every day. She's something called a design engineer; not the kind that drives the subways. I don't remember, but Dad tells me that mom used to work lots and lots but now stays home more because she loves Taylor and me. Dad does too but I guess he earns lots of money working.

Sometimes I feel a little sad. I don't really want to be like everyone else, but I wish that there weren't mean people to make me feel bad about not speaking. Mom and Dad tell me those people only make fun of me because they are scared. I don't really understand that, but I'm sure my parents are right.

My Dad's work name is Dr. Johnston. He's not the kind of doctor who helps sick people. He works on people's feelings. Something called a psychologist. It must be hard working on feelings. My teachers do that. Like last year, there was a big fight in our class. Not the kids, but the parents. I think it had something to do with mixing me and Tiffany with the reading groups, but I don't really know. Mom told me that it had nothing to do with us, that it was just grown-up problems. I wish that Dad didn't work so hard. When he comes home at night, he seems different than in the morning when we are having breakfast. Mom says it's just that he gets tired of helping people.

Mom is great. I have started calling her The Rock after some guy I see on TV from real old movies. If I don't understand something she'll always explain it to me so that I can understand.

She startled awake. Her shirt was soaked around the neck. Pia looked around and sadly remembered where she was. She searched for the dream, but it was gone.

23

Free My Daughter

"My name is Delores Miller Johnston," she read to the reporters assembled. "I am the mother of Pia Johnston. I am reading this statement to you today because the authorities will not confirm that my daughter Pia is about to be transferred to the Wind River Reservation in Wyoming or why that decision was made.

"Some of you know the story of our family, but for those who don't, here goes: Pia was imprisoned at Tranquility four years ago for no reason other than she is a non-speaker. At the time Pia was not an activist. Two years ago, I was shot by extremists during a peaceful protest of moms asking that their non-speaking sons and daughters be released. Despite President Sanchez's recent promise to release nearly all non-speakers, her administration is doing the opposite. Today, I demand that she keep her word and that we as a nation rediscover basic decency and respect for human rights.

"I and others have tried to work in good faith with the authorities including, at their request, refraining from protesting. I will end that now that the government has not kept its word. Let me be clear. The wounds that I suffered that day outside of the United Nations will likely never fully heal. But that will not stop me and others from fighting for our children. Today, I call on all Americans to stand up against injustice. Whoever you are, whatever your ideology, tell President Sanchez to keep the promises she made and free our children. I will take just a few questions and I ask that afterwards you respect the privacy of my son Taylor."

A familiar hand shot up.

"Mrs. Johnston, this is Vicki Hightower, CNN. When was the last time that you heard from your daughter, and how do you know that she is being transferred to Wind River?"

"I have not spoken with Pia in over two months. I found out just last night about the transfer through clergy, who have been helping parents such as me keep track of their children."

The next reporter didn't bother raising his hand.

"Taylor, this is James Francesco from Fox News. Have you spoken recently to your sister? What did she say? Is she being treated fairly?"

Delores intervened before Taylor could say anything.

"Mr. Francesco, please do as I requested and direct your questions to me. My son has been through a lot and is only fourteen."

"Okay, Mrs. Johnston then let me redirect to you. Is it possible that your daughter is one of the few detainees that President Sanchez classified too dangerous to be released?"

"No. My daughter has never been an activist, and our family has made it clear to the authorities that our only motivation is for her to be released so that we can be reunited."

"Okay but just a quick follow-up," the reporter persisted. "How would you know whether Pia is in fact not a threat given that you say that you have not spoken to her in several months?"

"Well, it's pretty simple. She has never been and there is no reason that this would change especially given that we had been privately assured by the authorities that she would be released. Let me further state that I believe the sole reason that the government is acting in such bad faith is because they see me as a symbol of resistance simply because I was seriously wounded and became a figurehead to some. I never chose to be seen in that light and have resisted making public appearances since that awful day."

"Okay, that's all folks, and we ask that you respect the family's privacy," a kind-faced older man interjected.

"Excuse me, sir, who are you?" James Francesco asked dismissively.

"I am the Reverend McDonald, and I'm serving as a spokesman for the family. That's all. Thank you!"

24

The Totali Treatment

(One week after Pia's transfer)

Sergeant Kenney

"Sergeant Kenney, please take a seat. How are you?" "Fine, Chief. Thanks."

"I hope that your wife and young son are doing ok, especially under these difficult circumstances. It has obviously been hard for you with your son, a non-speaker and all."

I stay silent, vowing to myself that I won't rise to his bait. "For the last two months, I have been engaged in high-level discussions with my superiors in the penal system and the intelligence community," Totali drones on. "I have called you here to inform you that those consultations have borne fruit and there are going to be major changes.

"My vision and that of my colleagues is that 18 months from now, we will be rid of most non-speakers from the camps. They will be sent to live in autonomous zones where each can self-actualize, or whatever it is that experts such as yourself call it. Of course, there will be a handful who despite our best efforts at rehabilitation remain simply too dangerous to be re-settled. I have agreed to take the lead in implementing a strategy for those few who simply can't or won't fit into independent living."

I think of Tommy, and how he doesn't need to "self- actualize" so much as to be left the hell alone to grow up.

"I hope that you will be gracious enough to acknowledge that I have been fair to you despite our differing philosophies," he sneers. I don't like where this is going. "But frankly, I don't care that you are not my greatest fan. You may not realize it Sargent, but you are not the only one with a family. You see I have two daughters at home, who thank god, both speak. Outside of my career, they are my life. And I want them to grow up in an America where they will be free to be who they want to be and not be commanded by some new order determined by non-speakers. More and more it will be up to me since my wife is very sick, not that it's any of your concern. I say all of this simply to say that it's time for you to get your head out of your ass and think of the bigger world.

"Even with your lefty ideology and dislike of me, I was easily able to put that aside until the riot a year ago. Before then, I didn't really question your loyalty to me or whether you would do your job. But I must be honest with you; that is no longer the case.

"As you know, I have been aware of your son's condition for quite some time. Despite your potential conflict of interest, I never used it against you. While it is true that I do not fully understand what makes non-speakers tick, I never believed that it should affect our supervisory relationship. Like you, I am a trained professional. Our job is to rehabilitate where possible while providing security for society where we can't. So, it saddens me to say that you and I seem to be going in opposite directions."

This motherfucker.

"I have in my hand a dossier on your recent performance," Totali said, brandishing a folder. "You will find outlined in it dozens of instances in which you chose to take action inconsistent with my example, probably because of your progressive view of rehabilitation. In other words, you chose your own ideology over prison system protocols. In more than a few instances, you ignored my direct instructions. Perhaps the most egregious example was your questioning of my treatment of inmate Charlene. You may consider me to be harsh or even cruel, yet let me remind you that everything that I did was consistent with the prison system's manual on levels of engagement. Once I and senior leadership determined that Charlene and others were an imminent threat to civil society through their revolutionary sentiments, everything that I did and ordered was proper.

Regardless, I am not here to explain myself to you but rather to say that you will be given a new assignment next week as part of the vision that I sold my superiors. While I have more than adequate cause to fire you, I have no desire to do so. Frankly, Sergeant, you are far too valuable to fire. Over the next few years, while we're crushing the terrorists per order of President Sanchez, I and other high-level folks will use you as a symbol of our new gentler and kinder treatment of compliant non-speakers.

So, here at Tranquility, you will remain, not as the top guy, but rather as a traveling symbol we can trot out for public relations from time to time. I know this change may sound unsettling, but I would ask that you consider your generous pension before doing anything rash. Life cannot be easy for the three of you considering that you and your [illegible] wife are trying to raise a [illegible] son. My replacement will be Jack Harper, a man for whom I have complete respect. As for me, I have been tasked with being a key agent in charge of counterterrorism. Do you have questions, Sergeant? No? Then, let me invite you to get the fuck out of my office."

Totali's words ricocheted around my brain. I'm about to let loose on him but common sense intervenes at the last second. I mentally formulate an unspoken retort.

Commandant Totali, I won't quit. But it is not that your pompous ass is right. Sure, I want to take care of my family. Who wouldn't? But the bigger thing is that I can taste and feel danger coming for all of us and there may be no place to hide. So, I am thinking that I need to hold onto the few remaining cards that I might be able to play. If there is no place where I can hide Tommy and Mandy, why not stay right here in plain sight?

As I leave his office, I think about the big changes that Totali was alluding to. Events over the past three years in the country and at Tranquility seem to have been constantly shifting in search of a landing zone. But my sense is that things might quickly deteriorate over the coming months. Sanchez, I think, intends to come down hard while trying to appear conciliatory. I am frightened but determined to protect my family. If things do completely unravel, I will protect them.

The big shots want to "use" me, the progressive black man, well so be it. But I will be using them, too. Perhaps I am just fooling myself, and I'm simply too scared to say my piece and quit, but it doesn't feel that way. Can I make Tommy and Mandy safer if I play by their rules? I don't know, but I feel certain that it is my best and maybe only play for now.

As for the progressive speaker movement, God only knows. I fear for that activist mother I saw on TV recently and her daughter Pia who was at Tranquility. She's probably safe short term but what happens when she's out of the news for a few weeks? But I can't save them and the others.

I need to keep my focus on my family, though. I especially worry about Mandy. She's a fighter, but that can cloud her logic. I know that sometimes she questions my resolve—not about fighting for Tommy and her, but taking a stand in general—but I feel strong; stronger than I have in quite some time. I never had many illusions about the American system. How could I, as a Black man? No, I see you America. I always have. I still have hope, but I don't have illusions as to how brutal you can be. I will need to be smart. No stupid risks in order to make myself feel like I am doing the right thing. I will protect my family AND get ready for the coming fight, but it will be on my own terms and timing.

For now, I am not going to try to win Mandy over to my strategy. My first, second, and third priority is to keep everyone safe. That means making sure that her activism doesn't get her jailed—a real possibility if she knows how bad things have gotten for me at work—and that Tommy isn't taken away from us and sent someplace for non-speakers. Whatever Totali has in that dossier on me, I know that he will use it when it best suits him to hit me where it hurts. Still, that's not my biggest concern; I can't stop worrying that Mandy will lose faith in me. Will she just count my taking Totali's shit as more evidence that I sometimes hide my head in the sand?

Maybe. But I fear that the alternative for the three of us is so much worse.

At least with my new job description, I will have lots of leisure time on my hands. I'll try and use it to my advantage. But first, I need to convince Totali and others that I will play nice. Yes, Sergeant Kenney will go out there and sell your lies to the public. I will bide my time, but only for now.

25

Badlands

The train stopped. It was still dark outside so Pia couldn't see much beyond the outline of a platform, but she thought that this must be Wyoming.

Pia had spent the last 48 hours in a sleepy blur for which she was grateful. She'd rather feel anything than the panic of two days ago. No one in the train moved, despite the fact that it had come to a complete stop. The guards remained impassive, and the inmates went back to sleep or at least pretended to.

Pia opened her eyes again thirty minutes later. She felt the sun through the glass. The landscape from the window on her left was beautiful, huge, and empty. There were so many shades of light, and the distant hills and mountains seemed to shimmer, fade, and change again in the blink of an eye. She imagined, not for the first time, wandering off to the distant mountains where she would make friends with the animals, build a perpetual fire in a safe cave, and live happily ever after far away from people.

Pia didn't think that she would get bored, not out here with so much to explore. She would transform herself from a New York City girl into a frontierswoman. And maybe in time, once the insanity passed, Taylor would join her. Pia didn't know whether her mother would be strong enough to survive out here, but by then Taylor would be a strong young man. The two of them would grow old in the foothills and mountains of Wyoming, isolated and content. Maybe they would find a way to secretly see their mother after things died down.

"Okay, settlers, time to move out," someone shouted, and just like that Pia snapped back to reality. The group was herded into vans. They were much funkier than the ones the authorities used on the front end of the trip, perhaps reflective of the poverty they were about to enter. The driver looked to be Native American, and most of those around the train station seemed to be as well. The occasional white guys appeared to be authority types with IDs hanging from their necks. They look bored.

It was time to complete the journey. The driver put the pedal to the metal, and off they went. The landscape remained stunning but the people the van passed looked impoverished; their structures barely houses. The weather was nice, mild, probably in the sixties with sunshine and little wind. But from what Pia had read, the weather in this section of Northeast Wyoming could be brutal so she was thankful that it was September.

Pia tried to study the route that the driver was taking so that she might reverse direction if the opportunity struck. One of the problems was that she could barely see out of the windows as the dust from the unpaved road was now enveloping the windows. Ninety minutes later they stopped at a community settlement. Pia realized that she had no restraints. She guessed it was because there was no place to go. No one cared if she did run away.

The van driver yawned, got out of the van, and headed for the main building. From the outside, it looked like some type of store. Pia waited for someone to tell her what to do, where to go, anything. She saw the driver talking to several people through the window until finally the door to the building opened and a large man walked toward the van.

"Good morning! Welcome to Wind River. My name is Hayatou. I am one of the Elder Leaders of the Wind River Reservation and this is my son, Betide. He is a non-speaker like you. I think that you know by now that the United States government has compensated several Native tribes to find you a home here on the reservation. We did not choose this for you. Your government did, and my people will do what we can to help you resettle."

Pia liked his directness and was relieved that he seemed nothing like the brutal, Machiavellian guards she had left at Tranquility.

"It won't be easy, but we believe that in time each of you will learn the ways of the land and how to survive. Your government has paid the tribes a reasonable amount of money to take you in. However, the arrangement is not for us to take care of you, to watch you, to guard or punish you. We have endured much since we were pushed off our lands over a century ago and now must focus on our own survival. Still, should you choose to remain, you will find many who are willing to teach you. Each of you must decide your own fate."

Hayatou gestured to ten medium-sized wooden structures and one much larger in the middle. From a distance, they appeared sturdy but quite simple. Metal structures escaped from each roof appearing to be exhaust for fireplaces.

"The Bureau of Indian Affairs contracted us to build the shelters that you see," he continued. "There is enough space to accommodate the two-hundred or so of you. There is enough food for sixty to ninety days, clothing to keep you warm, and other basic provisions. When I stop talking in a moment, each of you can take your belongings and go to whichever shelter you choose. As I said, you are free. Your new home is not like the camps you came from. No one will order you around. You will be in charge of yourselves. But other than the rations that the government has provided, your long-term survival is up to you. The food that you will eat once the rations are gone and the big snows fall will be up to you. Before that time, you may also want to make these basic shelters better or even build some new ones. Again, it's your choice. Good luck and I will check in on you again in about one week."

26

Camp 99

Charlene

I have stopped counting the days. Instead, I spend all of my waking time focusing on keeping myself sane. In some ways, I find it easy. The truth is I have always been fueled by anger. I depend on it to keep me motivated.

Many blame their parents for whatever shit they need to work out as adults, and I am no exception. When I was nine or so I played a game at home with Mom in which she was an unwitting participant. I pretended that she was a guard in a prison, and I was her captor.

That lingering anger from my childhood may have crowded out my overall development, but it serves me well here. This is not to suggest that I enjoy my time at Camp 99, or that I don't feel terror a lot of the time. But my outrage has served me well as a north star while I try to survive. I dream of revenge and justice, with the order of those two words always fluid. Commandant Totali and his merry crew would love nothing more than to break me and ship what remains off to some remote asylum. But he underestimates me and my burning inner core. He doesn't understand that I'm not scared of him, only of my inner weaknesses. On the inside, I am racked with worry. I can feel it in the knot in my guts and the quivering of my face.

It is my bad luck that despite being sent here once I recovered from Totali’s beating, he has been promoted. He now oversees one-quarter of the non-speaker camps and gets to roam as he pleases. He let me know just today that he set aside time for another one-on-one “session.”

At our last tete-a-tete, Totali introduced me to his new dog, Marshall. This particular canine was none too friendly, as his snarls indicated before he “slipped” from Totali’s grasp and took a large chunk out of my leg. As I was crying on the floor in shock and pain, Totali calmly explained that Camp 99 had undergone some painful budget cuts.

“So sorry, Charlene, but due to the financial shortfall, I cannot provide first aid at this time.”

With Marshall indicating that he was more than ready for another go, I agree to answer all of Totali’s questions.

“Who else was involved in the planning of the rebellion at Tranquility? Who from the outside helped? From the inside? I am also interested in our mutual friend Sergeant Kenney. You see, I have a detailed dossier on the good sergeant, so it will do you no good to cover up for him.”

“Totali, I know nothing about Sergeant Kenney. If you have a specific question about him, please ask it otherwise…”

Before I could even finish signing, Totali theatrically demonstrated extreme difficulty holding onto Marshall’s leash. So, I resumed signing. Fast.

"Kenney is seen as an honest guy. Your problem isn't him but the other staff. We bought shit from Davis, but I guess you already know that."

I give him quite a bit, of which less than five percent is true, and nothing is actionable. But I doubt that my veracity even matters to him. Totali gets joy from playing this twisted game with me.

"Okay, Charlene, sadly you have committed the cardinal sin: you've bored me. But I'll be back. I'll never forget you."

As the door closed after that visit, I cried into my hands with relief that the monster was temporarily gone. The gouge on my leg continued to bleed but I found enough crap on the floor to stuff the wound. Later that night, the prison nurse came to see me with antiseptics and wraps. Apparently, Totali had a change of heart and decided that he wanted more opportunities to play with me and perhaps even obtain some information that would please his bosses. My dying of infection at this time would be inopportune.

I do not think that Totali and his bosses have a deep understanding of our growing movement. They have unearthed small bits and pieces but don't have a full picture. Some who they have jailed are, in fact, key activists, but most are peripherals or even innocents. Despite having few resources compared to the authorities, we survive partly by using their hubris against them. I do not know how much of this comes from a belief that non- speakers are not their equals, and how much is just the arrogance of power.

Either way, I am thankful for their obtuseness and complete unwillingness to learn LOTS. I can say with some certainty that many guards and other speaking staff seem visibly uncomfortable with our brand of communication. While they mocked our signing, at least it was a communication mode they knew from popular culture and one that many understood. But this trend away from words seems to scare them.

Much of this is just speculation on my part. But I think many speakers, including the guards and staff inside Camp 99 can sense a future with them slowly losing control and they don't like it. For some, this discomfort translates to avoidance. For others, anger. How this phenomenon will play out over the coming years, I do not know. But there has been quite a shift from the early days of pitying us for our "disability" to resenting and fearing.

I will continue to try to survive here with my anger as a salve. It will help me manage my fear of Totali and what feels like the unending darkness of my captivity. But outside in the shadows, we grow more powerful. There are far more collaborators than the authorities imagine. I, for one, welcome President Sanchez's thinly veiled strategy of isolating us in faux independent zones. It gives us the physical space to plan a new country within the failed one.

My sources say that Pia has been relocated. I miss her and hope that she is staying strong. I can only imagine how she is feeling, having been sent thousands of miles from her family. Pia has an inner strength that she does not fully recognize. Perhaps it scares her for some reason, and that explains the reserve that I felt from her at Tranquility. Yet I hold her dear. The few days that I spent lying next to her in the Tranquility infirmary gave me the support I needed to survive and for that, I will always remain grateful.

Looking back to the horrible days that followed our spontaneous uprising, I am certain that Totali expected me to die quickly. How clever to place me next to Pia in order to show her the consequences of resisting, to terrify her by making her watch me perish. How disappointed he must have been that I didn't die. I assume that Totali will kill me soon enough, either intentionally or because he cannot control the monster within. It might happen via too much dog or excessive water. Who knows? What I do know is that such a small man will never break me.

27

Staying Alive

It had been four days since Pia was dropped at Wind River. She had gone from fear to euphoria to despondency, often in the course of one day. Pia tried to hold the thought that for the first time in years, she and her peers had control of their destiny, but it was hard.

The days were filled with disorganization and squabbling about even simple things like how to prepare meals. But on the fourth day, Desiree Johnson, the woman who had comforted Pia on the train, called a meeting. She had emerged as a de facto leader of the leaderless two-hundred.

"Okay, folks," Desiree motioned authoritatively.

The raucous group slowly quieted as a ripple from where Desiree stood to the very back.

"People, I think that it is obvious that we need to get our shit together," Desiree signed. "We can continue doing what we've been doing the last four days and we will likely be dead by the end of winter. I suggest that right now, we begin to organize ourselves unless someone has a better idea."

A person whose name Pia didn't know walked to the front and stood next to Desiree. He began communicating in LOTS. "The best way that we can organize is to figure out how to leave this place. Wind River is a designed death trap. We need to get to the cities where our people are organizing a future society. Here, we will just die!"

Snaps of approval began slowly and picked up steam.

A woman whom Pia knew as Tutela stood and the snaps died down. "And exactly how might we make it out of here?" she asked, alternately signing and using LOTS.

"We will figure that out," answered the young man.

"And what is to stop us from building a new society right here?" added Tutela. "Why do we have to go to the cities to do that? Here, we would be left alone to plot our future. We can conspire to build a creatively disruptive future and the authorities would be no wiser. We can make our own city."

The group appeared divided as a cross-current of signing and LOTS grew, and the meeting started to cascade off the cliff.

"Listen," signed Desiree. "We need to build everywhere— here, the cities, the suburbs, everyplace in America. But here we are. Let's jump on this opportunity. If our future depends on finding solutions for how to live differently isn't this as good a place as any to try?"

The young man stood and tried to interrupt. "Sit down, now, right now!" He sat.

Immediately, someone stood and communicated assertively using LOTS and nominated Desiree to be the group's leader. She was elected almost unanimously through a show of hands, with the young man and his proximate friends the dissenting. Without skipping a beat at the conclusion of the vote, Desiree signed "thank you, okay, what are we waiting for, let's organize our shit."

There followed a brief debate about the necessary tasks, with five working groups established to attend to them. Desiree advocated for a sixth special one to write some type of declaration of who the Wind River Two-Hundred were and what they stood for. The group assented, and to her shock, Desiree proposed that Pia lead that effort. Pia looked around hoping that someone would object, but folks seemed relieved that they hadn't been put in charge.

Pia sat back in her wooden seat and ruminated on the difficulty of her task. She assumed that she would have to recruit others to help since Desiree hadn't selected anyone else to participate. The five other groups would be well staffed, as the two hundred divided themselves roughly proportionately.

Pia worried about how much the diversity of communication styles might complicate life at Wind River, with its wide range from signers-only to militant LOTS disciples. She wished that she felt more optimistic about the future of the Wind River Two Hundred. At several junctures over the last four days, Pia felt that the group was on the verge of disaster, especially with the news that they had already lost two residents.

A young woman Pia knew marginally named Marguerite had wandered off at night and hadn't been seen since. Heptanoic, the head guy from the Bureau of Indian Affairs said that it was just a matter of finding the remains. Russell the Stoic, named for his too-serious demeanor, hung himself the third morning inside the makeshift outhouse. Someone found him and cut the rope. He still had a pulse but died soon thereafter while waiting for medical help that everyone knew would never arrive.

The relationship with their Native hosts had been generally positive. As Johnny Whitetail told them four days ago on the van, it was up to the new arrivers as to whether they would survive. He and his tribe would be here to help, he said, but folks needed to ask. Life was hard for the Native people whose families had lived here for generations. The land was beautiful but forbidding. Poverty ruled, so it was not surprising that the tribes had accepted the government's offer to pay them to accommodate non-speakers on their land. But the payment was for the use of their land, not to babysit the non-speakers.

The day after the big meeting, Pia asked about access to horses so that she and others might be able to travel. A Native man pointed to a midsized mountain.

"There is the nearest place, and you can walk there. But it would be a waste of time," he shrugged. "Look, our payment from the Bureau of Indian

Affairs comes with stipulations. First and foremost, we can't help non-speakers leave the reservation. If you want to leave, you have to start walking."

Later that afternoon it was time for the now-198 to hold its second meeting. Desiree started by proposing that Wind River establish an executive committee made up of the heads of the six working committees. Without any discussion, the motion was approved, which meant that Pia had an additional responsibility. Everyone then headed to their work group. Pia approached Desiree to ask for guidance.

"Hey, Pia," signed Desiree. "Judging by the look on your face, I am guessing that you are wondering about how to do your job, right?"

Pia nodded and smiled.

"Good question. The thing is, I know that we need to figure out the kind of community that we want to be and that doing so will be tough. You may not realize it yet, but you will be perfect for the job. It will take time, though, and that's why I didn't assign anyone yet to work with you. I suggest that you spend some time sitting in on the five working groups and getting to know people. What are they thinking? What do they hope life will be like here a year from now? Then let's talk."

"Okay, that sounds good," signed Pia, "but why me? We barely know each other."

"Well, I don't know, Maybe I just randomly picked you out of a hat."

Pia stared blankly at Desiree who began convulsing in silent laughter.

"It's because I watched you at Tranquility and saw that people respected you. They like you. The fact that you don't know this about yourself is interesting, but not surprising. Wind River is going to need you, all of what you have, even if you don't yet know what that is."

It struck Pia in that moment that Desiree sounded a little bit like Charlene. Why was it that people wanted to define her as something other than what she felt she was? It was puzzling and unnerving. Despite her annoyance, Pia admired Desiree's strength and the compassion she had witnessed on the train.

Desiree left Pia in a state of contemplation while she began rotating among the committees. Pia snapped out of what might easily turn into an hour of processing and followed Desiree's lead. She headed over to the meeting of the health committee, which was discussing a very basic task: how to keep everyone alive. The forty group members were communicating about how best to spread awareness about warning signs that someone might be in severe physical or emotional distress.

As folks bounced ideas off each other Pia was struck by the power of LOTS. She herself had struggled early on to feel comfortable with the new language and hadn't fully appreciated its nuances. But now she could see how the exaggerated expressions, raised eye brows, lips turned up or down, and finger gestures to others combined with lip-smacking, not only communicated ideas but seemed to deepen collaboration and ideas for how to solve difficult problems.

Next, she was off to the security committee, which was assessing internal and external threats. These included the climate, which was severe and daunting to address. As for possible assets, one or more of the committees would need to determine whether most of their Native hosts would be as hospitable as those they'd already met. Another wild card was that several mining companies operated on the reservation, with at least one being less than ten miles away. The workers for these companies were rumored to be heavily armed. Would the new Wind River residents come into contact with any of these workers as they dug for rare earth minerals? If so, was there any risk?

Pia tried to take it all in, but she couldn't get her mind off her charge, drafting a "who we are" statement. She felt that non- speakers, wherever they lived, needed to demonstrate not only that they could survive but that they were building something better than what they had inherited. Whatever the statement would be called (A New Declaration of Independence?), it would be vital to answer the questions: who are we, how will we govern ourselves, and what do we ultimately want?

Pia moved on to the two other committees. The food group should be feeling the heat, as the surviving 198 had but two months of available rations. Yet, Pia was distressed to observe bickering rather than substance, with the disagreement being whether the Wind River community should designate signing or LOTS as its recommended mode of communication.

Discouraged, Pia bolted after a few minutes to observe the governance committee, which might help her draft the declaration. This board had been tasked with making recommendations for how Wind River might govern itself beyond the vague outlines of having a leader and committees.

Pia imagined that the easy part would be agreeing to some form of democratic governance. The harder part would be to actually live under the agreed-upon terms. While 198 humans might seem few, their personalities and beliefs were diverse. That had also been the case at Tranquility, but differences had been tamped down since they were not free. Here, there were no guard rails. Freedom, or whatever one might call life here at Wind River, might prove the community's downfall

28

Classified Memo 1372

"This is Vicki Hightower, and we have some breaking news. Through confidential sources, we have obtained a shocking classified memo. It appears to be based on the work of the Non- Speakers Metric Conference a few months ago. For legal reasons, we can't share the memo itself, but we can outline some key details and figures.

"This first bullet point is already in the public domain:

- Approximately .09 of the planet's population, or around 720,000,000 people, will be non-speakers distributed across our planet by the end of the year

- "Within five years, by 2059, the global percentage of non-speakers will be .18, or 1,440,000,000 people.

- "Such a mathematical increase over the next few decades calculates to a non-speaking word-wide majority.

"So here now the bombshell! Our sources tell us that based on this data the United States government's interagency task force's current relocation plan will soon be increased by a factor of 10. This would mean that the overwhelming majority of non-speakers would be sent to remote parts of the United States, a clear break from what President Sanchez has been publicly stating. This dramatic increase is driven by the government's desire to keep the country governed by speakers.

"The memo goes on to provide scenarios based on modeling software. The consensus is that even after segregating large numbers of non-speakers in remote parts of the country, the only way that speakers would maintain governing control is for a high proportion of non-speaking re-settlers to die from natural causes each year. To be accurate, the memo does not advocate for anything other than letting the harsh conditions of these settlements run their natural course. Still, this must come as sobering to Americans, who, just weeks ago, heard President Sanchez assure the American people that her administration was working toward a humane path back into communities for all non-speakers."

"This news came on the heels of Wall Street completing its meltdown with an additional nine percent tumble that brought the Totali loss for the year to a staggering forty-nine percent. It is the worst crash since the Great Depression. Retirement funds have been wiped out. Banks have failed, and only the federal government's guarantee is preventing a Totali collapse of the financial system."

The news was a perfect storm of panic and despair. Protests increased, both from those who thought that the isolation of non- speakers needed to be isolated faster, in order to revive the markets, and those who called the government's plan a fascist concern for the economy over the lives of non-speakers. Campuses exploded, smoke rose from cities, and armed protesters, counter-protesters, and police in several cities shot and killed activists and innocents alike. It was sheer anarchy in many parts of the nation. Around the globe, the severity of the crisis varied but no place was untouched.

Ironically, places like Wind River were among the few communities not immediately touched by the crisis. It always took days for hard news to reach the reservation. And with poverty already the standard, there was not much to lose in a stock market crash. The federal government could still write checks to the tribes for hosting the non-speakers.

There was, however, one new risk at Wind River: A & R Mining Corporation had been teetering on the edge of going out of business for the past six months and this final economic nail in the coffin would mean that the large mindless ten miles from the camp would close. It would leave hundreds of miners and armed guards with no jobs and no immediate way to evacuate. At least they had plenty of supplies, including abundant amounts of beer, wine, and Vodka.

29

A Word from Our Sponsors

"This is Vicki Hightower reporting live from outside City Hall in San Francisco, where a large protest is underway with reports of scattered violence. Here's what we know: the reaction to the government's memo on its strategy for dealing with non- speakers coupled with the Wall Street collapse seems to have formed a toxic brew. Within three hours of the memo coming to light right here on CNN, a new coalition called the Committee to Restore Sanity announced a week or more of continuous protests around the country, with the stated goal to force the closure of the so-called autonomous zones and the immediate reintegration of all non-speakers back into their communities.

"Meanwhile, President Sanchez issued a statement this morning that she stands by her policies of assuring security for all law-abiding Americans while cracking down on the extremists within the non-speaker ranks. She strongly rejects the notion that the actions of her administration in any way vary from her public pronouncements to date. President Sanchez ended the statement with a call to lower the rhetoric and remain peaceful.

"Here at San Francisco's City Hall Plaza, the crowds are huge but peaceful. The mood, though, appears anything but calm. Chants are continuous and deafening, and it appears that the SFPD is having difficulty holding the line directly in front of City Hall. Over at the Bay Bridge, a march seems to be underway; over to you Peter Ventura."

The bridge stretched behind Peter, who was more fidgety than usual, looking around rather than at the camera.

"Thanks, Vicki. You sure have been busy recently at your anchor seat hah!"

"Certainly have," Vicki said with a tense smile. "What are you seeing, Peter?"

"I am situated close to PacBell Stadium looking up at the Bay Bridge, the lifeline between San Francisco to the west, and Berkley, Oakland, and everything else to the east. From my vantage point, I can see protesters fighting with police at the entrance to the bridge on the San Francisco side—hold on for a second. It looks like the police have started to retreat in the face of the surging crowd. I cannot say for certain, but it does seem that protesters have either seized control of the east side of the bridge or are close to doing so. It is an incredible scene here.

"I am just now getting reports from the control room that a similar scene is playing out on the Berkeley side of the bridge, where demonstrators are surging toward police lines. I can only speculate that protesters are attempting to cut off the bridge on both sides, which would paralyze travel within a good section of the Bay Area. That's what I know for now and will keep you abreast as events change."

"Thank you, Peter. Remarkable! Now let's cut to correspondent Susan Hernandez in St. Louis, where we are hearing about a standoff between protesters and counter-protesters."

Susan stood in front of a beige wall, a sharp contrast from the vista that had been Peter's backdrop.

"Sixty seconds ago, my crew and I were forced to retreat to safety inside a large office building. We heard several shots fired and witnessed people scrambling in all directions. There is no indication of who fired the shots, but seconds before they began, there were scuffles as several hundred counter-protesters charged the larger crowd of those supporting the non-speakers. I can see ambulances rushing to the scene, and there are unconfirmed reports of casualties."

"Thank you, and the news continues to grow grimmer with a truly disturbing turn of events here in Atlanta. Yazeed, what's going on?"

"Yeah, Vicki, thanks. This is Yazeed Moore reporting from the One for All community. In a brazen daylight attack on one of President Sanchez's model reintegration communities, the rightwing militia set ablaze this complex just before nine this morning. The fire destroyed what was considered a model reintegration community made up of eleven structures that housed families of speakers with non-speakers. As the occupants streamed out of the burning homes, they were set upon by attackers wielding bats, knives, and other weapons. There are confirmed reports of more than ten casualties, with that number expected to rise. No group has taken credit for this attack thus far. We have no reports of any arrests. Over a hundred fire trucks and police cars are here, and the authorities have cordoned off the entire perimeter. From here I can clearly see smoke still rising from the fallen structures. This is truly a sad day. Back over to you, Vicki."

"A sad and momentous day in our country's history, indeed!

We'll be following developments in these stories all day.

"In a few moments, I am going to bring in our panel of experts to give us some perspective about what all of this means— wait, okay, we are going live to the White House where Press Secretary Vanessa Briggs is about to address reporters."

The familiar scene of a White House press conference is overlaid with an unusually quiet solemnity.

"Good afternoon. President Sanchez has declared a state of emergency and called out the National Guard in all fifty states. She has taken this action in full consultation with the governors. This administration has done so reluctantly in response to the violence that has been reported in more than thirty states. President Sanchez wants to make it abundantly clear that violence is never justified, regardless of the cause. She asks all Americans to be peaceful and to return to their homes unless they are first responders or have some sort of emergency.

“The president will host a White House summit later this week to focus on anti-terrorism strategies. We will release the names of the invitees tomorrow with more details to follow. The goal of the summit is clear: to form a consensus for the way forward with reconciliation between communities. Okay, I’ll take your questions.”

30

Seargeant We Need You

Sergeant Kenney

"Sergeant Kenney, please stand by for White House Assistant Counselor Watkins," came the voice on the phone.

I was too shocked at the time to fully comprehend what was happening and why anyone from the White House would be calling. Ms. Watkins calmly told me that she would greatly appreciate it if I might come to the White House next Tuesday to participate in the first-ever summit of speakers and non-speakers. I think I stammered something like "I'd be honored," but I don't recall words actually leaving my mouth.

During the past few weeks since Totali read me the riot act and implicitly threatened my family, I had been sidelined. They would trot me out for occasional events, like meetings with low- level community organizers in New York State and New England. But to be honest, I have not minded it one iota, as it has allowed me to spend more time with Mandy and Tommy. It has been refreshing to get out beyond the penal system and talk to people from various walks of life, many of whom are not as jaded as the inmates or their often-angry jailers. Now, it may be that the folks I have met are sadly out of touch with reality, but if that is the case, I could use less reality.

After most of these get-togethers with well-meaning people, I wonder whether there are enough decent people across our country to pull us back from the ledge. The events of the last few days seem to indicate that the answer is no. For the past three days, nearly every large city in the country has been locked down, but even with that, large swaths remain in an armed standoff, with progressives on one side and National Guard units and right-wingers on the other. From the news reports, it looks like the nation is being jig sawed into puzzle pieces divided by ideology. I'm sure that the National Guard could break down the physical barriers that have been cobbled together between these districts if they were so ordered, but it seems that the president is looking to avoid further escalation. I'm not sure how she'll do that while she remains committed to crushing STAM and other militants. My worry is that the Atlanta attack will be copied in other places. I am actually amazed and thankful that hasn't already happened. Not yet, at least.

Mandy is scared. When I told her that I would be going to the White House, she reacted as if I had just said I was going to my execution. "Don't go," she pleaded. "They are just using you to justify their crackdown on militants and the more they suck you in the more dangerous things will be for all three of us. You are a relatively low-level guy, why in the world would they invite you if it wasn't to use you as a tool for their misinformation?"

"No shit, honey. Don't you think that I'm aware of the risks and am trying to navigate us through it?" But I caught myself before I got too defensive. "Look, I understand how you feel, but please trust me, Mandy. For now, I've got to keep my head down and do the government's bidding, like we planned. I won't step over the line. But we need to stick together for Tommy's sake and for our future."

Mandy started to answer, but she stopped, threw her arms up in apparent exasperation, and stomped off.

Later that evening, after both of us had calmed down we talked about a promising development that came serendipitously from a meeting in Bangor, Maine. The gathering was uneventful, but during the subsequent mingling, a woman introduced herself as Amy Fitzgerald and said that she was an old friend of Mandy's. Amy told me that she had lost touch with Mandy, but they had run together years earlier. She scribbled down her cell number and asked me to give it to my wife. So, I did. When I showed the note to Mandy, she lit up in a way that I had seen far too little of recently. She told me that Amy was a great friend and fellow activist who is as authentic as they come.

The following day, Mandy called Amy, and they agreed to meet in person in a little old East Village coffee shop. Mandy was excited. I was nervous. Was it a setup? Despite Mandy's absolute belief in Amy, it had been years since they had hung out together, and so much had changed. Was this reunion too good to be true? Or maybe I have grown so paranoid that I am no longer able to judge these things. But my deliberations and confusion were of no concern to Mandy, who took off in the midst of my fretting.

The four or five hours since she left have felt the way I imagine sitting on death row would. Time is standing still and racing forward simultaneously. One second, I feel accepting of whatever fate awaits us, the very next, I'm overcome by hysteria. I fall asleep finally, having exhausted myself, when the front door opens. Mandy. I dare not budge. Better to sit here and wait for her to find me. I convinced myself that the longer she took, the better the outcome.

So, I waited for five, then ten minutes. Finally, my self- control evaporated, and I launched myself toward the staircase. When I hit the last landing before the living room, I could hear Mandy crying. It's the soft heartfelt cry that I knew all too well. Mandy reserved it for special moments, good or bad. I sit down next to her and put my arm around her shoulder. I'll just wait.

Less than thirty seconds later, my love, my wonderful woman, looks at me and says that right now she feels more hopeful than she has in years. "Amy is exactly the same as I remembered her. Of course, she's been through the shit just like all of us these days. But seeing her Geoffrey, just seeing her and her continued fortitude reminded me that there is an army of good people out there."

Mandy and Amy had not made any plans; rather; there was an unspoken understanding to rekindle the friendship. Their fight for justice had been core to their relationship and would be again. Would they change the dynamics of society? Probably not. But they would rekindle their passion in the face of fear.

31

The Storm

The news of the national protests took two days to reach Wind River. As word moved among the 198, electricity replaced the languidness of everyday life among the non-speakers. It was the best thing most had heard in months. While the governance and work group structure seemed to be functioning reasonably well giving the community some confidence that they might survive the winter and beyond, there had been collective despair about the lack of outrage from speaking society that they had been sent to live— or die. Where were all their allies? There had been a collective feeling of being forgotten. Then, the news arrived, first via their Native neighbors and then from the primitive radios that got decent signals on lucky nights.

Maybe the 198 weren't alone. Decency might still prevail, even if justice remained a far-off goal.

The national uprising brought a burst of energy. It spurred forward Wind River's decision to test what the collective jokingly referred to as its Pony Express. The name was meant to poke fun at their own primitive capacity to communicate with anyone, or in this case, the other non-speaker autonomous communities. Desiree and the executive committee hoped to launch it this week, to begin exchanging information with the ten or so other autonomous communities within Wyoming. The idea was to rely on travel and trade between the reservations. Desiree had met with leaders of the tribes to ask for help. She offered to compensate them with food and other enterprises once the 198 became self-reliant.

The executive committee met yesterday to drill down on the plan going forward.

“If we can make Wyoming work,” said Desiree, “what do you think about next trying to reach out to other communities in New Mexico, Arizona, Colorado, Utah, Idaho, Montana, and the Dakotas?”

Pia smiled and others clapped back, partly because the idea was motivating, but also because it seemed amusingly out of reach. One of the committee members, Harold, signed to Desiree admiringly that she was “ballsy.”

Desiree turned serious. “Establishing a nationwide communication network will be a tremendous challenge with clusters of non-speakers scattered across fifty states. Keep in mind that that’s why they sent us here. Wind River and the other enclaves were chosen for their remoteness and size. The government looked for good places to make large numbers of people disappear.”

“Is anyone thinking about how to contact the more populated parts of the country?” Harold asked. “Obviously, their situation is quite different. But if we are serious about building a national network, we would have to reach areas where the majority of non-speakers still live. We would need an entirely new strategy since the challenges of distance and integration among speaking society are so different. I wonder what we need to communicate in compact areas with a mix of non-speakers and speakers."

June, who Pia barely knew despite being her peer on the committee, jumped in. "I wonder about the psyche of these communities after the slaughter in Atlanta. My guess is that the non- speakers and their families felt safe surrounded by institutions like the police. Must have been quite the shock to be attacked and killed by supremacists while the authorities took their sweet time to react."

Next, the group discussed the necessity of activating speaking allies. They would vastly outnumber non-speakers for at least the next few decades. How much risk they would be willing to take to protect and support non-speakers as crackdowns got tougher?

Over the course of many work group meetings, Pia had increasingly evolved into using LOTS as her go-to communication mode. At first, she was reluctant because she wasn't as comfortable using it as she was signing. But over time, she pushed herself because it was becoming the tool of choice—and because she began to see its power firsthand. There was something about LOTS that demanded collaboration. You could sign while only half paying attention, but if you tried to do so with LOTS, you'd lose the stream of communication and wouldn't be able to jump back in. Pia wondered about how LOTS tracked with prehistoric communication methods. Were there any similarities? She thought to herself how ironic that modern society had evolved language and technology to the point that it often seemed that no one was really listening.

Pia retreated to gather her thoughts, as she often did after such meetings. Today marked the one-month anniversary of the group's arrival. She felt more confident that the community was slowly figuring out how to survive. The governance structure was beginning to function. It was now the middle of November, too late in the season to plant anything, but at least the food committee had solid plans for the spring. Nascent medical services and other vital infrastructure were being established step by step. The work was slow and methodical, but at least the 198 were making some progress. And no one else has died after that first horrible week.

Pia continued to marvel at the paradox of the place. In many ways, the mountains and valleys were beautiful beyond words. Yet the surrounding poverty was stunning. The natives had survived with seemingly far less than even poor American communities. Utilities such as internet were spotty at best. Most of the housing was substandard. Twenty-first-century amenities that most Americans would take for granted were largely missing.

Pia dreamed about seeing the mountain flowers that would bloom in the spring if she and the others could survive that long. But for now, it was time to batten down the proverbial hatches as they were being told the first real blizzard of the season was less than a day away. It would be a good test of how far her community had come in a month. They would measure by whether the population remained 198 once the storm passed.

In preparation for it and the long winter to follow, the work groups had subdivided into smaller teams. They tied down anything that might be whipped by the wind, gathered enough firewood to last three months, centralized emergency medical and other supplies, and established an internal communication network so that if anyone got in trouble, they could get help.

As Pia looked up at the sky, she saw that it had already turned the snow color that she loved as a kid. New York City did not have many good snowstorms, but the occasional big one announced its imminent arrival with its own special sky colored with ice and snow crystals. It would slowly sink lower and lower until it was on the ground, quickly transforming the city. Gone would be the greyness of winter, the garbage, and grime replaced by a winter paradise visited by squealing children and liberated adults.

Pia needed to get her tasks done in the next few hours, and then maybe take a walk in the hills to watch the further lowering sky before dark. Tomorrow would tell just how prepared the community was. There would be many other storms before spring. If Wind River autonomous was to survive over the next few months, its members might get to meet their sisters and brothers from other camps. Maybe, Pia daydreamed, the various non-speaking communities would organize a group adventure and hike to the middle of Wyoming.

32

Evolution Number 9

Pia stumbled upon an interesting statistic. According to the United Nations, in 1990, there were 95,000 people alive on earth who were one-hundred years or older. In 2050, there were roughly 900,000. By the turn of the century, a mere 50 years from now, that number would skyrocket to twenty-five million. Pia's point was that things change. Humanity changes. She didn't pretend to understand what the hell was behind the non-speaker phenomenon. It was safe to say that no one did, not even the best experts, and it seemed as though people had stopped trying to figure it out. Amid the uprisings and the stock market crash, Pia couldn't remember the last time she heard that old argument about whether or not people like her should be "cured." Pia always knew her position in that argument. She thought the growth in the number of non-speakers was the thumb of evolution pressing down on civilization. Her father would have had lots of opinions, and his memory made her shiver.

What lay ahead? Pia and most of her peers believed it was likely that, in time, the entire human civilization would evolve to be only non-speakers. That appeared to be the conclusion of the intelligence community. Why else would they and the politicians be so freaked out? If the current non-speaker numbers were to remain relatively constant as a percentage of the population of non-speakers, they'd be no threat. At some point, likely sooner than later, non-speakers would rule the earth as a majority, and further down the road, as the only humans.

If this was inevitable, what were the implications? There was no way to know. It seemed a stretch to believe that non- speakers were innately better than speakers because they happened to be on the tip of the evolutionary spear. But Pia did believe that non-speakers had an opportunity to do better, to create a more equitable and less destructive civilization. They had to prove it, beginning here.

Pia understood that evolution was nature's way of moving things along. Exactly what advantages non-speakers possessed that would equip them to survive in the future was not clear, but she did have a few observations. At Tranquility, it appeared that groups of non-speakers were able to communicate and organize themselves quite efficiently. Charlene and her group almost never signed, yet they seemed to act as one. At times, it seemed as if they were a single organism with multiple appendages. The engaged and collaborative nature of LOTS was definitely a factor, but Pia wondered if non-speakers had a greater fundamental ability to understand each other's moods, expressions, thoughts, and energy.

Members of the non-speaker Wind River community seemed to have some of those same abilities, but they remained to be further honed. Pia was struck by the magnitude of the task, especially when they had the more immediate, daunting challenge of surviving one winter. She continued to worry that too many of her peers were focused on more ideological issues than tackling the basics of growing food, fixing things, keeping each other alive, and proving to their Native brothers and sisters that they could be good neighbors.

Pia knew from her time at Tranquility that the non-speaker movement was no more monolithic than the speaking society. There were literally hundreds of ideas about the best way for non- speakers to build the movement to establish a society of and for the future. And this did not even take into account the differences among speaking allies. Perhaps the quintessential question was whether non-speakers should live alone in their own zones or integrate into society.

But there were other question marks, with the always- persistent debate about language a hot topic. Is signing bad, or necessary? Some non-speakers seemed so attuned to others that they were almost like mind-readers; would future generations have that ability? Pia believed that these questions wouldn't be answered in her life, but she wanted to be part of helping to address the many challenges, existential and practical.

Fresh news had arrived just hours earlier about the deepening rebellion around the country. As bits and pieces of information reached Wind River well after the events went down, she felt the frustration of the forced isolation but nonetheless, exhilaration. Breathless news reports from the first raucous days of protests had simmered down, but then the camp was electrified by news that very few of the protestors appeared to have gone home. The Bay Bridge remained closed. Major sections of many cities across the nation remained in the hands of the movement, with troops in place to keep separate the non-speakers and their allies, and the Speakers First crowd. Some of the news outlets were focusing on Sanchez's White House conference, but to Pia and her peers, it seemed a cruel joke, nothing more than a public relations stalling tactic.

The heads of the committees had an interesting meeting with Wind River's Native leaders. The Bureau of Indian Affairs had gotten a whiff of the agreement struck with the two tribes to help the 198 communicate with other non-speaker settlements in Wyoming. The bureau told the tribes that the government would withhold the promised compensation if they violated their contract, which included strict prohibition against helping non-speakers with travel or communication beyond the settlement.

Those at the meeting were not surprised and thought that they would all disperse after exchanging resigned pleasantries. But instead, both groups lingered. Pia didn't know why, but the tribes did not seem in a hurry to end the meeting. So, everyone stayed and communicated through a combination of signing, interpretation, and lots of gesturing. It did not change the tribes' position that they couldn't jeopardize their sizeable compensation package from the feds. But for the first time since their recent arrival, Pia felt growing warmth between the two groups. Pia couldn't point to anything specific. But maybe some of the Native people were feeling what Pia was: a sense of camaraderie based on being screwed over by a common enemy. She wondered how that connection played into her questions about a future of non-speakers. For now, though, Pia knew she couldn't get preoccupied with these existential thoughts. She kept her eyes on the practical tasks of surviving the winter while trying to build on the good will with the Tribes that she felt.

33

Sergeant Kenney Goes to Washington

Sergeant Kenney

The cliché, "What a long, strange trip it's been," doesn't begin to do justice to what I am experiencing. My iPhone alarm pops to life at six and interrupts a decent sleep. I immediately recall that I am in a Holiday Inn in downtown D.C., and not my own bed.

With a mixture of dread and curiosity, I put on my finest garb for the White House and gulp down a cup of coffee made from boiling tap water and a packet of Green Mountain. And then, I just sit here staring at the hotel wall while waiting for the call that I am told will come.

By seven, I am getting edgy and worrying if I have somehow screwed up the logistics when the phone rings. "Sergeant, I am Secret Agent Foley. Welcome to Washington. Please meet me downstairs in the lobby. I will be holding a black umbrella. Do not bring anything with you, including your phone."

I hear a click on the other end and head downstairs.

I've been to D.C. several times before, but there would have been no reason to have been inside the White House unless I had been lucky enough to draw the hard-to-get tourist card.

But here I am – end route to my first White House visit. Our car pulls up to the guard gate fifteen minutes after we leave the hotel. Foley exchanges laughs with the officer in charge before we proceed to the circular driveway in front of the building. There, we wait while other invitees pull up and enter the building. A few faces look familiar on TV, including Secretary of Defense Pulmonary. I remain in the car with Foley, who offers no explanation as to our status, so I assume that the Secret Service is prioritizing based on security status. Five minutes later, Foley says it's time to move and launches himself out of his seat, opens the passenger door, and leads me through security.

Once inside, I'm escorted to a room full of chairs, with a podium and flags on the front. I recognize it from TV. I find a seat and look around the room to see if I've met anyone before, knowing full well that it's quite unlikely. The seats seem to be occupied by two different types of people: those who look slightly uncomfortable in these surroundings, and those who project an air of importance. The former, those in my category, crane their necks, searching the room, probably trying to get a read on what they should expect. Meanwhile, the comfortable class chats with each other or stays busy on their phones. Foley insisted that I leave my phone at the hotel, a fact that reinforces my second-class status.

So, here I remain for what seems like days until someone approaches the podium and says that President Sanchez is happy that each of us is able to attend. She proceeds to lay out the schedule. In five minutes, the president will address us, and at the conclusion, she'll take questions and comments. These had been pre-arranged, so we were told not to raise our hands. We're assured that we will be given ample opportunity to share our perspectives after the opening session when there will be breakouts chaired by White House staffers. With that, the press is escorted in. Less than a minute later, President Sanchez enters to a large round of applause.

I am not embarrassed to admit that I am in awe of the moment. I'm hardly one of Sanchez's fans, but still, here I am in the White House, about to hear the president address us. How very strange under any circumstance, but even more so given the events of the past month. If you had asked me what lay ahead after Totali read me the riot act, this would not have made the list.

I would like to be able to report back the president's words, but they are either forgettable or I'm too distracted by the pomp and circumstance to pay sufficient attention. My one takeaway is that the White House's agenda today is to put the proverbial lipstick on the pig. The nation is reeling, if not in full free fall. The economy collapsed, and people are living in the streets in numbers unparalleled at least since the Great Depression. And now, there's widespread violence and disruption across the country. What to do? Of course, hold a political event and try to spin things.

After the presidential address and canned questions and answers, we're off to an extremely large conference room with tables arranged in several concentric circles. I'm in the outer ring, with the other nobodies. In the inner circle sit the big boys and girls, an array of White House staff and two cabinet members, the secretary of defense, and the interior.

While I contemplate the lack of power that my seating infers, Secretary Palma Nari begins by saying that, at the president's request, she and Secretary Lindsay will chair the meeting. They'll be assisted by the White House staff gathered around the center table. Each of us has been invited, we were told, because we have something to contribute to the national conversation. We might have ideas about how the country can come together around a plan that encompasses restoring the rule of law and economic recovery. Palma Nari turns the proceedings over to Precious, a White House staffer who assures us again that while she will call on certain individuals, everyone will be given an opportunity to contribute.

Precious Stevens, the assistant to the president, moves into facilitating, saying what a truly diverse and knowledgeable cross- section of America we represent. For forty-five minutes, she focuses on the security threat presented by people labeled radical non-speakers and their anti-establishment allies. It's rough to hear, but not surprising. I daydream about getting home and seeing my family when I startle upon hearing my name.

"Sergeant, are you with us," Precious says, as some giggle. "Sergeant

Kenney, I was hoping that you might share your experience as a leading administrator at Camp Tranquility when a small radical element rioted during those infamous days. What lessons did you learn about how we should think about restoring a culture of law and order?"

I feel my head swim in a sea of confusion, and I feel sick to my stomach, so much so that I might pass out. Heads turn in my direction as I clear my throat, buying time to get my shit together. I sort out my options in what feels like several awkward minutes but is really just seconds. I tell myself not to overthink it, just give them something, as I very slowly get to my feet.

"My name is Sergeant Geoffrey Kenney, and I have indeed had the privilege of working at Camp Tranquility, which, as some of you know, was opened three years ago to serve as a temporary home for approximately four-hundred and fifty non-speakers. I am proud that I and my fellow staff have been doing our very best at Tranquility. It hasn't always been easy. We sometimes have struggled, but I will say that there is a commitment by those who run the camps to seek workable solutions for all. The riot was a low point, for sure, and those responsible have been held accountable. Thank you."

I see a Precious frown. Not with her mouth but with her eyes. "Sergeant, can you tell us more about how you identified the ringleaders? Given that one of our main tasks today is to determine strategies for isolating and eliminating the few radicals among the many non-speakers, I think we'd all like to hear how your team did that in a real-world situation. How can we prevent this from happening in the future? What are your recommendations for dealing with some of these very same forces who have taken to the streets so violently the last week?"

I know that I need to offer up some red meat, but at the same time, I think of Mandy and Tommy and don't want to say anything that will make me a sellout in their eyes. It's bad enough that I'm even here.

"Well, these are all complex issues," I stammer. "Clearly there were ringleaders at Tranquility, and an ongoing challenge was to find ways to identify them. One of the lessons we learned is to better train our guards to understand indicators for potential danger than to invest too much in clandestine raids and eavesdropping to identify possible radicals."

"Thank you, Sergeant," Precious says coldly, still clearly dissatisfied with my answer but not willing to invest any more energy in me.

I zone out until it's time to go back to the Holiday Inn, where I grab my shit and head to Reagan International. I don't think that I've ever been happier to have wheels up than this exact moment. At least for today, I can return to Mandy and Tommy. I'll just have to wait to see what lies ahead, but I can't shake the feeling that my options are narrowing, and my morals or livelihood is at risk.

34

Homeward Bound

Sergeant Kenney

I'm so relieved to get home that I forgot Mandy took Tommy by train to Bridgeport to see her old friend Amy. This is Mandy's second visit for what seems to be an amazingly quick rekindling of an old friendship.

According to Mandy's note, she and Tommy should be home by six, so I pour myself a scotch, straight up for maximum impact. Just as my belly is warming to this most welcome substance, I hear the lock turning, and in bounds Tommy. He leaps through space and onto my lap. It feels good.

"Honey, I want to hear all about D.C.," Mandy says over his head, "and I have lots to tell you as well, but first I need a long and very hot shower."

Tommy and I hang on the couch signing back and forth; he has lots to report about his excursion. What is it about trains that tickles the imagination of kids? Tommy is most intrigued by the conductor, who mysteriously appears and disappears.

"How did he keep track of who paid as people were constantly getting on and off the train?" he wants to know. And of course, the snack bar was a big hit. Tommy signed all about the delicious donut that he had on the way to

Bridgeport.

Feeling that he had accurately briefed me on the train trip— with only sparse comments about Amy and her daughter, Cecily— Tommy stops signing and nestles under my arm pit. He does this in his Tommy way, with maximum pressure on my rotator cuff; I could tolerate the discomfort for days because I love his warmth and smell. So, here we sit, suspended in happiness, with no outside world, no White House, no national crisis, nothing but Tommy and me.

A few ticks later from our grandfather clock, Mandy emerges looking pink and happy in her PJs. Despite me feeling exhausted, she looks awfully good. She snickers and looks away having picked up my signal. Mandy, hardly a drinker also pours herself a scotch and suggests that I put Tommy to bed. It takes my tired son less than five minutes to nod off, perhaps to the memory of rushing trains. I leave Tommy to the safety of his dreams and head with anticipation to our bedroom.

"Okay, tiger," Mandy says teasingly to me as I enter what I hope will soon become the magical land of romance. "Let's hear about your day, and then I have lots to tell you."

I spill my guts about how I felt the White House staff had used me, how it was becoming harder to be in rooms with people who talk so callously about non-speakers. But I spare Mandy the details about my unsatisfactory answer to Precious's question, given that I want to move quickly past earlier today and focus on now. To attempt a romantic, segue, I make a sitcom-sounding comment, "and how was your day dear?"

Her expression tells me that she has something less playful to talk about. I know from Mandy's first reunion with Amy that she was involved in some pretty high-level activism, but exactly what, I did not know.

"Honey, Amy is in pretty deep with a coalition of major religious and civic organizations." Her description reminds me of what I read about the Civil Rights movement of the 1960s, during which Black churches and other well-respected institutions were major players shaming America to do right. I can only guess how the politics play out, but it sounds like President Sanchez would have trouble dismissing the groups Amy works with. The president can't label church folks terrorists like she has those poor souls locked up in camps.

The more Mandy talks, the more it seems that Amy has leverage and knows how to use it. She told Mandy that her coalition has the attention of the administration because Sanchez and her cronies do not yet feel they have public or corporate support for what many think is their ultimate goal: isolating all non-speakers on rural lands. Amy told Mandy that the coalition is leaning heavily on business leaders to stand for the rights of non-speakers. Apparently, it is having an impact as the S&P 500 crowd and big tech are worried about how the turmoil tearing across the country is impacting their bottom line. So, while ideologies may have hardened, corporations are driven by wanting to remain profitable.

Despite their leverage, Mandy says that Amy is worried that the administration is ready to crack down on non-speakers using what she called an Apartheid-like strategy. To date, the coalition estimates about a quarter-million non-speakers have been sent to one of the tribal areas from the north, the Dakotas, Wyoming, Idaho, or in the southwest of Arizona and New Mexico, and extending as far east as Oklahoma. The coalition's number stunned me. Is that possible? And how, sweet Jesus is the government removing people? It all sounded too crazy to be true.

I don't want to hear much more, as I feel the initial rush from the scotch wearing off and the lust for sleep overtaking the lust for my wife. We agreed to talk again in the morning, but then Amy dropped one last gem on me. In case I don't comprehend how polarized America is becoming, Mandy reports a dramatic rise in the number of speakers immigrating to Native lands to join their non-speaking family members and even friends. These numbers seem to have spiked after the attack in Atlanta and have continued to increase. This matches what I have been reading over the past month on the web, where there is more and more chatter advocating for progressives to abandon the cities for the reservations to build an alternative to modern America.

I sleep like the dead, but the spell is broken seven hours later by the TV set, turned up loud. Mandy is staring at the screen.

"What's up?" I ask, simultaneously studying her expression. "Well, you must have made quite an impact yesterday at the

White House," she says sarcastically. "Sanchez just announced that after a week of consultations with citizens and experts culminating with yesterday's event, she is ready to offer the nation a practical path forward."

"Fuck me," I blurt as I study the TV screen for clues and quickly check my phone for headlines. The *Times* has one of the biggest electronic headlines that I ever saw.

Sanchez Announces Three -Pronged Law & Order Program

- **National Guard units to protect law-abiding non- speakers and detain known radicals**
- **Justice Department to establish a special office to prosecute seditions**
- **Administration finalizing land purchase with 15 tribes and Governors of 11 Western States to help non-speakers and others choosing to relocate**

"What does this mean for us?" Mandy shouts "Is the government moving us?"

I don't have an answer or even a clue, so I just put my arm around her and we both stare straight ahead. But my gut tells me that there won't be many more quiet moments like this for a while, and I'm not wrong. The response from the resistance takes less than two hours. An umbrella organization that includes Amy's coalition announces its principled opposition to the president's plan while keeping open the possibility of negotiations.

As I read more detail about Sanchez's plan online, I noticed just how ambitious it is in terms of purchasing additional space on Native lands and in adjacent, sparsely populated areas. When Mandy and I finish watching TV and scouring the internet, we find each other's hand and walk quietly into Tommy's room to watch him play quietly with his toy trains, still excited from yesterday's trip. We hope he can stay this way.

35

Mining for Survival

Winter continued its march, alternating clear, bitter-cold days with frequent snow squalls and an occasional blizzard. To Pia's relief, the 198 remained alive and able to go about their day- to-day tasks. Wind River had even gained three new arrivers— speaking brothers and sisters of two of the camp's non-speakers. They had traveled from California for three days over the highway, rural roads, and snow-covered trails in a four-wheel-drive Jeep. Their unexpected arrival caused a stir and a bit of controversy, forcing the executive committee to take a formal vote on whether they could join the community. The verdict was that the newbies would be allowed to stay for now. Pia saw their arrival as a hopeful sign.

News continued to trickle in about the continuing political standoff on the streets of America, alongside stories of economic misery. With the order in cities collapsing, Pia wondered if Wind River might be safer than one of the non-speaker urban enclaves. Resources were tough here, but at least the players were clear: the residents, the Natives, and the land.

Days and even weeks had begun to pass quickly, which was good. Life on the reservation had fallen into a pattern for the non- speakers. Meals were communal and typically combined nourishment, community building, and the practicality of daily life. Often the executive committee would bring issues to the floor toward the end of breakfast, lunch, or dinner, either to inform or seek ratification. More important issues were reserved for formal town meetings at which a two-thirds vote was required to take action.

But most of the day was spent working. Pia's body and even face began to slowly transform under the physical demands. Thin, tall, and delicate looking when she entered Tranquility, muscles began popping from her arms and her face became harder.

Everyone had tasks that were overseen by either the five working groups or specially assembled work teams. Between gathering wood, hunting, fortifying existing buildings, or starting new structures, there was more than enough work to go around. Life was hard but, in some ways, uncomplicated as the non-speakers went about the business of surviving interacting with each other, sometimes the Natives, and always the land. But that changed.

While everyone knew about the mining company, until yesterday, it had been invisible despite the fact that it lay only 10 miles away. That ended when a small non-speaker work group was out gathering firewood in the hills and encountered security agents from the mine. The two guys were riding snowmobiles, following the tracks of a bear that had been breaking into mine food supplies that were stored outside. At least, that's what they told the Wind River work group.

The leaders' committee already had lots of items to discuss at today's meeting, and it now had one more. The two security guards had made a strange yet intriguing proposition. *Were the Wind River inhabitants looking for work?* As usual, Desiree opened the proceedings by asking for additions to the approved agenda and quickly moved to discuss the unusual encounter.

"Here's what I know," reported Desiree. "Sheryl from the work group told me that both men were well-armed and wore mining company IDs. She and the others believed the men's story about following bear tracks and thought that the encounter was happenstance. That said, I think that we need to be very careful here."

"What are your worries?" Pia asked.

Tally rolled her eyes at Pia and started to sign aggressively in Pia's face when Desiree held up her hand.

"Hey, it's a legitimate question," gestured Desiree, "and by the way, whatever your issues might be with Pia, fix them." She looked around at the whole committee and communicated slowly, for emphasis, that everyone in the group didn't have to like each other, but she did expect mutual respect.

"Now, as to Pia's question, here are my concerns: are these two men even who they say they are? Probably, but we need to find out. Was it really an accidental meeting and does that even matter? Most important, were they just blowing smoke up our collective asses about work, or is it real? What kind of work?" And oh yeah, by the way, what about the rumors that we heard from the natives that the whole operation was in some type of financial trouble?

“Thanks, Desiree, that makes a lot of sense,” Pia said.

Her antagonist just looked away, still doing little to hide her dislike of Pia. Henry from the committee proposed that Desiree speak to the members of the tribe about what had happened and ask for their advice. This resonated with the group and a plan was put in motion.

Two days later, Desiree took Pia with her to walk to the tribal headquarters to see if anyone might be around to speak with them. It was only a mile-and-a-half walk, but the snow was nearly two feet high, and the snow shoes made walking slow and tiring. When they arrived, there was no one inside so they decided to sit down and wait.

“Pia, I have wanted to talk to you about our committee.

Since we have to wait anyway, this seems like a good time.” “Sure,” Pia signed to Desiree.

“What do you think is up with you and Tally?”

Pia looked away not sure that she wanted to have this particular discussion.

“Do you know that she has been lobbying others in questioning why you are on the committee?” Desiree asked gently. “I don’t get it, Pia. You are obviously a very good and principled person. But being ethical doesn’t mean that you shouldn’t fight back.”

Pia looked up at Desiree with watery eyes. "It's not that I think that I shouldn't fight back, it's that I don't understand what it would even be about. I have never done or said a negative thing to Tally yet she seems to hate me. You ask me why, hell if I know. I just know that she does. Why do you think she's got a hair up her ass about me?"

"Well, my guess is that Tally is an angry person who has got more than a little bully in her. And she has chosen you as a convenient target. Now I am taking a not-so-wild guess here in saying that you have probably been the victim of this kind of behavior before, right?"

Pia nodded her head yes with a look of embarrassment. Truth be told, she was tired of playing this role.

Just then, Hayate and Heptanoic walked in and did a double take seeing their two visitors. Heptanoic, a huge man with a long flowing pony tail nodded and both left to change out of their winter layers, as in the headquarters were still warm, red-hot wood embers glowing in the fireplace. Hayate opened the door and hooted to get someone's attention, and in a few moments Hasanov's son, Betide, entered. Hayate, a short stout man in sharp contrast to Heptanoic, gestured and the five sat down on the floor near the flickering fire.

"Friends, thank you for all of your hospitality," signed Desiree. "We come to seek your advice."

Desiree proceeded to repeat the facts and questions from the executive committee. She and Pia then sat patiently while the two host adults conversed at great length.

"Tread carefully," Hitomi advised. "The white man's enterprises over the years have been at best a mixed bag for our tribe. If we had Totali control over the reservation, we'd get rid of the mining company and ban future ones, but we don't." He paused and looked around. "But this doesn't mean that they might not be useful to you in the short term. You need white man money, right?"

Desiree nodded yes.

"Okay then. Listen to what they have to offer. Just keep your eyes open on all sides of your head."

With that, all three Native men rose, and Betide wished Desiree and Pia a safe trip back. Pia looked back at Betide as they were exiting and was struck by his immense Doe-like eyes. They were even more expressive than usual. Was there a message in there? Pia wondered if the son was underscoring his father's advice. Be careful.

36

The Offer

"Be on the lookout," Desiree informed the groups working on the perimeter of the camp. "We want to make contact with the armed security staff from the mine. If you see them, be courteous and cautious. Hand them this note inviting their leaders to enter the camp to meet with me and the executive committee."

A week later, the note was passed. Two days after that, two miners showed up after lunch and asked for Desiree.

Informed of their arrival, Desiree came out to greet the two strangers. She waved them inside to the room where meetings were held and gestured for them to sit and wait. Less than ten minutes later, she returned with Henry from the committee and Oscar, one of the three speakers who had recently joined Wind River's ranks. Working through Oscar, Desiree welcomed the two and asked that they introduce themselves.

"My name is Wayne Catcall. I am the chief of security for A & R Mining Enterprises, and this is my lieutenant, Tookie O'Brien. Thank you for inviting us to chat. The reason that we are here is to ask for your help in monitoring the southern border of the mine. We would obviously pay you for your efforts. A & R has a number of security concerns, and we are limited in the number of men we have who can respond. Our property line is huge, and even with snowmobiles, O'Brien and I continue to be concerned that we cannot provide sufficient coverage."

Desiree faced Oscar and signed for what seemed to be longer than usual. Oscar began interpreting but Desiree had to jump in and sign some more to clarify the message.

"Okay," said Oscar, "I think that I have it. First of all, Desiree thank you for your offer. She has a few questions and concerns. Number one is what type of monitoring are you talking about. What would we be looking for? Number two is what would be the risks, and what are you offering in exchange? Finally, how, if at all, do the tribes factor in? Why haven't you approached them? After all, we are new here, and they know the land."

Catcall looked at O'Brien before answering, which raised Desiree's radar.

"Great questions Desiree! What you'd be looking for is basically anything and anyone that shouldn't be wandering around at our border. That would include large four- and two-footed animals. As my men probably told you last week when they met your work group, we have had problems with nuisance bears getting into our supplies. But we also have had issues with some of our men getting drunk and stumbling off. We've lost three that way to hypothermia the past two winters. By the way, I'd appreciate you treating all of this as confidential. The bottom line is that the mining company just wants to keep things safe for everyone. Incidents are bad for business.

"As for the tribes, let's just say that they aren't always thrilled with our presence. I get it. So, we try to stay out of their way to lower the possibility of problems. As to compensation, how would two-thousand dollars a month sound? In exchange, you would guarantee that your teams would fan out northeast, north, and northwest at least twice a week. Once per week, a designated person from your group would meet at a prearranged place to report on anything unusual that you saw."

"Four-thousand!" signed Desiree.

"Excuse me," said O'Brien, speaking up for the first time. "Four-thousand dollars. It sounds like a lot of work."

Cascall smiled and shushed O'Brien.

"Wow, I can see why they made you a leader. I'll tell you what: I can do three-thousand, but that's it. Do we have a deal?"

With that, Desiree stood and walked over to Cascall, who rose to meet her. They exchanged gazes, with Desiree's particularly intense. She then broke the temporary awkwardness by extending her hand to Cascall. The deal was on.

After the meeting, Desiree summoned Pia and asked Henry to stick around.

“Pia, I have an important assignment for you and Henry. He will explain the details to you, but the gist of it is that I want both of you to liaise with the designees from the mining company. It is an important and sensitive assignment, so I am counting on both of you to be smart.”

With that, Desiree left to find other members of their committee to brief them on developments.

37

Free STAM

Charlene

"It is an honor to meet you Ms. Charlene Vicnacious."

Those words ushered in a strange visit from the American Red Cross. Five weeks earlier, I began a hunger strike. I decided that since Totali intended to kill me anyway, I would do what I could to grab the initiative and turn it around on him. But I need publicity. Otherwise, it's like the old joke about the bear shitting in the woods. So, I bribed my most trusted guard, and he smuggled word out to a coalition of progressive organizations and church groups. When Totali was informed that I was refusing food, he must have been amused. That was until he began to read about it in the papers. Soon other imprisoned STAM members had joined in, and Totali had enough. He ordered guards to force-feed me. A few days later he paid me a visit.

It immediately felt different from our previous sessions. In the past, he typically let me know in advance that he'd be stopping by in order to scare me as much as possible. But this time his demeanor was more cerebral and less visceral.

He told me that the Red Cross would be paying me a visit very shortly.

He was concerned that I might stumble in my communication with them.

"I am not here to play games with you, Charlene. Let me explain your options so that you can make the best decision. I fear that your isolation may have clouded your judgment, and that is why I am investing my time in you today," he said in his trademark affected monotone. "I know that you fancy yourself some type of heroic figure, a revolutionary of sorts. But let us examine your situation with cold, hard facts. One, you are currently a prisoner of the federal penal system with no guarantee that you will ever be released. Second, I am in charge of this facility, and therefore in charge of your fate. Lastly, one of the reasons that you are here and will remain here until I and the authorities decide otherwise is because of your dear friend and lover LJ."

Hearing those words had its intended impact. Totali had saved his best for last. I turned away so that he would not see any tears that might escape. I did my best to remain impassive. But this sadist would smell my pain.

"I can see that I have upset you, Charlene. That, of course, was my intent; but not because I enjoy seeing you in pain for its own sake, although I do. The reason I am advising you to keep your fucking mouth shut is that things have gotten a bit frayed, and we, the authorities, need to get normalize everyday life—help America get back to being America, everyone happy and making money, that sort of thing. You have a role to play, a real role. As the true patriot that you are, I am confident you will help.

"I am talking win-win here, unlike your previous pathetic attempts to create some sort of idealist utopia for non-speakers, especially you and your queer comrades. Forget about all of that, or even better, think about what it means that barely two years after you told LJ that you loved her and wanted to spend forever with her, she was spilling her guts to the FBI. She turned on you and others pretty easily and early. She was very helpful as our paid agent once we placed her with you in Tranquility. You see, Charlene, I have human nature on my side. The survival instinct is strong in all of us. It certainly was in LJ. She was a great asset to us, but unfortunately, as it turns out, not much in love with you. She told us everything that you had shared with her about growing up and feeling unloved by Mommy and Daddy. How sad. I have it all here in this file. It paints an extensive and interesting psychological profile of you, the weak insecure wannabe revolutionary. We have more, lots more that I will share with you in good time. But for now, I would like you to think about the future, your future. It is possible that if you play your cards right the powers that be might consider letting you go; but only of course if you help us with our little problem of turning down the heat.

Perhaps in time, your kind will rule the world. The science and the math suggest that might be the long-term outcome. But those days are a long way off, and for now, I and my fellow speakers are in charge, and we will remain in charge well beyond your pitiful life. I, for one, intend to live a long happy life not ruled by mutes such as you.

I am going to leave you now so that you can think through your options. If you choose to cry to the Red Cross, I fear that you and I cannot live together here for much longer. While I would have no trouble ending you right now, that might be messy from a PR standpoint. I will hope for the best, but prepare for perhaps a sloppy end to our relationship."

With that, I prepared for the Red Cross visit. I'm led out of my detention block and brought to the administration building. The fact that they put me in an office with just one guard and no handcuffs concerns me. I try convincing myself that it might be good and that perhaps I'm even being released. I feel a rush of hope for the first time in months. But it's quickly dashed by my introduction to the three who enter.

Denise McGruff from the Red Cross goes on and on about my alleged fame within the movement for a bizarre twenty minutes. It's all patronizing bullshit, but I don't interrupt. Her little soliloquy buys me time to figure out what the fuck is going on.

"The purpose of the delegation's visit," she explains, "is to ensure that you are being treated well. Are you receiving adequate food, housing, and medical services?"

Despite my best effort to suppress a laugh, or maybe because of it, a snort escapes. Not wishing to be rude, I try to disguise it as a sneeze. The delegation tastefully gives me cover by saying "God bless you." I think it's obvious that I had not answered their question about my treatment and expected them to ask again.

But they didn't, and it only confirms that McGruff and the company are looking for a graceful way to discharge their task and leave. I could tell them the truth about the brutality and murder within these walls, but for what purpose? Would the Red Cross endanger its position as the go-to American charity by advocating for someone like me? I doubt it. So, I smile back and sign that life here is bad, and that I shouldn't be in prison for trying to better my circumstances when I was wrongfully detained at Camp Tranquility, but that I'm being treated okay. They smile, make some more small talk, and in less than five minutes, they are out the door. I think I made my point, and I got the publicity that the movement needed. I'll drop my hunger strike now so that I can live and fight another day on *my* terms.

38

Love Hurts

Henry and Pia went about their mission with gusto. They both viewed it as important for their community and a break from the daily monotony. There were already twenty folks assigned to the wood gathering teams that would also be patrolling the perimeter, and Desiree suggested that the number be doubled.

Two days later, the duo met with the thirty-nine souls who would shortly be dispersing in five northern vectors to begin monitoring the land. Henry explained that each group was to go about the task of gathering firewood while recording any unusual sightings of man or beast.

"With the recent thaw and melting of the snow, your main job is to find as much wood as possible so that we can stay warm all winter, but in the process jot down what you see and where. Do not take any action. Your job is simply to report back to us. Okay?" Henry was surprising Pia in his role. Usually quiet and reserved and physically unremarkable, he seemed to be thriving on the job.

With that, the five teams went off in five directions separated by roughly thirty-five degrees on their compasses.

The week passed without any team reporting sightings beyond rabbits and coyotes. As arranged, Henry and Pia made their way to Signal Rock at the appointed hour to meet with A & R's representatives. They made it a point to arrive thirty minutes early to scout for possible danger signs and escape routes. Better to be safe. Thirty-five minutes later, they spotted snowmobiles rapidly approaching and came out from their cover to greet the men from the mine.

John Ringo and Larry Fontaine introduced themselves. Neither could sign, but Wind River came prepared. Henry brought out a pad of paper with a pen and began scribbling a few notes which would be pretty simple since there was in fact, nothing to report. As he was writing he looked up and noticed Ringo gazing at Pia who was alternately averting her face from Ringo's eyes but shyly glancing back at 15-second intervals. Less than two minutes later Henry handed the paper over to Pia who read it and nodded her head in agreement. She then passed it over to Fontaine. After both A & R men reviewed the paper, the four agreed to meet again next week at, the same time and place.

Henry and Pia began their slow snowshoe-footed walk back to camp. The sky was crystal clear with the kind of deep blue that was almost blinding. Henry kept looking out of the corner of his eye at Pia, who was either unaware or uninterested in her peer's attention.

Finally, Henry and Pia stopped to rest. Henry faced Pia unsure of what to do, and then he finally gave Pia the well- understood mute shrug: "WTF?"

Pia feigned innocence, but Henry wouldn't have it.

"Pia, you know that we can't have any contact with these men beyond passing notes, right?"

"Of course. Why would you say that?" Pia signed. "What are you talking about, that Ringo guy? Sure, Henry. He and I are going to hook up here in the snow and raise a family of bears together, okay?"

Henry just shook his head but decided that he had done his job warning Pia.

When they arrived back at camp, Desiree was pacing. It was unlike her, as even in times of crisis she project calm. Not now. She looked at both, nervously waiting for a report. Pia told her that nothing happened; the two mining guys showed up a little late, got the report, read it, and left. They'd all meet again next week. Desiree looked at Henry who simply nodded, seconding Pia.

That night, in her cot Pia thought about Ringo. She shared the medium-sized building with twenty others. The walls were covered with animal skins to keep the heat from the fire inside, but even with this relatively new feature it still got cold at night. The combination of being close to other cots and the cold air motivated Pia to slide as far under the blankets as possible as she did, and her hand slid down her thighs. Pia groaned lightly and turned over to muffle her sounds on her pillow. She was surprised when an orgasm rippled through her body. It was not her first but was the best. In fact, Pia was still a virgin, a secret that she guarded given how unusual it was for a twenty-two-year-old woman.

Pia, Henry, and the other thirty-nine continued this work routine for the next three weeks. On week two, Fontaine handed Henry a sealed envelope with three-thousand dollars inside. It would enable the community to buy more food from the tribes. Things were looking up.

The various committees were going about their tasks with increased purpose. Their vigor was fueled by a combination of confidence that Wind River would survive and excitement that the movement in the country was growing. The non-speakers could see possibilities for the future, if still but a glimpse.

Pia had recruited one member from each committee to begin drafting a statement about who the inhabitants of Wind River were, as a community. Thus far, the group had generated five draft statements, all of which they soon threw into the circular file. It was tough work, all agreed. Everything they came up with sounded either like a collection of clichés or emergency instructions for evacuating a plane. Finding balance was tough, but the group pressed on.

The one fly in the ointment for Pia was that Tally not only continued but ramped up her animus toward her. Worse, Tally seemed to have won over a small but growing number of allies who seemed to view Pia as a hopeless dreamer who endangered the community's future. It was all very baffling.

Despite this, Pia had rarely been happier. Twice, sometimes three times per week around two a.m., long after everyone had gone to sleep, she snuck out of camp and walked north. Waiting there with a tent, blanket, and wine was none other than John Ringo.

39

Pia on the Road Again

Pia and Henry, having overseen their assignment with A & R with aplomb for the last two months, were asked to represent Wind River at the first meeting of the autonomous zones to be held at the Acoma Pueblo Reservation in New Mexico. The goal of the big meeting was to begin connecting all of the autonomous zones in the west. Eventually, they would bring in non-speakers from the urban enclaves in the east and Midwest. Over the past month, there had been considerably more news, mostly positive, in and out of other autonomous zones and some urban enclaves. There was a sense, still fragile, that a network—if not a new nation—was slowly taking root.

News also included a rare letter from Taylor.

Hi, sis, sorry that I haven't written more, but there's a lot going on. I am good. School sucks, but my friends keep me from going nutso. One reason I've been busy is that Mom's not in great shape. I don't know exactly what's wrong, because you know The Rock, she won't say. I even tried reaching her doctor, but they won't talk to me without Mom's permission. Maybe she really is okay and just slowing down. But she's too young for that right? Anyway, I'll keep an eye on her and let you know if I find out anything. Love you!

Pia thought about how vibrant Delores was before the bullets had pierced her. She feared that her mom would never again be that person. Pia could only imagine the toll it must be taking on Taylor, seeing their mother in a weakened state after losing his dad not many years ago.

But what options did Pia have if her mom nosedived? She must consider everything including the possibility of getting Taylor to Wind River. She wondered what life might be like for him on the reservation with almost all non-speakers and a million miles from the life he had known in New York. Perhaps she could somehow leave Wind River, and she and Taylor would move into one of those protected joint speaker-non-speaker communities.

She found it a paradoxical sign of the times that, in the midst of the government's crackdown on non-speakers, the pushback from progressives had created more possibilities for them to connect, as would be discussed at Acoma. But it came at great potential risk. There were increased reports of extra-judicial killings executed by a shadowy combination of vigilantes and law enforcement. Few of these found their way into the press, although the *New York Times* was currently running an investigative piece on the matter.

Pia thought back to that day years ago on Canal Street when the presidential order came down. If she knew then what she did now, Pia didn't think that she would have wanted to survive. She simply wouldn't have had the strength to continue. She thanked Charlene for helping her get through Tranquility during that first terrifying month and helping her grow.

Her friend was often in Pia's thoughts, particularly the yin and yang that defined their relationship. They were so different and yet similar. Each carried a huge rock on their backs, yet both strove to lighten others' loads, albeit in very different ways. Charlene was driven by anger and Pia by hope, an asset and curse for each. Pia desperately wanted to see Charlene again. She would ask her for advice about how to deal with her new nemesis, Tally. Pia chuckled to herself imagining the exchange would end with Charlene saying something like "toughen up girl!"

40

Perhaps I Wasn't Clear

Sergeant Kenney

I'm sitting at home still trying to interpret Sanchez's new executive orders when the phone rings, and I'm told to put on my uniform and report to Totali's office ASAP. When I arrive, Totali is standing with his back to me and peering out the window.

"Good morning, Sergeant. How was your trip to D.C.?" "Fine, thank you."

"Good. Okay, let's get down to business. Please take a seat and review the file on my desk with your name on it, and then let's talk."

I begin reading.

"What is this all about, Chief?"

He ignored me, and I kept reading. My handshakes with anger as I turn the pages.

Finally, Totali wheels around with an impassive, businesslike expression, the polar opposite of the blood that I feel rushing to my face. I start to rise from my seat and move in Totali's direction. He stands his ground with his hand up in warning.

"Careful, Sergeant! I advise you to think very carefully about your actions today, as they might prove to be life-altering, and not only for you but for your wife and son."

I sit down in my chair, but for the first time, I began contemplating how to kill someone.

"As you can see from the file, I have more than enough evidence to have you and Mandy arrested. That would obviously require child services to take custody of Tommy. When I gave you your assignment over a month ago, I thought that I was clear that your role was to be a useful mouthpiece for me and my bosses. Yet, I heard yesterday evening from a White House staffer that you whiffed on softball questions during the conference. Is it so hard for you to understand that all that was required was to label Charlene and her cabal the terrorists that they are?

Anyway, Sergeant, I am sick of playing nice with you. Either you get your shit together right now, or you and your family can say goodbye to your cushy lives. Am I clear, Sergeant? This will be your last redirection."

"Okay," I nod, too afraid to say more, because I might end up with my hands around that motherfucker's neck.

"Good. So here is what you are going to do: clean out your locker because you will be exclusively working from the road at this point. I promised the White House that you would be more cooperative going forward. Sanchez is moving to finally end this mute uprising around the country, and she wants to deploy useful idiots such as yourself to speak to the press about the threat posed by these revolutionaries. Beginning next week, you can expect to spend most of your time in Motel 6's in glamorous locales like Bismarck, North Dakota. But before you leave, I want you to visit Charlene in her cell. I promise that if you fuck me again, Mandy will end up looking even worse.

"And, oh yes, I forgot to mention that the promotion I have been waiting for has come through. I will become a special assistant to the undersecretary of Homeland Security specializing in counterterrorism. I have been promised lots of running room to crush the STAM uprising. I intend to succeed and certainly won't let you get in my way. You see, Sergeant, unlike you, I have a rosy future. If I do my job right, who knows? Maybe even Sanchez will notice, and eventually, I can grab a cabinet position."

Two guards walk me to Charlene's cell. I'm prepared for her to look bad but not for what stares back at me. Charlene's face is so swollen that I barely recognize her. One eye is completely closed, and the other a slit.

"My God Charlene," I utter, despite having steeled myself before entering. "I am so sorry. Why did Totali do this to you? Jeez, sorry for even asking that," I stammer realizing how incredibly stupid the question sounded.

But Charlene gives me an injured-looking smile on the left corner of her mouth and slowly signs, "Hunger strike."

I don't know what I can do, so I simply sink into the seat next to the bunk. I knew that Totali had beaten her about the face intentionally to make a point. Most of the beatings he and other guards had administered in the past were less obvious. This one was a message. I received it loud and clear.

"Charlene, is there anything that I can do to help? I ask, again feeling stupid and helpless with my words.

She looks around to see if any guards are watching. Seeing that the coast is clear, she motions for me to get closer.

"Get this out."

I don't understand but then I feel a piece of paper in her palm which I fumble with for a moment and then pass into my pocket. I look back at the opening to her cell and am relieved that the two guards were busy discussing what bar to go to after work.

My heart's pumping, and the next ten minutes feel like hours. I keep my hands away from my pocket, just wanting to escape the walls of the camp and Totali's immediate grasp. When I get to my car in the parking lot I still don't dare to go to my pocket. I drive. A few miles away, I pull into a Dunkin parking lot. Still, I look around, shaken by the last hour and the explicit threat to my family. Finally, I dig out the note and open it. At first, I could barely read it. The words appeared to have been written with some sharp object, not a pen, and in blood.

Tot. murdered EW & TT

I keep trying to interpret the meaning. Finally, I get it. *Totali murdered Ellen Wilson and Tammy Teeks*. I know of the two. Each had been reported to be seriously ill over the past month, and they were transferred temporarily to the infirmary before supposedly being sent to local hospitals. If Charlene was right, they never got there.

41

At Acoma

Henry was startled awake by the slamming of the brakes. He nudged Pia several times until she agreed to open her eyes. “Okay, Mr. Henry and Ms. Pia you will be sleeping in tent number nine.”

They stumbled into the huge temporary structure, and Pia collapsed onto the first cot that she saw. There would be time in the morning to unpack, but for now, she was so tired that she just wanted to close her eyes and sleep for days. Her head had other plans, though. It was full of questions and internal narratives that she couldn’t extinguish. Pia replayed incidents of Tally baiting her. She thought of Desiree pushing her to stand up for herself and Charlene’s constant nudging to the same end. Was she really someone who lived in the clouds and couldn’t or wouldn’t assert herself? Her head filled with recollections of friendships as she tried to accumulate a lifetime of evidence to discount such a verdict. But for every instance that the defense presented a memory to demonstrate beyond a reasonable doubt her ability to stand strong, the prosecutor soon provided a compelling counterargument. How cunning and remorseless was her mind. But this is how it worked, how it always has operated. Her head contained a rich library of a lifetime of tapes of discussions that she had with herself and others. Over and over again, she replayed them, especially at night before giving in to exhaustion.

Lately, Pia thought a lot about her family and what life was like before her father killed himself. Why hadn't she sought more answers about what happened to him? She tried to make sense of it all by telling herself that her father's role as a therapist forced him to absorb other people's angst and depression and it broke him. But she knew in her gut that there was more to it. Truth be told, her father was always a bit depressed. He tried to hide behind his practice and adult responsibilities, but she saw now how her Mom resented how much he withdrew from the family. Taylor saw the family dynamic for what it was. Why didn't she?

Pia was always the stable one in the family. Taylor, while nerdy, could be quite emotional. Mom was Mom, a force of nature. Good ol' Pia, though, could be depended on to never get too high or low. If Dad was especially quiet at dinner, she would try to smooth things over for him the rest of the night while never asking if anything was wrong. Perhaps she sensed that he carried inside him a considerable hole, and she hadn't wanted to dig it up for fear that the source of his unhappiness was unfixable.

Regardless of her internal scars, Pia had found strength at Wind River and was committed to trying to be a better person and a stronger leader. She had a clearer sense of the former than the latter, which remained a bit of a puzzle. Pia knew there must be something in her that Charlene and Desiree caught a glimpse of, but she herself didn't see or understand it. Her peers chose her for leadership roles like attending this conference. She owed it to them to step up and work with Henry to bring back something of value. She committed to spending the next few days watching others and perhaps trying new strategies to see how they fit. Hopefully, the high stakes would force Pia out of her comfort zone. Can events help a person overcome fears that are holding them back, even those that haven't been clearly identified? She laughed to herself that perhaps she should go see a movement psychologist. Finally, she had adequately exhausted herself. Sleep was now within reach; time to shut down her head. In the morning, she would join Henry and begin experimenting to see if she could find a better leader within.

42

The Long Way Home

Sergeant Kenney

I lean on the gas and speed home. It feels like the walls of my chest are closing in on me, like a shrinking room in a horror movie. I cannot hold a thought for long as I drift in and out of panic mode. Mandy is right. We are in danger. What should I do? What is the plan? I punch myself in the leg in anger over Totali's complete depravity and stupidity. Yeah, what's the plan, Mr. Got it All Together? How stupid and naïve I have been thinking that I could wall us off from all of this.

When I get close to home, I call Mandy and ask her to meet me in the vestibule outside of our house. I fend off her question as to what's wrong and reassure her that I'm okay. Just do it, please! When I enter, she's standing there, looking apprehensive and cracking the door to look back at Tommy.

"Honey, we've got to run." I blurt out. "Why, what's happened?"

"You and Tommy aren't safe. I don't know how much time we have, but it is much less than I thought. We need to make plans to leave and hide."

Instinctively, Mandy opens the door again to look at Tommy. He's immersed in one of his games.

"Okay, honey, let me contact Amy. She has offered to help in the past. Do you think they are listening in on us? Is that why you wanted me to come out here?"

"I don't know, hon. But after today nothing is off the table."

43

Getting Down to Business at Acoma

Pia sunk deep into a dream state. She was back in New York sitting at the dinner table with her dad, mom, and Taylor. Everything seemed normal except Taylor kept looking away and averting her eyes. She made faces at him but nothing. Soon she was standing up and waving her arms wildly, but Taylor didn't see her, and her parents seemed oblivious.

"Taylor, Taylor," she tried yelling but of course, she could only sign or "express" the words. "Taylor, I'm over here why won't you talk to me?" She heard a sound, a strange one, and looked around to try and see where it was coming from. She felt shaking and finally opened her eyes to see someone standing by her side.

"Good morning," the stranger signed, "my name is Sleeping Horse. You are a good sleeper to block out the blowing of the goat's horn."

She glanced around and remembered that she was at Acoma Reservation. Next, she looked around to find Henry, but he must have already dressed. She quickly slipped into her overalls and warm socks, while looking around at the ten or so remaining stragglers. A huge young Native man entered and stood at the door making eye contact with Sleeping Horse. After looking at each other and exchanging a series of gestures and facial expressions, Sleeping Horse stood and waved for Pia and the others to follow.

The weather was sunny but cold and the distant hills looked so sharp and clear that they must have been drawn with finely sharpened pencils. The land here was also beautiful, but very different than Wind River. Pia remained transfixed by the hills and nearly stumbled over her own feet. The attendees meandered forward, and within a few minutes, she came to a huge tent. Inside it looked like a small city and Pia noticed that it was actually filled with many smaller tents, giving it the feel of small alleys with connecting rooms. Conferees were sitting to the sides on mats, their legs crossed. There were a few chairs toward the center, and these were occupied by those Pia imagined to be the ringleaders of the event.

The smell of food hit her brain and Pia realized how hungry she was, having not eaten since she and Henry left Wind River. She followed her nose until she came to a huge circular wooden table that easily accommodated more than thirty hungry customers at a time. The food, some type of porridge, was tasteless but hot. Pia sucked it down like a milk shake with liquid oozing from both corners of her mouth. She noticed that the person to her left was smiling, so Pia cleaned herself with the corner of her sleeve and smiled back at her.

Pia felt good being here. She didn't know why, but she did. People seemed relaxed, and that was a state of being that had been hard to come by at

Wind River until just recently when it became clear that they would probably survive the winter. The sound of the goat's horn blared again, and Pia wondered how she managed to filter it from her dream. The three people who were seated in the middle of the main tent stood and began communicating. The two on the sides were signing, but the young woman in the middle was using LOTS while making eye contact around the room. Pia glanced at her neighbors to see their reactions. She could feel a positive vibe.

Pia looked around for Henry but couldn't locate him. She glanced back at all of the faces and was so immersed in their expressions that Pia missed some of what was being communicated. But she got the gist and headed to the sign-up sheets posted on the walls of the main tent. There were ten categories and two days to cover them all. She decided to head first to a session on sustainable economies which was in the far tent. This was Pia's first conference of any type. Her only frame of reference was hearing her dad talk about medical conventions, but those seemed very different based on his description. He usually brought home cool gifts, like play stethoscopes, and gave them to Taylor and Pia.

Darius, the leader of Pia's session began. "Welcome everyone," he simultaneously signed and used LOTS. It surprised Pia, because on Wind River the default was signing, even though a growing number preferred LOTS. The group decided that hybrid was fine. They broke into five groups of three and began sharing what each community had been doing to develop sustainable economies.

In Pia's group, there were a few awkward moments before someone stepped up.

"Okay, I'll break the ice. My name is Francine, and I'm a member of the Washoe Tribe of Nevada. We are committed to honoring our own Native non-speakers while we work toward the long-term goal of building a sustainable integrated community without any animosity with traditional speakers. We sell items like clothing made from local materials. Regional markets buy them from us and have been doing so for decades. But now, with changing times, we are rethinking how to continue doing so but under the new normal.

"My tribe agreed, after a lot of heated debate, to allow the Bureau of Indian Affairs to settle white non-speakers on our reservation. Some of my tribe volunteered to train the new arrivers but to be honest, there were problems. The cultures and experiences of the Natives and whites are so different that despite good intentions from both groups, there were clashes of expectations early on. I am sad to report that, in one instance, there was a serious fight between several Natives and whites resulting in a death. Both people took the sadness and trauma from that event and redoubled their commitment to making their vision of an integrated community work. Over the past two months, great progress has been made."

Pia decided to talk about Wind River's enterprise, scouting for the mine. In the middle of her description, she noticed that Francine's expression was one of puzzlement. She looked at her other group member, Thomas, who was a non-Native living at Gila River. He looked nonplussed. Thinking that she must not be clear, Pia stopped and signed asking whether Francine or Thomas had any questions.

Thomas shrugged.

"No," signed Francine, "but please be careful. These mining companies on Native lands have a terrible reputation."

Francine's comment struck a defensive chord as Pia thought of Ringo and gulped. She quickly finished up.

Next, it was Thomas's turn.

"Gila River is very large, much bigger than Wind River. But I think it's as much a curse as a blessing. The government provided far more food and supplies than it sounds like you have at Wind River." Thomas looked directly at Pia to accentuate the point. "But I think that it has contributed to a false sense of security. Too much time had been spent debating governance and putting off developing future enterprises."

Pia tried focusing on Thomas's story, but she couldn't shake Francine's comment. She was happy when the day ended, and it was time to escape to her tent. Despite her obsessive thoughts about Ringo, she again slept the sleep of the dead.

Day two had been advertised as different. The conferees would dive into envisioning the future. Despite her assignment at Wind River to draft a future-looking vision, Pia continued to dislike this type of debate because she thought it too theoretical, and people presumed to know more about the variables than she thought possible.

Thankfully, the discussion leaders framed the proceeding with an understanding that they were not going to try to make big decisions today. Pia found the most provocative part of the afternoon a presentation of projections by two scientists, one a speaker and the other a non-speaker. Both agreed that the numbers were clear, even if the underlying reason was not: unless some sort of cure was found and widely adopted, non-speakers would be the majority of the world's population in no more than ninety years and perhaps as few as fifty-five. The percentage of non-speakers born had continued to geometrically increase as predicted and there was no longer any scientific basis for doubting the future. However, the two scientists engaged in an interesting intellectual tussle to close. The non-speaker argued that humanity is in the midst of a historic evolutionary change to human DNA. No, posited the other scientist, it was too early to know that.

At the end of the day, Henry found Pia and suggested that they debrief. Pia agreed, but she had her own agenda.

"Henry, someone said something that I don't really get. This Native woman in my group the first day warned me to be careful of the mining company. It was weird since it seemed to come out of nowhere. What do you make of it?"

"Pia, I have no idea, I wasn't there and don't know the context. But I'm glad that you brought it up. I'm begging you to stay away from John Ringo. He scares me."

"How can I stay away from him, Henry? You and I are the liaisons."

"Pia, you know exactly what I mean."

44

All the News Fit to Print

Sergeant Kenney

"Sergeant, thank you for coming in. I can only imagine that doing so was not an easy decision. My name is Joseph Nightingale, and I am one of the attorneys for the *New York Times*. I was called in by the folks you talked to, two of our very best investigative reporters. Let's start with the main points we covered in our call with you. Please tell us if everything that I outline is correct and add whatever context and details you think are important."

And just like that, I'm taking the dive. Is this typically how people make life-altering decisions? One balances at the edge of a diving board for what feels like an eternity until they allow a gust of wind to blow them off. For me, the gust was the threat to Mandy and Tommy. I no longer control events. Perhaps I never did. The developments of the past month have been more bizarre than the wildest thriller. And yet, it has been my life.

Today, I finally reached my calm place, a location that I have not occupied in quite some time. It felt possible to take the plunge. I picked up the phone and called the *New York Times*. I had no clue as to who to ask for, so I just started talking, first to the operator who quickly redirected my call to the next level. Four calls later, I was speaking with Joseph Nightingale and two reporters on speaker phone.

We agreed to meet later that afternoon at the offices of the *Times*. I told Nightingale about the handwritten note that Charlene had handed me. He explained that it was one of many legal issues that he and the *Times* needed to wrestle with. But he assured me, the paper is definitely interested in running my story, assuming that they can verify my information.

"Sergeant, please excuse me for being redundant, but I do want to make certain that you understand the potential ramifications. We very much want to run with this story because of its obvious significance, but you very well might become a government target. Do you understand that?"

"Yes, Mr. Nightingale, I am prepared. I think that the government may have me in its crosshairs anyway. Whatever I do is a risk, and at this point of my life, I am just as concerned with keeping my self-respect."

I proceeded to tell the *Times* trio everything, including what I knew of Charlene and the others who had been at Camp Tranquility. Lastly, I showed the group what is likely to soon become a well-known note, which they examined with great interest.

Afterward, I find the closest bar and order an Old Fashioned, drink that I haven't had since college. I try to remember the last time I went to a watering hole, and for the life of me, I can't. Is it possible that it was all the way back when Mandy and I were first dating? The memory joins with the growing warmth in my stomach, and the next thing I know, I'm reaching for my cell phone to call my wife. I almost hang up before she answers, but then I tell her what I had just done.

"Of course, you did," Mandy responds. "That's the man I married."

"Have you been able to reach Amy?" I ask.

"Yes, Amy told us to sit tight, and she would get back to us by the end of the day."

After I tell her some of the details of my meeting with Nightingale, she again says how proud she has always been of me and that I am the strongest man she has ever known.

Fast forward to the next morning, and I'm on a conference call with several staff members from the *Times*. They probe even deeper into details, such as what Totali's role had been at Tranquility, the names of other camp officials who might be able to verify aspects of my story, and the chain of events between me and the White House.

Jackie Chen, who identified herself as the lead reporter on the story, jumps in. "Sergeant, we are planning to publish the first of three stories in this Sunday's paper."

I gulp, I hope unseen. "Great, but do I need to get a lawyer?"

Joseph Nightingale jumps in. "Yes, Sergeant, that would be wise. To be

Totalily transparent, my job is to ensure that the paper won't be sued. Your exposure is beyond our purview."

With that, Nightingale tells me that he's about to text me the names of two attorneys whom he would highly recommend. "And by the way, Sergeant, these guys charge a lot and sometimes seem to be doing little, but trust me they are good."

With that Nightingale laughs to no one in particular, a quirk that I picked up on before and am now starting to find a bit irritating.

The next morning, Aide Allman called from the White House. "Sergeant," he announces with great flair, "I am sorry to say this but you have disappointed all of us at the White House and are likely in violation of your oath as a public official."

"How so?" I ask, trying to sound as neutral and clueless as possible.

"Let's stop playing games, Sergeant. We know that you have been speaking with the press."

"Okay, fine. Then I have nothing to say other than I am in the process of obtaining counsel, and please don't contact me again. Have a great day," I say serenely as I hang up.

I met with attorney Germaine Miller a few hours later. We quickly agreed that she and her firm would represent me and that the arrangement would be pro bono.

"My firm has a strong commitment to finding just and lawful means to resolving the current crisis. Additionally, Burns and Belinda LLC has a historic commitment to civil rights causes, and the partners believed that you, as a high-profile African American officer, deserve the very best of representation."

I don't know how to take her last comment, but that aside, I leave feeling equal parts grateful and scared. I imagine that I'm in for the fight of my life.

The *Times* editors emailed me my quotes and the facts attributed to me to check before it all appears in a front-page article tomorrow, in the Sunday edition. I print it and assume my quiet place lying on the living room couch.

Time seems to collapse, and amazingly it's the next morning and there's the paper in front of me. Searching for the article feels like going to the mailbox to find an acceptance or rejection letter from the college of your dreams. I frantically search for the big takeaway, unable to read it in order to fully absorb the story. Like a laser beam, my eyes focused on two headlines.

Extra-Legal Procedures at Camp Tranquility

A Pattern of Misinformation from the White House

45

The Bridgeport Experiment

Sergeant Kenney

I am certain that no one followed us. Not even the best tail would have been able to keep up in the harrowing traffic that is the daily nightmare of I-95 between New York and Bridgeport. Between the mammoth eighteen-wheelers and weaving passenger cars driven by seemingly crazed people, no one would find it possible to track a small vehicle ahead of them for more than thirty seconds.

Mandy and I hold hands when I pull into downtown Bridgeport just as the morning rush hour is slowing. We have an address, so I leave the rest to GPS. Amy had assured Mandy that our new home in the gated community would be safe. Still, with all that had happened in the last seventy-two hours, I could feel the tension in Mandy's hand, and I assumed she could feel mine. Several turns later, residential homes started popping up, and I soon came to a street that was barricaded with a huge traffic bar blocking access. A young African-American woman bounds out from her booth and asks where I am headed.

After we convince her that we have a legitimate address and purpose, she returns to her booth and raises the bar, allowing us to pass. I look back to see the gate closing and wonder if access from every conceivable entrance is similarly restricted. I make a mental note that once settled, I'll drive or walk the entire twenty-two square blocks that Mandy told me makeup Free Harbor, the unofficial name for this seventeen-thousand-person community.

I have so many questions about Free Harbor that I overwhelm myself, which has unfortunately become my recent MO. I make myself stop, but not before listing my most significant concerns. Is everyone here a "friendly"? If so, how did that happen?

Were people forced out so that those wanting to live in an integrated so-called progressive community could do so? Who guarded the gates? What was the stance of the local police about Free Harbor? *Stop,* I tell myself again.

We come to the address, 362 Fairgate, and I pull into a parking spot next to the apartment complex. Here I sit, scanning the many windows, while Mandy dials Amy. Three minutes later, a side door opened and out bounds Amy, beaming. Mandy jumps out of the car, and the two old friends embrace. For a moment, I think that Mandy has forgotten about us until she breaks away from the embrace and grabs Amy's hand, leading her to our car.

"Amy, this is my son Tommy, and you've met my wonderful husband, Geoffrey."

"You can just call me Sergeant," I say with a straight face.

Mandy elbowed me and laughed.

Amy leads us upstairs. There appear to be four units in the building. She places a key in the door and opens it to what I pray will be a new, safer life. The apartment is small and modest, but who cares what it looks like? We made it. I'm free.

Amy gives Mandy a brief tour, while Tommy and I head for the window to check out the neighborhood. After the walk-through, Amy gives Mandy another hug and turns to tell me she's so happy we're here and that my family is safe.

"You must have so many questions but for now I just wanted to show you around. Perhaps tomorrow, you and I can talk about Free Harbor, how it came to be, and how it works. But for now…" Amy stops midsentence, gives me another hug, and bounds out.

"Wow," I say to Mandy, "your pal sure has a lot of energy."

"She is wonderful. I know that she's my friend, but I think you two will really hit it off. Amy has stepped up big time finding us this place in less than two days. In some ways, she's like the mayor of Free Harbor. She knows everything about this community, so I think she will be able to help us get settled. But the hell with all of that right now, sweetie. Let's have breakfast. You must be hungry."

"Famished!"

After we finish our runny eggs and toast, Tommy and I build some Lego structures together while Mandy reads on the couch, occasionally looking up and smiling at me. She looks even more beautiful than seems humanly possible. But as happy as I feel, I can't keep my questions at bay. Eventually, I told Mandy that I wanted to walk the neighborhood and would be back in less than two hours. She looks at me quizzically but doesn't object. Without waiting for her to do so, I'm out the door, with a quick glance at Tommy who is still too tied to his Legos to notice that I am leaving.

I head north away from the guarded gate we had entered hours ago. With no specific destination in mind, I let my instincts as a retired lawman guide me. I want to explore the entire perimeter, but that might be too much for today, so I set my sights on getting a sense of who lives inside this supposedly protected community. The streets are relatively empty, which might be partially due to it being a weekday with school in session. But as I keep walking, I get the impression that no one lives in many of the apartments. I check for the usual signs of occupancy: mail hanging out from boxes, deliveries left outside front doors, newspapers, and anyone coming and going.

Finally, I come upon an older Black man leaving an apartment with a quart of engine oil in his hand as he walks toward a parked car.

"Hey, buddy," I half shout to get his attention, while being sure to display my warmest smile. "How ya doing?"

The man smiles back and waves me over to him.

"What can I do you for?" asks the stranger, who quickly puts out his hand

and introduces himself as Myles.

"Nice to meet you, Myles, my name is Geoffrey Kenney. The thing is that I just moved in here, and I am trying to get a lay of the land. I have been walking for about ten minutes, and one thing that I noticed is that it seems many of the apartments are empty. Am I right?"

With that Myles snickered. "You really are new here. Look, I've got to put some oil in this old piece of shit and then drive to the 7-Eleven to get some milk. If you have fifteen minutes to spare, why don't you just hop in? I will give you the skinny on this place."

So, just like that, my new friend and I head for the convenient market. As we drive, he points to a few apartments and says that he knew the people who had lived there, but they had all been bought out within the last two months. Myles must see my confusion at the term "bought out" so, he explains that the coalition for something—he could not remember the name—was snatching up property, albeit for a fair price.

"Whoever they are, they have been buying up most of the homes so that mutes and their families might take their places."

The term, "mutes," stings, but Myles means no harm, and I need to hear more. We arrive at the store, and I decide I want to walk home, to explore more. Myles invites me over to his place later in the afternoon; I quickly accept.

As I leave the 7-Eleven, I can see another guard house with a security person in it, so I head over. I find a young Latina inside and say hi. She looks pretty indifferent to her job, judging by the headphones she's wearing, the dark shades over her eyes, and the rapt attention she is paying to her iPad. After several attempts to get her attention, I tap her on the shoulder, and she shoots upright, startled.

"What the fuck man, don't sneak up on me like that dude." "Sorry, ma'am but I couldn't catch your eye."

"Wow, so I'm a mam now. This job must have aged me more than I knew."

For a moment, she just stares at me, and then she lets out a cackle indicating that we're cool.

"Hey, I just drove through another gate hours ago, and I'm trying to figure out how to get in and out of this place. How many gates are there and how does security work?"

She looks at me, seemingly trying to determine if I'm serious or just messing with her. I explain my situation without giving too much away—I just moved in today, and I'm very cautious when it comes to the safety of my wife and kid—to put her at ease while assuring her that I am not a cop. The latter, of course, is now true.

Her name is Demitri, and she's been on the job for just ten days after being hired by a security temp agency. Free Harbor, she believes, has ten or so entrances, although it's an open secret that one could find a few unblocked streets here and there, where you could just drive in without being stopped. I ask where one of those open entrances might be so that I could save time in the future, but she just points north. With that, I thank her and head back toward my new apartment.

Something isn't adding up for me. The lack of real security, for starters. Why did they hire some second-rate rent-a-cops, rather than relying on the army of progressive volunteers who were manning the barricades in other enclaves? Buying long-term residents out so that they could establish this supposed safe haven seems at odds with a supposed social justice agenda. I try to stop myself from thinking these thoughts. I have been here for all four hours, and the last thing that Mandy will want to hear is me questioning her judgment and that of Amy. I can wait and get settled in a bit, but at some point, I will need answers.

I arrive at our apartment and find Mandy and Tommy on the floor completing the great Lego project.

"So, Sarge, how was your adventure?" "Fine."

"Fine, that's it?"

"Yeah." Because at this exact moment in time, seeing my two loves relaxed on the floor and having fun is enough.

46

Back on the Reservation

Pia returned from Acoma with a new resolve. She had been told so many times by different people she respected to step up but until now those had been empty words. Now, she felt it.

That night she snuck out of camp as planned to meet John Ringo. When she arrived at the tent, she could see that he had already helped himself to the wine. Ringo jumped up to greet her, but Pia put out her arm to keep him away.

"What's the matter?" Ringo asked with a laugh and a bit of a slur. "Aren't you happy to see me? It's been forever."

"John, I just came to tell you that we are done. I can't keep doing this. It's bad for everyone, including you. If I get caught, I'll be done at Wind River. If you do, you'll get fired. We were crazy to do this…"

Before Pia could finish signing, Ringo pushed her down and rolled on top giggling. He was either drunker than Pia realized or just didn't care. He tried pulling down her pants as she pounded on the sides of his head with both fists. He didn't stop. In a last desperate attempt, she channeled all of her energy into her right leg and violently kicked Ringo in the groin.

"Fuck, why did you do that, you bitch?"

Ringo remained on the floor of the tent but soon began chuckling. Pia looked down at his figure and, with a rush of anger, kicked him in the ribs. Ringo groaned, and Pia ran out into the cold.

The following day, Pia met with Henry to discuss what they would report back to the executive committee about what they had learned at Acoma. After finalizing their talking points Pia looked at Henry. "Thank you."

Henry squinted, his shy, polite way of communicating which became even more exaggerated when he didn't understand something.

"Thank you for your advice and your patience. I have fixed the problem."

Now he understood.

That night, as always, the camp quieted by nine and fell silent less than one hour later. Pia lay in her bunk reviewing the day and thinking about the report on Acoma that she would deliver the next day. Mid-thought, she was startled by a racket outside.

"Piaaaah! Piaaah!"

She ran outside to see a figure riding through camp on a snowmobile.

"Piaaaah!"

Now, half of the camp was awake and outside their bunks. Pia ran toward the dark figure and realized in horror that it was John Ringo.

She made a beeline toward him, but he was driving the snowmobile too fast and haphazardly for her to reach him.

"Piaaaah!

Just then, Pia saw Desiree running toward Ringo with her hands in the air gesturing to him to stop. But Ringo was craning his neck in all directions trying to find Pia. He didn't see Desiree standing directly in front of him until it was too late. Pia heard a thud and saw her friend fly through the air. Ringo swerved upon impact and hit two other residents before crashing into the side of one of the buildings. His snowmobile rolled over and came to a stop. Ringo lay unconscious in the snow. Dozens of people rushed to help Desiree and the two other fallen residents. Pia stood in shock, unmoving.

47

Murder at Tranquility

Sergeant Kenney

The story hit the other major news outlets like a lightning bolt. I started preparing for whatever blowback would follow.

There is little time to lose, as I assume the White House— or at least Camp Tranquility—is preparing a counter-offensive. What will be everyone's reaction to my complete break with the program? I'm not sure how much I even care at this point. Mentally, I've moved beyond fear for my personal security, as long as my family is kept safe.

I sit transfixed next to Mandy as *Facing America* leaps onto the TV screen. Its host, Tubi Garfield, breathlessly tees up the story announcing its impressive array of guests who will help us understand all that was in the dramatic *New York Times* exposé which includes allegations that prison officials murdered at least two detainees. We will hear from the Reverend Samuel Bilarous head of the Coalition for Equity and Fairness and Cyndi Watkins, the director of Homeland Security. The Reverend was first up and lit up the air with the most damning items from the *Times* piece.

"The government is routinely torturing non-speaking resistance leaders.

One, but only one, an example is that of Charlene Vicnacious. I fear for her life because the authorities are growing desperate trying to silence dissent." He proceeds to hold up a blown-up replica of the handwritten note that Carlene had handed me.

"Frankly, if not for the heroism of everyday citizens, in this case, Sergeant Kenney, the authorities would have already murdered Ms. Vicnacious," he concludes.

Now, it's time for the counterpoint. Enter Ms. Watkins, who immediately executes a skillful misdirection by announcing that the *Times* had come up empty on the real story.

"What the reverend has failed to mention is that at least fifteen members of STAM have long been involved in a broad- based conspiracy to overthrow the legitimately elected government of the United States. While I am not free to share details today, I assure you that later this week, what I am saying will all become crystal clear when the Justice Department releases details."

"What the fuck," I mutter and Mandy reaches out and grasps my hand.

Tubi Garfield presses the director, who continues to demur in the interest of national security. However, she feels perfectly free to share one tidbit.

"The government's case will include proof that the source of the *Times'* story was, himself, part of the conspiracy. The public will be able to judge for itself the veracity of the plot once it's safe for the government to share more of this highly sensitive information."

With Tommy in the other room, I suppress my urge to scream. I look at Mandy, who maintains the same steely look that I interpreted as courage many times before.

"We need to be prepared," I say. "Now that the White House has thrown down this conspiracy gauntlet, it won't stop."

Mandy looks at me. "Well, at least for the moment we are safe here at Free Harbor. Whatever happens, I won't allow the three of us to be separated."

I feel like we were trading roles.

"Honey," I say sadly, "please do not make promises. You have been teaching me that. It won't make us safer. You are such a strong woman and you have made me stronger. So yes, I am so glad that we are together. But there are no assurances that we are safe here."

With that, she tears up and tells me, her voice shaking that I have shown the world the man I am, that the man she has always known me to be.

"I married a young man who was hurting but had the inner strength that you are now projecting," she continued. "You are that same man today, only better. Tommy and I love you and always will."

Hearing these words from Mandy feels good. The past few months have been hell, yet today, I feel more centered than I have in quite some time. I am

Geoffrey Kenney, and I will stand up for myself and those who I love. I will not be intimidated.

48

Run

Two of the Wind River residents who had been designated as camp paramedics attended to the three victims, leaving John Ringo lying alone in the snow. After finding that Desiree had no pulse, one of the paramedics began CPR. But it was of no use. She was dead.

The other two suffered broken bones, but nothing life- threatening. Four residents dragged Ringo, still unconscious, into one of the bunks and chained him to an iron frame. Two other residents headed for the tribe's headquarters to get help. Henry grabbed Pia's arm and led her back into her bunk.

Nearly every resident of Wind River was now outside wandering in all directions, some with a purpose and others aimlessly, in grief, as news spread that Desiree was dead. One group was milling around her body crying. People quickly learned that Ringo was from the mine and that he had been screaming for Pia, but why? It didn't take long for a story to emerge. With it, the camp grew even angrier at the killer chained in a bunk, and many started to turn on his presumed lover. Residents piled on to build a narrative, some of it real, much made up. Fury spread like a virus. Tally did her best to disseminate it throughout the camp.

"Where is that cunt?" she signed. People began gathering around her.

"Pia got Desiree killed."

Pia was too stunned to notice the gathering mob outside of her bunk. Henry, who was pacing the cabin, immediately picked up on the danger. "Pia, get dressed. We have to move."

Pia looked up at Henry not comprehending.

"Pia, move your ass. We gotta get out of here, *now*!"

He grabbed her arm, opened the back window, and hoisted her up. She climbed out into the snow with Henry right behind.

"This way, Pia," he signed tugging her away from the camp. "We have to get to tribal headquarters."

The pair walked for less than five minutes before they ran into the two residents who had gone for help, now accompanied by Ahyato. Henry signed to the two residents that Pia was in danger. Ahyato, a non-signer, understood. He reversed direction and led Pia and the group back to tribal headquarters. Meanwhile, the bedlam was growing in the Wind River community. A group of at least thirty were combing the camp for Pia, but she was nowhere to be found.

"Let's get that motherfucking miner," signed Tally. "We'll make him tell us what he and Pia had going on."

The crowd surged toward the bunk where Ringo was chained.

Activity buzzed at tribal headquarters. Word spread quickly throughout the Native village about bad trouble that involved the mining company and dead white people. The head of the Native police, Ehtahlet, had been awakened, and he was on his snowmobile racing toward the Wind River community. When he arrived, he saw a group of at least ten dragging a white man out of the bunk and into the snow. Someone kicked John Ringo.

Ehtahlet was scared. The last thing the tribe needed was an incident involving the miners. He reached for his rifle and fired into the cold night air. Everyone stopped what they were doing and turned toward him.

"Move away from the miner." He advanced toward the mob pointing his rifle in their direction. People scattered. Ehtahlet grabbed Ringo by the shoulders and tugged him forward twenty feet. He turned back toward the mob and told them to move back. No one budged.

Ehtahlet fired into the air again and shouted "*Do IT*" People moved away.

He propped Ringo onto the back of the snowmobile and secured his semiconscious body with rope. Ehtahlet glanced back to make sure that no one was advancing. He hit the gas, and off the two went.

The interruption seemed to break the adrenaline spell that had been cast on the residents. They realized they were exhausted and cold. After another few minutes, they slowly headed back to their bunks.

Ehtahlet was met at tribal headquarters by five others, who dragged

Ringo into a secure room and locked him inside. It was now one in the morning, and it wouldn't be light for several hours. Nothing else could be done tonight.

49

Get Out!

Not many residents slept that night, but at least they stayed indoors until the first light. Henry had returned to the village by three a.m. By six, most people were awake. Henry spread the word for committee members to meet, but he quickly learned that Tally had beaten him to the punch. He hurried to find where they had gathered.

"Hi, Henry," Tally signed with more than a hint of sarcasm. "Welcome back, and I hope that your miner friend is safe."

"Tally, stop," signed a member of the committee. "We need to figure shit out. There's no time for your drama."

Tally looked annoyed but complied. Henry saw his opportunity.

"Listen, we need to be leaders now, not flame throwers. Our entire community is at risk. The tribe is upset, and who knows what the mining company will do. Either we get our shit together, or someone else will come in and tell us how to live, whether that be the feds, mining company, tribe, or some combo."

Tally jumped in. "Yeah, all well and good but first we need to know exactly what happened and what you knew, Henry. You and Pia had a huge responsibility, and you blew it. Why should we trust you now?"

Henry looked at Tally and then at each member. While a respected member of the committee, Henry had been more a follower than a leader. But he knew that this was the moment of truth.

"I will tell you everything that I know, and then the committee can decide what to do next."

Carefully, slowly Henry explained that he suspected but did not know for sure that Pia was romantically involved with Ringo. He had warned her several times to keep her distance from the man. But it wasn't until he and Pia returned from Acoma that she let him know she had ended it.

"That is the truth, every word of it," he said. "Now, it is up to you to decide what you want to do next. The last thing that I will say is that, in my opinion, we need to get Pia out of here ASAP. Her presence is a danger. As for Ringo, the tribal police are in charge. We need to respect whatever decision they make unless we want to get into a conflict with them."

Henry slumped back into his seat. Tally fumed but didn't come back at him.

"Yes," signed another member. "I agree. Priorities number one, two, and three are to get Pia the hell out of here."

Everyone but Tally started to nod in agreement. Defeated in her attempt to exact some type of retribution, she sulked.

The group designated Henry to communicate with Pia that she would be sent packing immediately. He would also serve as the liaison to the tribal police and the mining company. Once the meeting adjourned, Henry hurried to the tribal headquarters. Henry had always looked older than his actual age of 23. With dirty blond hair and an already razor-thin face, the events of the past day combined with a lack of sleep seemed to have added twenty years to his appearance. Bags sunk from his eyes and cheek bones bulged from his gaunt face.

Pia was sitting in the administrative office with a tribal policeman whom Henry didn't recognize. She was drinking something hot, and he saw the ribbons of steam that circled her eyes, but Pia didn't seem to notice much of anything as she stared into the distance.

"Pia," he signed. Seeing no response Henry felt a surge of rage. He shook Pia violently, harder than he intended, to get her to snap out of it and pay attention. She began weeping. The soft tears turned into a torrent, and her body shivered with anguish. "I am sorry, so sorry, Henry."

He sat down next to her and put a reassuring arm around her.

"I know Pia. What happened was a tragedy, and while you certainly share some fault, you are a good person. No one could have anticipated this. But right now, for your safety and everyone else's, we need to get you out of here. Okay? Do you understand?"

Pia nodded, yes.

"Good. Here's what we are going to do."

Henry told Pia about the evolving nationwide transport network that was now operational, something called Light Rail. The word "light" was to acknowledge, that unlike the Underground Railroad on which it was based, those caught were unlikely to be murdered. Rather, the consequences would be being returned to jail or to Wind River. The Light Rail was, in reality, an interlocking network of people, safe homes, and vehicles that transported people between the rural non-speaking communities and urban enclaves. Henry explained that the developing infrastructure might eventually become crucial in the movement to unite non-speakers and progressive speakers.

Henry went on to explain how it all might work for Pia. She would remain here at tribal headquarters until details were worked out—pick-up and drop-off points, handoffs, and lodgings.

Henry stopped himself, realizing that he had strayed. Pia didn't need to hear all of this as her far-away gaze indicated.

"Anyway, the point is that we are committed to getting you safely off the reservation. If we can arrange it, you will be going home to be with your family. I can't promise it but that is the plan for now."

So, Pia's eventual departure was set. Time was of the essence. The longer Pia remained, the greater the risk to her and the community. After Henry left, Pia began thinking of the possibility of being reunited with her mom and Taylor. But strange as it seemed, she didn't feel joy about seeing her family. She felt very little. Despite considering herself a hopeful person, to a fault, she could not at this moment look forward to the future. So much had happened over the past few years that she simply yearned to be left alone somewhere remote. What would the world feel like devoid of other people? Would she miss them? Or would the chirping of the birds and the sound of the wind suffice?

Four days later, two hours before dawn, she lugged her large duffel bag through the dust and tossed it into the back. Pia didn't recognize the driver, and neither of them seemed interested in introductions. He hit the gas, and the van rumbled forward on the unpaved road that twisted up the foothills. Pia looked back at the primitive buildings that she had called home. She tried tricking her mind, substituting a feeling of accomplishment to replace her guilt and sadness. But this was not how she had imagined ending her time at Wind River. She had grown here and had made a real contribution to helping the community survive the winter. But in the end, she had blown it.

Part 3

Great Expectation

50

Get the Job Done

During the first leg of her evacuation from Wind River, Pia was weighed down by guilt and self-loathing. She was single- mindedly focused on the debacle she had brought down on the Wind River community and its consequences. Ironically, the real threat lay two-thousand miles away in a small drab office in the administrative office wing of the White House. There, Special Assistant Joseph Totali sat awaiting specific direction from the undersecretary for Homeland Security.

"So, chief, let's get down to business."

"Thanks, Mr. Undersecretary. One small thing, if I may? Would it be okay to refer to me as the special assistant instead of the chief? I know that it's a small thing. Running prisons was great, but I'd really like to focus on my new position."

"Fair enough, Mr. Special Assistant. For this meeting, should I call you Joe or Mr. Totali?"

"Joe is fine."

"Okay, Joe, let's get started. What do you have for me? Bear in mind that the president has given us explicit instructions to spare nothing in our fight against terrorism."

"First, let me assure you, Mr. Undersecretary, that I am the man for this job. In some ways, you might say that I have been preparing for this assignment my entire life. Over the past few years, I have been monitoring the expansion of STAM, with an eye on its leadership, including Charlene Vicnacious. I believe that she is one of the top three or four in the entire movement. Her network of wannabe revolutionaries is well-organized and relies on sympathizers for weapons, communication, and funding. In my time at Camp Tranquility, I witnessed firsthand how Vicnacious and other militants paid off some of the guards. That's how they were able to smuggle weapons, perpetuate violence on those considered prisoner collaborators, and communicate instructions freely to outside militants. In short, STAM is very dangerous, and we underestimate it and its leadership at our own peril."

"Okay, fair enough, Joe. So, what's our plan?"

"Mr. Undersecretary, I think it's pretty straightforward. We need to eliminate STAM's leadership, including but not limited to Vicnacious. But as importantly, we also must root out the collaborators, who are many. For example, I believe that my second in command at Tranquility has morphed into a STAM sympathizer. I tried using him for a while as a tool, but he has now gone completely off the reservation and is talking to the *New York Times* about so-called atrocities committed against prisoners.

"I am also monitoring the western reservations, as I fear they are becoming breeding grounds for new insurrectionists. We have paid informants among all of the tribes to help us keep tabs on potential threats. As an example of what we are looking for, a prisoner of interest has fled the Wind River reservation after an incident that we are still investigating. I only bring this up because this particular individual is the daughter of that woman Delores Johnston, who was shot years ago and became a symbol of sorts to the progressive movement. But more concerning is that the escapee has connections to Vicnacious from her time at Tranquility. You add it all up, and what I see is the need to be aggressive, very aggressive, to cut off the head of the snake and its offspring."

"I got you, Joe. This all sounds very promising. As I said, the president is adamant that we get things under control by eliminating as many terrorists as possible. Of course, discretion is key. We don't want the president to have any fingerprints on aggressive policing. That's your department. But between you and me, you have lots of running room to get the job done. Given the high priority that the president is placing on your task, if you pull it off, I would not be the least bit surprised to see you tabbed for an even higher position within the administration."

"That's great, sir, and I won't let you or her down. How should I keep you apprised of my progress? Should we meet regularly?"

"No, Joe, that won't be necessary. In fact, it's best for me to stay distant from your work. I am going to designate one of my staffers to be your liaison.

He will help you with any resources that you might need, logistics, manpower, special weapons, that sort of thing. Any questions?"

A small frown of disappointment clouded Totali's face, and he muttered, "No I get it." While he searched his mind for possible follow-up questions, the undersecretary quickly stood and left the room. Totali was left to ponder not just how he'd track down Pia, but also the next move along his career pathway.

51

Sally Parker

Once Pia was evacuated from Wind River, the driver began winding his way through the foothills until they hit the highway. As they passed prototypical American signs like Stuckey's Restaurant & Gas Pia allowed herself for the first time to believe that she was headed home. Her taciturn van driver rendezvoused with his handoff just outside of Powder River, Wyoming. He sat mummy- like in the front seat as a thirtyish-year-old woman with braids got out of her parked Toyota RAV4 and made her way to the passenger door. She opened it and signaled for Pia to follow.

Her name was Sally Parker, and she was the opposite of Pia's quiet van driver. Sally grew up in Chicago and ran some kind of design studio. Her father was a cop and her mother a lay teacher at a Catholic high school in the suburbs. Sally was the palest person Pia had ever seen and looked like a combination of different eras. She had big hair like something Pia had seen in old movies. But her clothes were trendy. Pia pegged her as being in her mid-thirties but Sally was overweight with a large round face that made it harder to judge. As she spoke, simultaneously signing to apparently show off her skills, it became clear that Pia would learn everything that there possibly was to know about Sally and her world, whether or not she wanted to. It was okay, Pia rationalized because listening to Sally would help pass the time over many miles of asphalt between here and New York City.

At first, Pia was simply being polite, but her interest grew as it became clear that Sally and her family defied stereotypes. Sally had said that her cop dad was a law-and-order guy, so Pia assumed that he opposed Sally's volunteering as a driver of illegal human cargo. But she was wrong. Mr. Parker, it turned out, hated the policies and practices toward non-speakers, because he believed such treatment to be un-American and against the teachings of the church. So, when Sally told him that she was going to drive a government exile home to New York, he sat her down and spoke in great detail about how she could keep safe during the journey.

Mrs. Parker shared her husband's beliefs but was frightened for Sally and tried to talk her out of going. But in the end, she signaled surrender by pressing her mother's crucifix into Sally's hand and whispering in her ear to keep safe. The next morning Sally jumped into her Toyota and headed west on I-90. She was determined to make a trip of it and see the sights on the way to the prearranged meeting place. Despite living within a day's drive of the great American plains and the foothills of the Rockies, Sally had never wandered that far. This was her treat to herself. She was happy to take a risk to do the right thing, and why not explore at the same time?

So before picking up her precious cargo, Sally would visit Badlands National Park in South Dakota. She was intrigued by its exotic-sounding name. Sally loved weird geography, and what could be stranger than an attraction named Badlands. She traveled all day and found a motel just before dark about thirty miles outside of the national park. How different everything was out here, Sally thought, including the lifeless buck mounted on the pickup truck in the motel parking lot. She was famished, so after finding her room she walked across the street to a diner. The waitress gave her a friendly hello and asked what she would like.

Still, Sally could not help but feel alone so far from Chicago and on her own. Her father had warned her to keep her head on a swivel and be aware of her surroundings. Do not, under any condition, mention a thing about what you are doing or where you are going, he said. This struck Sally as obvious and unnecessary advice until she remembered that her tendency to overshare was sometimes her undoing.

After a heaping meal of meatloaf, mashed potatoes, and peas Sally had headed back to her motel to sleep. She needed to wake up early the next morning to make it to the rendezvous on time. The light on her phone was blinking, which surprised her since only her dad knew that Sally would spend the night at the A & S Motel, and she had spoken to him less than one hour earlier. So, with some trepidation, she dialed her father, who immediately answered the phone.

"Sally, I am sorry to bother you, but I just learned that there was an incident at the Princeton truck stop about an hour outside of Chicago. I heard it on my police scanner just after we spoke. I have not told your mom because she will likely freak out. From what I gather, there was a shooting and two people were dead with three wounded. The report indicates that it had something to do with a dispute between a non-speaker and a vanload of young men. That is all that I know, but my worry is that once this hits the airwaves, everyone's antenna will be raised that much more. So, as careful as I am sure you are being, double it. Got me?"

Sally promised her dad that she would, and also that she would keep the revolver that he gave her safely in its lock box unless her life was on the line.

Whoa, thought Pia. *Did she just say gun?* Sally finished by mentioning that this was the reason she did not make it to the Badlands and instead made a beeline for Powder River, Wyoming. Pia felt her stomach knot up. She double-checked with Sally to make sure that she had not misheard about the gun. Sally confirmed it but assured Pia that she had it safely stored in a hidden compartment of the car.

Perhaps sensing Pia's unease, Sally grew quiet for the first time and turned on the radio to a country music station. About forty- five minutes later, Sally asked Pia if she would like to call home using a burner phone. Pia asked if Sally was serious, no longer trusting Sally's judgment.

"Is it safe?" Pia asked.

"Sure, but call your brother at this number. We gave him his own burner since he's our conduit on the other end."

Pia examined the phone and looked up again at Sally. "He's expecting your call."

Pia dialed, not believing that she was about to hear Taylor's voice for the first time since she was returned to Tranquility before being transferred.

"Pia, is that you?" answered a voice that was not quite the Taylor she remembered. Of course, he was growing up.

She tapped yes, using a version of Morse code that the two of them used to play.

"I can't believe it. It's real. You are coming home. The last two days have been a bizarre world. I was walking home from school on Wednesday, just like I always do. I stopped at that bakery where you and I used to pick up bread or a goody to bring to mom. I wasn't paying attention, and all of a sudden, this young woman asked me whether I had ever tried the cookies in the far corner, and if yes, how are they? Pia, are you still there?"

"Yeah, buddy, I'm here," she tapped.

"Anyway," Taylor said, "the next thing she says is 'I wonder whether Pia likes these?' Then, she looked around at the others in the store, quickly handed me a note, and disappeared. I looked down at the piece of paper and began to open it, but I thought it would be better to run home first. I was freaked and decided that I would open it with Mom. But halfway home, I caved and ripped it open. It took a few seconds for the message to move from my eyes to my brain. But once it registered, I blasted through the door and handed mom the note."

Delores had sat on the couch, opened the note, and read it with her jaw opening wider and wider. *Pia has left the Wind River Reservation and is traveling home to see you. She is safe and being escorted by STAM security. Destroy this note after reading it. We will contact you again with details. Her trip will take about six days. We will help you make arrangements to move to a protected enclave in the area.*

"Where did you get this?" Delores had asked her son.

"I explained to mom what happened in the bakery," Taylor told Pia breathlessly, "and Mom came over and hugged me. She asked me over and over if it was true. I said yes, but until now I didn't Totalily believe it. I love you, Pia."

There was silence and Pia thought she heard sniffles. "I love you too, Taylor," she tapped out slowly.

"Okay, that's enough for now, Pia." Sally reached over and took the burner out of Pia's hand, placed it down next to her, and reached into her glove compartment. Out came a small hammer which Sally quickly used to obliterate the phone. She rolled down the window and tossed it onto the rapidly moving asphalt.

52

I-80

Pia was unnerved by the shooting in Illinois and discovering that her escort was packing. For the past few hours, Sally and Pia had been scanning the radio for news of any trouble spots that they would want to avoid. The pattern over the past few years had been that trouble spread like a virus. News of one event often seemed to spark other violence. Some of it was typical copycat behavior, while at other times, the law of social physics was at play: action leads to reaction.

The last mileage sign that Pia remembered seeing was North Platte on I-80. Sally decided to stick to the main interstate, thinking that the threat of being spotted was low and worth it to avoid possible yahoo trouble spots if they traveled the backroads. The two were making good time and should make it to the New York area in two days. Pia asked Sally if she knew the plan for the final handoff, but she shook her head. Pia had a strong sense that Sally knew more than she was saying. Still, Pia tried to convince herself that Sally's withholding was for her own good. Henry had told Pia before she was shuttled away from Wind River that her family would be living in a new safe location by the time she arrived. Details were still being worked out, but Henry assured Pia that all would be in order by the time she hit the East Coast.

Pia was still badly shaken by her role in Desiree's death. It was a burden she was sure she would carry forever. Yet, the farther east she and Sally traveled, the more excited she became about seeing her family. Pia continued to peer out the window, checking highway signs for distances to each goal. Once she passed one, she established new metrics, next up, Des Moines. At the same time, she was fighting sleep. She imagined living in a new home with mom and Taylor. She saw images of a place with blinding white sun streaming through dirty windows. Mom and Taylor were sitting on the couch in the diffused light.

Pia was startled awake by glass shattering on the passenger side less than a foot from where she sat. Sally swerved violently to her right just as they both heard a *pop, pop, pop* sound.

“Get down Pia, someone is shooting at us.”

Pia dove to the floor and covered her ears. Sally pulled off into the breakdown lane and reached for the box that contained her gun.

“Motherfuckers,” screamed Sally. Pia remained on the floor with her hands still over her ears, though the shooting had stopped. “Stay down Pia. It’s lucky that we’re on a busy interstate because whoever that was might have been able to finish the job if there were no other cars around.”

After several minutes, Pia heard Sally speak into her new burner phone. “Victor 1, there’s been an incident. Please advise as to any changes to the plan.”

The two sat there for two minutes until the burner rang, and Sally answered it. She listened and nodded before hanging up and smashing the phone with the hammer.

"Okay, Pia, there's a new plan. We'll be meeting another car at the first rest stop after Omaha, okay? I am sorry about all of this. I know that I could still get you there safely, but I don't make the rules" Sally said with tears of disappointment rolling down her face. "You know, I think that I deserve some credit for deciding to take the interstate, which turns out might have saved us."

With that Sally patted the gun, which now sat in her lap.

Pia slowly made her way off the floor while continually checking for suspicious cars. Not another word passed between the two for the next ninety minutes as they closed in on the designated rendezvous spot. Sally was more collected but still appeared distraught. Finally, Pia decided to say something. "Sally, I just want to thank you for helping me and saving me back there. I can't thank you enough!"

With that, Sally smiled but it looked forced. "You're welcome. I just wish the others would realize my value." She continued to massage her gun.

Just calm down. Everything is okay, Pia told herself. She would soon be in another car heading toward her final destination. Pia hoped that her new driver would know the details of how and where she would reunite with her mother and Taylor.

Less than fifteen minutes later, Pia saw the sign for the rest area and Sally pulled into the right lane. Sally pulled past the big central building and circled the parking lot. Pia could only assume that she was looking for a particular vehicle, as she continued to inch forward while peering out her window. Suddenly, she slammed on the brakes, and the car lurched to a stop. A young African-American man, probably in his late twenties, slowly emerged from his car. Sally unfastened her seat belt and raised her gun.

"Sally, what are you doing?"

"Protecting you, that's what I am doing. I don't know this guy. It could all be a setup. This is my mission, and I will carry it out."

"Sally, please!"

Sally pushed Pia hard against the passenger door and jumped out of the van with the gun by her side. The young man slowly approached but jumped back when he saw the gun.

"Jesus, stop," the guy mouthed to Sally, evidently hoping not to attract attention. "Take it easy. What are you doing?"

"Identify yourself right now or get back in your car and drive away," shouted Sally loud enough that a family emerging from their van looked over. Pia held her breath not knowing if they had seen the gun and would call the cops.

"My name is Larry 17683, and I am lost."

With that, Sally shoved the gun into her pants and came over to Pia's door signaling to get out.

"He is the real guy, Pia. Good luck."

Pia rushed over to her new escort and Sally got behind the wheel and took off. Larry, or whatever his real name was, shook his head in disbelief over what had just happened. He put his arm on Pia's shoulder to indicate everything was okay. "We need to move," he said. "I am worried that someone has called the cops, and they might be looking for our blue Honda Accord. The authorities probably wouldn't appreciate the combination of a gun, a white woman, and a Black man. Let's hit it!"

53

Moving on Down to the West Side

Weeks later, Taylor would recount for Pia the crazy few days he and Delores spent relocating in anticipation of her return. Their new home was within something called the Free Zone, an eight-square-block area on the southwest fringe of Greenwich Village. Known as FiZ for short, it sprung to life nearly eight years ago, before anyone could predict the current crisis. Partly as a result of its longevity, FiZ had metamorphosed several times. Befitting its locale, it was first known for its sexual and lifestyle diversity, and more recently as a safe haven for non-speakers, their families, and progressives. The Golden Gate uprising, the term now used to refer to the upheaval that followed the release of the infamous government memo, further invigorated FiZ.

Mom and Taylor were told that they were to move to this rendezvous spot because it was one of the few places that STAM could, to a degree, guarantee their safety. There was no way in or out without being screened by a ragtag army of progressive militants, New York University student volunteers, local residents, and supportive ex-military. The NYPD and other authorities that might otherwise be a threat to Pia's freedom had largely ceded control of these blocks. But that didn't preclude occasional incursions into FiZ by elements suspected of being para- government, including a recent one in which seven people were shot and two killed.

Delores and Taylor had quickly gathered their stuff and moved in one day. They kept most possessions back in their home off Canal Street, given that they planned to split time between both. Pia, of course, would have to learn to live full-time within FiZ, but at least they would have her back. Taylor was excited about Pia but worried about his mother, who seemed as confused as she was happy by the speed of events.

The wait for Pia was excruciating. Taylor and Delores had heard nothing about where Pia was or when she would arrive. Taylor found it hard to think about school or much of anything other than his sister. Meanwhile, Delores seemed weighed down by everything that she had gone down over the last few years.

As Taylor was anxiously awaiting Pia's return, Larry 17863 was traversing the backroads of Pennsylvania and monitoring his police scanner. He gave Pia a handheld radio and asked her to listen for news about the incident at the rest stop. One of Pia's eyelids had slid down and the other was about to follow when a radio host's announcement of "breaking news" shocked her awake.

"We have just learned that federal prosecutors will charge Charlene Vicnacious and fourteen other STAM members with a plot to overthrow the government of the United States. This comes on the heels of the explosive *New York Times* exposé on the treatment of prisoners and the announcement last week by the Justice Department of an ongoing investigation into all aspects of the case. Vicnacious is being transferred to Washington D.C., where she will be formally indicted. That is all that we know at this time but more to follow."

Pia banged Larry on the shoulder and signed for him to pull over.

"What's wrong?" he asked slowing to a stop on a small dirt pull out.

Pia signed him the news, including that she was a fellow inmate and friend of Charlene's.

"This is terrible. Poor Charlene. They won't stop until she is either dead or Totalily broken. I cannot believe all of the shit that keeps piling up."

Larry shook his head sympathetically. "I know this sucks Pia, but we need to get back on the road or we might be joining Charlene in jail or dead. And by the way, my STAM comrades have reason to believe that there is at least one informer among the Wind River community and that the authorities had been tipped to your movements. So, we can't take any chances."

With that, Larry took off.

"They are never going to stop are they," signed Pia. "Even if we make it to New York City, I won't be safe. Desiree was right about everything. We need to fight if we are going to live. Fuck it. I am going to fight."

"Pia, I don't know you and your back story but I do know this. Your only chance is for me to get you to the designated safe zone. All of this other drama can wait. So, for the next 12 hours I need you to keep your eyes and ears open and your brain clear. Can you do that?"

54

Doubts

Sergeant Kenney

"Good morning, Sergeant, this is Joseph Nightingale from the *Times*, how are you?"

"Hello, Mr. Nightingale," I reply. "I'm hanging in."

"Fair enough. We have a few questions for you, and perhaps you for us. Might we proceed?"

"Sure, let's do it. My wife, Mandy, is going to join me unless you have any objections."

"No, that's fine." Nightingale giggles. His laugh still drives me nuts. It almost sounds creepy, and I wonder again if I can even trust him. But it's probably just a harmless quirk.

"First of all, Sergeant, given the government's allusion to further indictments being possible, are you concerned that they will charge you?"

Mandy and I look at each other. I know my wife, and I can tell that the question agitated her. She's ready to pounce. I shake my head at her, and Mandy swallows her words.

"Well, Mr. Nightingale, I'd say, no I don't expect it, as I have done absolutely nothing to warrant it. But that said, I have little faith at this point in our legal system, so who knows?"

"Is there anything, Sergeant, that you haven't told us that the government might use to indict you? Even if you consider it small, we need to know. Please understand that we all stand by your story and have an ethical responsibility to print the truth. But that's the thing. We need to be sure that the *Times* is not walking into an ambush here. So, please think carefully about whether there's anything that you might not have shared with us."

"I shared everything, folks. All that I can hypothesize is that Totali might have manufactured something to add to his bullshit file on me."

"Wait a minute, sergeant," Nightingale says, "what file?" "I believe that I mentioned that once or twice when Totali was trying to intimidate me to go along with his sadistic program, he talked about a file on me that he said could use at any point to fire me. But it was all bullshit."

"Did you ever look at what was inside?"

"Yeah, briefly. He took it away before I could see much. As I said, it was crap. Innuendos and he said/she said, third-hand accounts from other guards that I was supposedly helping some of the inmates."

"Which inmates, Sergeant? Was Charlene Vicnacious one of them?

"Well, yes. She was Totali's main target, but as I said, any indication that I was in her pocket is Totalily made up."

"I understand, Sergeant, but in these times and circumstances, who knows how the government might choose to use such information? I wish that you had told us all of this before."

"There was nothing to tell. As I said, none of it is true. There was nothing to tell."

"Okay, Sergeant, thank you for your time. You'll be hearing from us soon. Have a nice day."

Mandy and I look at each other.

"Those feckless assholes," she says. "What do you think we should do?"

"I think that we need to start thinking about a plan B and C. This place isn't safe regardless of what Amy says."

"I don't know about that, Geoffrey. Maybe we need to start thinking about cutting a deal."

"Cutting a deal? What deal, and with whom?"

"The government obviously," Mandy says, now looking annoyed.

"Are you serious? Do you think they would even stick by it? I can't believe you of all people would say that. What are you thinking?"

"Let's just drop it, Geoffrey. All I'm doing is what you always do think of options, all the different ways that the three of us might survive. I'm not proposing anything, just thinking out loud. But I guess that you are the only one allowed to make decisions for this family."

55

Keep Your Head Down

Larry cut the engine and shook Pia. She barely stirred. He shook her again.

"What's the matter?" Pia muttered.

"Nothing. We are here. You are home. You are safe."

Pia held her breath as if the sound of air entering and leaving her mouth would give them away. She kept her head down while trying to keep an eye on the passenger window to get her bearings. She knew that she was in New York because she could hear and smell it. Pia felt the car back up and saw the lights from what looked like basement apartments. Were mom and Taylor close by? What was happening?

Someone opened the door.

"Pia, you need to keep the blanket wrapped around your head. The guy at the door will lead you inside, okay? Congratulations, you made it home."

Pia did as she was told and followed the stranger inside. As soon as she passed into the vestibule, she turned to thank Larry, but he was already gone. The new mystery escort led her upstairs. Pia held her breath as she climbed the few stairs. It was hard to believe that in a few moments, she would be with her mom and Taylor. The next chapter of her life was about to begin.

56

Joan of Arc was Overrated

Charlene

It's impossible to sleep during this six-hour journey from the grasp of Totali into the hands of my new captors. The leg irons and cuffs that the FBI agents fastened to my body ensure that I won't be able to nap. Instead, I looked for markers through the tiny rear window to determine where we had just been. Maybe that will help me figure out where we're going. The six FBI agents sit silently on the opposite side of the van and remain so when I ask them about my final destination.

It must be well past midnight when the van comes to a stop. The FBI agents spring to their feet and open the door. A few minutes later, they returned and led me to the rear door of a building, a federal lockup in Alexandria, Virginia. I maintain the same expression that I learned over my years of captivity: blank. Initially, it was just a strategy to reveal nothing to my captors, but now I feel like this is really who I am on the inside.

Even though my face doesn't show it, I am frightened. I had steeled myself to die at the hands of Totali, with the only question being when and how. But this new turn of events is scarier. It has a different type of finality, one that I had not prepared for. I'm haunted by a sense that I have blown it, that I have never really lived. I try to shake the feeling from my head by scolding my brain for concocting a silly drama. Yet, I can't. At this exact moment, all that I can recall from my entire life is conflict and heartache. Now I'm afraid that I have failed at life's most basic elements: finding someone to love, someone who would love me, someone who would make me more human.

But the world will see nothing of my struggles and who I really was and am. Instead, they will see a made-for-TV drama. I imagine my trial, and how I will be portrayed. For some, I would play the role of heroine, a modern-day Joan of Arc. For others, I'll be Charlene Vicnacious, supervillain and traitor to America. But what I feel right now is far less dramatic than any of that. I feel all alone.

How would I live if, magically, I was freed? Who would I be? I don't know. I try imaging myself living with someone like LJ, but who wouldn't betray me? I had loved her and imagined that she loved me. Would that be possible with someone else, or was I too far gone to open myself up again? I try to transport myself into a normal future, but there's nothing there. So, I change the topic like I'm changing the channel inside my brain. Instead of trying to figure out love, I wonder if the government might offer me a deal and what it would be. But it really doesn't matter. What would I gain from accepting any plea? In exchange for not executing me, the best they would offer is the opportunity for me to spend a few more decades locked away with my haunting thoughts. No, thank you. I retained my dignity, and I intend to keep it. Even if the image that popular progressive culture had created of me was one-dimensional, I am proud of the stands that I took and my refusal to buckle. If that's all that I have, so be it. It's something, maybe even a lot.

I think back to the days in Tranquility. Compared to what came later, it now seems like a day camp before that crazy day when Pia's mother was shot. I often think of Pia, despite the fact that we only spent six months together. There was something about her that sparked my curiosity. We were different—that was obvious—but there was something else whether that be a reminder of my sister or the surface innocence she projected despite the hurt.

If she and I were free, I think that I would want to sit down with her and try to figure out the attraction. It certainly was not sexual. There was something about her pain that stirred me. Hers was restrained, somehow elegant. Mine was visceral and overwhelming. Was it possible that if we spent enough time together, we might heal each other? No, that was stupid. But still, there was something.

57

Sweet and Sour

The weeks since Pia got out of a van and into a Greenwich Village apartment hideaway had sped by, while also moving at a snail's pace. Pia felt absolute joy one minute and emptiness the next. She was confused and unmoored, even while reveling in the embrace of her family.

Pia's first few days with her mother and Taylor were wonderful and surreal. She felt safe from the world in their tiny apartment. It was like a dream, and dreams are not to be disturbed by reality. The three never thought about going out during those first few days. When Pia was not hanging out with her family, she spent much of her time looking out the single window overlooking the street. She tried to imagine what life was like out there, and how the good guys kept the boogie man outside the gates.

Pia often replayed the moment when she first passed through the door into her new life. Her mom screamed. Taylor tried to muffle his joy into the palms of his hands, afraid that the authorities would somehow be alerted by his shouts. Pia cried so hard that she vibrated and almost stumbled to the floor. She laughed at the memory of the tall, incredibly skinny escort who whispered so urgently for everyone to please move inside. He looked more like a character from a touring carnival than someone assigned to security. Pia's first reaction, once she composed herself that day, was that Taylor had morphed into a man, and her mom aged two decades. Pia had stared long and hard at Taylor.

"What," he said, "did you think that I would stop growing just because you weren't watching? And look at you Pia, all pumped and hard looking."

They both laughed.

That first day, the three talked for as long as they could, until Pia's emotional fatigue had triumphed over the adrenaline rush. She headed to the cot in the living room intending to wake early to continue catching up. But she was exhausted and didn't wake from a deep, dreamless sleep until late the following afternoon. Mom was doing something in what passed for a kitchen, and Taylor was gazing down at her smiling.

"Morning, sis," and with those words, Pia and Taylor began to explore a new groove of sibling banter.

She felt like the clichéd older relative but could not but keep thinking how quickly he had developed into a young man. Taylor broke the spell and started the conversation. As strange as it might seem, after years apart, she could not think of anything to tell him. So, Taylor began filling Pia in about his school and friends. "Stuyvesant HS is intense, not in a good way, but I've been able to create guardrails with a small group of close friends. We've got our own world that keeps us sane." Pia thought to herself thank God that he still has his geekiness. But he was different. He had an edge. Or had it always been there, and Pia had never noticed?

As they talked, the newer Taylor began coming into focus. He was confident in who he was. She was struck by that quality because it was one, she had been chasing. *My little bro no more,* she thought to herself.

Taylor was also angry. Not in the way that some people take license to constantly vent about the unfairness of their lives. He was angry about the people in charge. Pia asked him whether he had plans for college, and he just rolled his eyes at her. Pia gave him her best quizzical face, but rather than laughing as he had in the past, he just looked away.

"WTF Taylor," she signed. "Hey buddy, lighten up."

But her deflection fell flat, and Taylor just looked at her with an expression that she had never before seen him wear. Pia still felt his warmth and love but also his almost dismissive anger.

"What is it?" Pia signed.

Before she finished, he moved next to her and put his arm around his sister, but rather than helping it made her feel uneasy.

Later that day, the three were drinking coffee in the kitchen with the radio on in the background. Delores was joking about her myriad of medical issues. She had four different specialists, seven medications, and three hospital locations that kept her busy.

"It is my full-time job," she said with a smile that could not cover up the deep fatigue etched on her face.

Pia asked what the doctors were saying. Delores looked at her, and then at Taylor, and said in a soft voice that there were medical issues associated with the shooting years ago that had gotten worse.

Taylor looked surprised, and something else—pissed. The siblings exchanged glances. Delores, reading the atmosphere, expanded upon the bomb that she had evidently just dropped on her son.

"Taylor, I am sorry if I haven't kept you apprised of all my medical issues, but really, what would have been the point? It's been years since the shooting, and you have grown into a young man. You have a life. And now Pia is home. So, I am doing great. I don't know how much time I have, nor do my doctors. I want to live my life free of medical drama. And you and now Pia do not need to be sitting around worrying about every change in my condition. Do you understand?"

"No, mom, I don't understand because what you are saying makes no sense," Taylor fumed. "But why start now? We never talked about anything real as a family in the past. Not dad's depression, not about how much danger Pia was in, not about pretty much anything."

Taylor looked at his mother who sat stone-faced, and then back at Pia before doing a one-eighty. Delores went in the opposite direction to escape into the farthest corner of the apartment.

Pia started after her mother and then thought to herself, *Fuck it, I'm not going to continue to play the adult child role and smooth things over for everyone. I'm going out.* Without telling either Taylor or Delores, Pia was out the door.

She had only been out into FiZ a few times and had never wandered far. She was curious about life beyond the boundary of her new enclave and decided to explore the closest border, which was on the north side. When she arrived, she found apartment buildings bordering the city beyond. She could hear the sounds on the other side and wanted to see for herself, so she continued along the border until she came to a heavily armed gate that looked pretty well secured.

"Hi, may I ask you a question?" Pia signed, looking at one of the dozen or so armed guards, a thirtysomething dressed in army fatigues.

"Only if you can convince me that you are not a cop or some other government toad," said the man, without smiling.

"Fair enough, but how can I prove it to you?" He continued to eye Pia suspiciously until his gaze was broken by a large bang beyond the gate. Pia turned her head to see a car explode into a ball of flames and people running away. It was followed by the sound of shattering glass and people piling into the few stores still open.

Looters emerged less than sixty seconds later; arms loaded with small electronics. Sirens blared, and cop cars screeched to a halt trying to block the perpetrators from escaping. Next came the sound of gunfire. Before Pia could react, she was tackled. Struggling to breathe under the guard's weight, she tried in vain to push him off. A few seconds later he rolled off.

"I seriously suggest that you get the hell away from this area unless you want to end up dead," the guard said. "Shit like this goes down here without warning pretty much all the time. I don't know who you are or what you want, but consider yourself lucky that you are on this side of the divide."

With that, Pia turned around and headed back to the apartment. She didn't want to face the shit storm with her family but was resigned to deal with it. She quickly covered the five blocks, turned the key in the lock, and entered, bracing herself for the next act of family drama. Instead, she found Taylor and Delores watching TV.

"We have breaking news," said the talking head behind a news desk. "Charlene Vicnacious and fourteen other members of STAM have been formally charged with capital treason. Over the past year, Vicnacious has become one of the recognized leaders of the militant non-speakers movement, so these charges are not a Totali surprise. Our news team will keep you updated as events develop."

58

Utopia Tilts

Sergeant Kenney

To my surprise and delight, our community meeting to discuss increased security led to a consensus about how we'll keep Free Harbor safe for the next few weeks. But we need to move quickly—everyone agrees that Charlene's indictment will mean more violence from both sides. Our first steps are walling off sections of our building so that no one but the fourteen of us can go in or out. The other task is far more challenging: bringing in supplies and weapons at night until we have enough for at least sixty days. Clandestine trips outside of Free Harbor would be a necessity.

I'll be the lead for tonight's excursion, along with two of my neighbors. I'm on edge. We have limited knowledge of conditions outside over the past twenty-four hours but there was nothing that we can do about it. The three of us will be armed and our arrangements with our supplier are solid. We pay in cash, plenty of it, and with that comes a certain degree of loyalty.

My nervousness about the planned supply run is somewhat lessened by the feverish pace of the construction. What we lacked in building expertise, we make up for in redundancy. So, our barrier walls might not be up to industry standards, but we built two back- to-back, just to be safe. Our small community includes three other children in addition to Tommy so we turned construction into a game. The kids were tasked with decorating the walls once they dried, and now we call that area the children's zone. Their laughter as they paint and color the wall—always forbidden at home—helps lighten the mood for all of us.

Just before midnight, Frank, Camille, and I set out on what I hope will be the last of our supply missions, at least for the next month. I go out first, while the other two cover me from behind the threshold of the building. Our car is hidden away under tree branches in a utility area twenty yards away. I move a few feet at a time, and when I reach halfway, I signal for my friends to follow.

We slowly climb into the car and wait to see if anyone is watching. About ten minutes later, confident that we were alone, I turned the ignition key and held my breath. Still, no one around, so we slowly roll the car out from under the greenery and head for danger.

We reach the southeast guard gate, wave at the security crew, and pass through. We come to a large fire in a nearby dumpster surrounded by a group drinking beer and randomly throwing bottles. Other than them, the streets are quiet, and we'll soon be at our destination. As we passed under I-95, we heard what I hope is the backfire from a truck. We all jump. A minute or so later, we turn into an abandoned industrial park and crawl up to a loading dock, turn off our lights, and honk twice. Nothing. We wait, and five minutes later, honk again. Still, no one comes out, so we can either go in, which we've never done before, or go home empty- handed. I slowly get out of the car holding a handgun. I look back at my two neighbors, who are pointing their rifles out the back windows, trying to cover my approach to the dock.

"Roseman," I yell in the direction of the door by the dock, hoping to get the attention of our supplier. I say his name again, but still nothing, so I signal for one of my friends to move closer.

I'm going to go inside. I push the door open and hug the wall to my left while my eyes adjust to the dark. I hear nothing so continue inching my way along the wall.

"Roseman where the fuck are you?"

I'm ready to give up when I hear some muffled sounds coming from the other direction. I inch my way back toward the door, open it, and wave Camille inside. She and I head toward the sounds until we see a dimly lit office about thirty feet ahead.

"You stay here," I tell her, "and guard my back. If anything goes wrong, do what you can to cover me, but then get out of here and head back to Free Harbor with Frank."

She nods. I hold my breath and go forward.

I get within arm's length of the office door, crouched down below where I could be seen, and knock. Someone opens it, and I stand up to see who it is, pointing the gun right at the figure and asking what happened to Roseman. The man lights a cigarette, revealing the gaunt smug face of a stranger whom I had never seen before.

"Roseman went out of business, homes, but luckily for you, I have taken over. You got the money?"

I hope that I'm still being covered from behind. I tell the stranger that I wasn't stupid enough to come in carrying cash, but I assure him that I have it.

"Great," he says, "let's do business. Before your Mr. Roseman retired, he kindly left me a list of customers. What is your name?"

"Dude, you don't need to know my name. Here is the list that I gave to Roseman. Do you have the shit or not?"

"Calm down homeboy, of course, I have your stuff. But where is the money?"

"Meet me outside by the dock with all of our supplies, and you will get your money, every cent of it."

With that, I inch backward and feel relieved when I hear him moving in the same direction. We come to the door, Camille opens it, and we both high-tail it back into the car to wait. In less than one minute, the door to the dock opens, and a small group starts pushing out our supplies. They load everything into the trunk and back seat, leaving the three of us huddled together in the front nervously holding our weapons.

"That's it, homes, now the money."

I hand sixty twenties to him, and we speed away. I hope that this is it. I tell myself that I'll never go back to that place. After a few minutes, we approach the dumpster fire, which has only grown bigger and rowdier. I let out a sigh of relief knowing that the security gate is just thirty seconds away when I hear a pop and my side window shatters. I swerve to the right but keep driving.

"Shit, is everyone okay?" I shout.

59

He's Dead

Sergeant Kenney

Camille runs inside to get help, and I start to drag Frank's limp body toward the apartment door. Mandy, Dr. You, and others rush out to help.

"Honey, were you hit?" Mandy asks as she helps me push Frank through the door, simultaneously checking my body for blood.

Once inside, we place Frank on the bed. Dr. You rips open his shirt to find bullet wounds in the chest area. She frantically begins CPR, stopping only to listen for a pulse. After several minutes of this process, she drops her head and utters the words everyone knew were coming.

"Frank is dead."

Mandy cries and others scream, but I can only stare, numb to all that has happened.

In the morning, three of us, fully armed, go back to the security gate to see if there's anything to learn. The post is abandoned. Whatever security there had been is gone. The street outside the gate, where the shots seemed to have come from last night, is eerily empty. We returned to the complex and shared the news.

“Thank God that you were so insistent about walling us in here,” says Mandy.

I tell everyone that for now, I think that we are safe but much of the area directly outside Free Harbor has been overrun with looters. I don’t know if anyone else was hurt or killed, but we are on our own until things calm down or we find a way to sneak out.

60

Mother Nature

The government refuses to comment on a story posted by the Sunshine Radicals. The article appears to include some highly classified and potentially explosive information, all of which was later confirmed by other anonymous sources:

General Augustus, Chairman of the Joint Chiefs' of Staff facilitated a top-secret meeting last month deep in the belly of the CIA headquarters at Langley, Virginia. The general shifted his eyes around the table looking for something, anything, to answer these questions.

"You are the CIA's best scientists and analysts," he said, "and our task is clear: to make sense of the new data. Why has there been such an alarming acceleration in the percentages of non- speakers being born? Why are these new numbers at odds with what most scientists, including you all, had predicted? Here are the facts as I understand them. Please jump in if I get anything wrong. First, the new numbers indicate that non-speakers will likely become the majority of the population in the world by 2071 rather than 2094. Second, there is reason to believe that the rate might increase again, perhaps by a factor of one point five to three. Is that right? McKenzie, as the top CIA analyst here, please highlight the potential impacts of these data. "

"Thank you, General," the analyst began. "The most obvious is that the initial fifty-year cushion had created enough psychological buffer between the now and then that there was little panic within the general population. Something fifty years away struck most people as beyond their lifetimes or attention spans. Sure, there was concern, but no immediacy, no existential panic.

Most importantly major multinationals were not running to cash out. But the new projection of 2071 might burst Americans' psyche.

"My analysis, therefore, is that the United States government needs to begin planning tomorrow for a multitude of impacts in the medium- and long-term. To state the obvious, if the United States is to survive as the leader of the world, it will need to do so first with integrated leadership consisting of speakers and non-speakers, and eventually only the latter. We need to build a heterogeneous leadership structure and extend it to all American institutions: the military, civil government, police forces, civic, everything.

"We also need to factor in the psychological realm. The CIA's top social scientists have produced several papers over the past few years trying to pinpoint the stressors and how to best manage them. While it remains impossible to predict impact with certainty, it is clear that the nation's top leadership must pay acute attention to managing generalized and specific psychological stresses unlike anything the United States has experienced. Imagine the actions and reactions as speakers approach and then achieve minority status.

"From a strategic standpoint, the obvious answer is to immediately begin co-planning with the growing non-speaking population to ensure a continuation of the American way of life both here and in the influence, we project around the globe. We need to establish a strategic American partnership between speakers and non-speakers that ensures a peaceful passing of the torch while protecting the rights and property of living speakers. Our intelligence analysts have been studying how other countries have been preparing for the eventual, be it 2096 or five years from now. Many are frozen by deep political divisions. But a few, like Australia, are already moving toward a smart integrated strategy. All the while, we in the United States are unfortunately bogged down. So, gentleman, it is here that our agency has its work cut out for us."

"Thank you, McKenzie," the general resumed. "So, there it is. We all know that our politicians and their parties are best suited for planning for the next election cycle and a little more. Matters have only been exacerbated by the announcement of the capital trial of the STAM- 15. President Sanchez has staked out her most extreme position to date. It will be difficult to get her to shift, certainly in the short term. Nevertheless, it is what we need to do. I am open to your thoughts and questions. Jones, how about you?"

"Well, sir," the junior agent began, "I think that we have our work cut out, but frankly, we have little choice. We urgently need to start advocating within the intelligence community for partners. I believe that many share our stance, but getting anyone to put their careers at risk is the challenge."

"Thank you, Jones, that is spot on," said the general, as he saw a hand go up. "What is it, Edgars?"

"Thanks, general. These data speak for themselves. All we need to do is get them out and be ready to explain what it all means. That is our job."

"Fuck, yeah, why hadn't the rest of us thought of that Edgars? It should be easy. I'll get right on the horn with the president."

61

We Gotta Get Out of This Place

Sergeant Kenney

One of my favorite books growing up was *Tale of Two Cities* and the line "It was the best of times; it was the worst of times." I can't get it out of my head as Mandy and I watch events unfold. The worst of times was easy to identify, as America continued its slow but steady slide into anarchy. The best was less tangible but lay with hope for a better future as we read about non- speakers and then supporters starting to shape a future America. From the rural west to the big East Coast cities, new communities were popping up that were rejecting the brutality of Sanchez's America, while looking to build a future made up of progressive speakers and non-speakers. Some of the new communities floundered. Disagreements among allies flourished and threatened the entire movement. Yet, there was hope in the air.

But Mandy's and my optimism for a future in which Tommy might grow up in a healthy environment continues to be dampened, not only by the news reports we read but by what we witnessed firsthand, most horribly Frank's murder. Free Harbor is especially vulnerable because, in the rush to build it, many obvious security issues had been overlooked. The surrounding community is rapidly descending into anarchy, and rather than new residents flooding in to fill Free Harbor, many are leaving.

I've been thinking about all of this since the shooting but hadn't brought it up to Mandy. But then she surprised me.

"Honey," she began hesitantly. "I have been thinking that we should leave here, and that was even before the shooting."

I held my breath not wanting to interrupt. "Why Mandy?

Are you sure? Where do you think that we should go?"

"Well, I don't exactly know, Geoffrey. There are places that seem safer like that Fuzz, or whatever they call it."

"I think you mean FiZ, for Free Zone," I laugh.

"Yeah right, that's it. And there are others. I think that we should look into them."

I'm surprised but happy that Mandy seems to be separating her loyalty to Amy for our well-being and knew that one of those communities would offer a better life for Tommy. Beyond that, I'm beginning to appreciate that a worthwhile future depended on all of us slowly, perhaps painstakingly, building a new way of living. This is what swims through my head as I drift off to sleep.

I awake to see Tommy sitting on Mandy's lap by the computer, the morning sun streaming in.

"Geoffrey, come look at this."

I sidle up beside her and see on her screen a web page titled Free Zone America.

"Honey, I found an interesting one in New Haven not far from Yale. It is only four- square blocks, but the description sounds perfect for us. What do you think? Should we check it out and how?"

"Yeah, Mandy, I think that we should investigate it and every possibility including whether we could get there safely. But I have an idea. Do you remember that young woman from Tranquility I told you about?

"Anyway, I didn't want to upset you, but last week, Nightingale called. At first, I was pissed because I thought it would be more of the same with him protecting the *Times'* ass at our expense. But he gave me a heads-up. Turns out that our old friend Totali is heading up some secretive unit within Homeland Security, and he suspects that it may be involved with some extra-legal actions."

"Extra-legal, like what?"

"He didn't know and therefore couldn't say, but reading between the lines, he may have been hinting at assassinations."

"Was he talking about you?

"Again, he didn't know, but he called to warn me, so I'd say he at least has reason to suspect that."

"Fuck, fuck, fuck. Oh, my God, do you think that's what happened to Frank? They were trying to kill you?"

I give myself some time to recover from Mandy's startling conclusion, and then I text Pia. She takes about an hour to respond.

"Hello, Sergeant, it was quite a surprise to hear from you. It's been a while. The last time I think was just before they sent me away to Wind River."

"I remember that," I text back. "I still feel guilty for not giving you more information about what Totali and his bosses were planning. But perhaps I can somewhat make it up to you and ask you for a favor in return."

"Go on Sergeant."

I text Pia about our situation, and she says that she knows nothing about other places but will try to find out. She promises to text me back ASAP.

"And what about Totali?"

"Pia, I can't tell you the source of this information, but I trust it. If it's correct you and I are in imminent danger. Apparently, Homeland Security has set up a hit squad. I know this may sound crazy, but you and I may be on the list. As a matter of fact, they may have already tried to kill me but missed."

There's a long pause between texts, and I start to worry that I scared off Pia.

"Thanks, Sarge," a new message pops up. "I appreciate it. I'll get back to you if I can find information to help you get out of Bridgeport."

62

Moving Day

Sergeant Kenney

Six days after I texted Pia, we were ready to leave. She had passed on information about a community in Rhode Island and said that her source was reliable.

I see the truck labeled Acme Meats pull up around three a.m. The driver turns off his lights and engine. Mandy and I have hardly slept; we've been peeking through the window for the last hour. We had packed all of our bags before going to bed but only after we knew that our neighbors, especially Amy, wouldn't drop by. It was tough, but I convinced Mandy that out of an abundance of caution, we should tell no one. Mandy feels guilty about Amy, but she knows it's necessary. Once we're safe, she knows she can reconnect with Amy and ask for forgiveness. I don't think she'll need to beg— my leaving will keep the people of Free Harbor safer too.

"Tommy, let's go," I say as I shake my sleeping son. I took his hand and did one final check of the apartment to ensure that we had taken all that we could and needed. With that, we quietly make our way downstairs through the security door in the new wall that we built just weeks ago. During the day, I still have vivid memories about the night Frank was shot, and I have nightmares about it when I sleep. Rushing off into the outside world once again makes me shiver. But I can't let it show. I smile at Tommy as he holds my hand and urges me to swing him. I do.

Tommy and Mandy hide in the vestibule as I peek outside and carefully make my way to the cab of the truck.

"Hi, Vincent, good to see you," I tell the driver, on whom I've never laid eyes before.

"You too, Paul, is your cargo ready?" Having passed the security check, I signal for Mandy and Tommy to step out, and they move quickly to the truck. I opened the back for them, found a few seats with seat belts, and helped fasten Tommy's. Vincent explains the details. Mandy and Tommy will remain in the back until we arrive at our destination in southern Rhode Island. If they need anything before then Mandy will knock twice on the back of the truck close to where I'm sitting. We estimate the trip will take two hours if we don't encounter obstacles along the way. It's a big if.

Vincent is carrying an automatic handgun. He hands me another, saying that he's only doing so because I am an ex-cop with firearm experience. He turns the engine key but keeps the headlights off, and we creep toward the abandoned security gate. All is quiet, so we slip out to the streets and soon find the entrance to I-95 north. The plan is to stay on the interstate, if possible, which means traveling through a few coastal communities, first in Connecticut and then Rhode Island. Those are the likeliest to be problem areas, but it's all a crap shoot.

As we approach New Haven, I can feel the hairs on my neck standing on end. In a few miles, we'll reach the turnoff where I-95 continues east toward Rhode Island and I-91 heads north to Central Massachusetts. New Haven has been in the news recently with random violence including multiple shootings and arson, some on or close to the highway. I notice Vincent patting his holstered gun. I hope the frigid predawn temperatures will keep more of the bad guys indoors. There are in fact few cars on the road and campsites by the sides, which is good. Vincent moves to the left lane when the split between I-95 and I-91 is less than one mile away. This spot is often backed up, but this morning it's smooth sailing.

I look back at the New Haven skyline once we're on the bridge. I can see scattered fires, likely from people who are unhoused trying to stay warm. All in all, things look quiet. There are no large cities the next forty miles, but lots of strip malls with on and off-ramps every few minutes. Near these, the danger is greatest. Vincent keeps looking out his window and at the rear-view mirror, while I keep watch on the right. About thirty minutes outside of New Haven, I hear Vincent yell, "Shit!"

I jump to attention.

"What is it?" I ask, not seeing anything.

"Up there on the median strip, some jackoffs are building a fire. It looks like they are burning an old car. Hang on, Paul, I am going to get into the breakdown lane and speed up."

I pull out my gun and hold it in position.

"Okay, here we go, I am going to floor it. Hang on."

Just then a Molotov cocktail flies across the front of the cab, narrowly missing Vincent's window. He swerves violently, and we scrape the guardrails, causing sparks to fly. We fishtail as another fireball is hurled from behind, but this one falls harmlessly to the asphalt.

"Hold on, Paul, let me pull over once it looks safe, and you can check on your family."

I'm worried about Mandy and Tommy, so I bang twice on the back panel. No response. Growing more concerned, I knocked again, but still nothing. We couldn't stop until we were in a safe place, which turned out to be a dark, quiet spot about five miles up the road. I run to the back and yank open the door. Mandy and Tommy are both lying on the bottom of the truck motionless.

"Vincent," I yell, "help!"

I bend down next to Tommy, who is bleeding from the head, but at least he's breathing. Vincent checks on Mandy.

"I think she's just knocked out. I don't see any injuries. How is your son?"

“Tommy, Tommy can you hear me” I keep yelling but he doesn’t respond. Just then, I heard Mandy’s voice.

“What happened? Are we there?” Mandy sees Tommy in my arms, covered in blood, and the sight snaps her out of her fog. She rushes over and takes him from me, crying and rocking him.

“We have got to get him to a hospital” she shouts. “Where’s the nearest hospital?”

Vincent says to hang on, as he calls his network to find out where’s safe to go. Mandy continues to scream while she rocks Tommy, so I get behind the wheel and shout for Vincent to get into the back of the truck with my family. I slam the driver’s door and hit the gas heading north, looking for the omnipresent hospital signs that dot interstates. Sure enough, five minutes later, I see one and take the off-ramp. We’re about fifteen miles south of New London. I screech up to the emergency entrance and bang on the door. A nurse and a security guard open up, and I yell for them to help my son.

Once inside, they put Tommy on a gurney and wheeled him into the ER. Mandy won’t be deterred so they let her follow, while I wait outside with Vincent.

“Paul, I am so sorry,” he says.

“My name is Geoffrey, please just call me that.”

"Okay, fair enough, Geoffrey. But listen, I cannot stay here. I spoke with my people, and if government agents come my cover might be blown. That would endanger many others. But I promise, I will check in with you. Once Tommy is better, someone will come back to take you to Rhode Island."

Neither of us, certainly not me, wants to say the word "if." But it sticks in my head. Terror is too weak a word for what I'm feeling right now. But as the minutes and then an hour tick by, the adrenaline starts wearing off, and exhaustion takes over. I fall asleep in a waiting-room chair.

It's still dark outside when I wake up, but I can see the sky lightening around the parking lot lights. I want to sit right here and never move. I tell myself that Tommy will be safe if I don't move if our whole family just stays right here.

That feeling of stillness is quickly pushed out by anxiety, though, so I walk toward the nurses' station. I was trying to find someone who might update me on my son's condition when Mandy walked through the door, looking blank and exhausted. I'm paralyzed with fear that horrible words will tumble from her mouth.

"Sweetie, the doctor's relieved pressure on Tommy's brain from blood and swelling. They told me that the next twenty-four to forty-eight hours would be critical. He is still unconscious, but that is not necessarily a sign that he won't recover."

“So, he is okay, they are saying?” The words feel stiff and awkward coming out.

“They’re saying there is some hope. We won’t know for a while and just have to wait and see.” Mandy takes my hand and we start walking back to the reception area. “Once Tommy wakes up, he is going to still need medical attention for some time, so we need to figure out what to do.”

Those words hang between us until an ER nurse comes out into the waiting area. Mandy pops out of her seat.

“Geoffrey, this is Geraldine. She was in the operating room earlier and has kept me informed.”

“Hi, there, Mr. Kenney,” the soft-faced older woman begins. “I know how scary this is for you both, so I just wanted to tell you that Tommy is doing better. His vitals have gotten stronger, and he is showing some signs of coming out of his coma. So, we are guardedly optimistic. But it is going to be days before we can even talk about a recovery program for him. Mandy told me in confidence about your situation, and I want to help if you will trust me.”

I look at Mandy with confusion. Why would she tell a stranger our situation? I apologize to Geraldine, saying that I need a few minutes alone with my wife to talk. The nurse seemed unfazed and walked a respectful distance away from us.

“What are you thinking, honey?” I ask. “Why should we trust this nurse or, for that matter, anyone else? What is stopping them from calling the cops to report an accident to a child?"

"I just do, dear," Mandy juts out her chin. I can see how strongly she feels she did the right thing. "Please trust me, as I do you. Geraldine lives a few miles north of here at Groton Long Point. She said that we could stay there and that we would be safe. It is a progressive enclave with mixed families. She seems taken with Tommy and wants him to get as much care as he needs before we put him back into a car. That makes sense, right? Don't we want him to fully recover before we risk moving him?"

I agree, but I'm still worried. I try to quiet my nerves because we don't really have any options. Tommy should not be moved for quite some time, and here we are, alone in a hospital that's as far from where we came as it is from where we're going. I feel as if I'm slowly falling, unable to intervene in events or to accept my fate. Perhaps I am simply tired from the cumulative stress of the past few years.

With the decision made, Mandy and I let Geraldine lead us to visit Tommy in the ICU. It's the first time I've seen him since he was rushed into the ER. My sweet boy looks the way he does each night after he falls asleep, only now he is fighting for his life. Mandy and I hold each other silently, and I concentrate on sending my boy silent messages of love. Tommy will recover. I know it. The alternative is unthinkable, and therefore not possible.

63

Groton Point

Sergeant Kenney

For the week since the crash, and the more hopeful two days since Tommy woke up, Mandy and I have been sleeping in Geraldine's basement. When we're awake, we're at the hospital. While Tommy's prognosis is hopeful, the doctors say he will need extensive rehabilitation in order to fully recover. The hospital is working on the how, when, and where.

When Tommy first opened his eyes, I felt relief that I could not put it into words. Mandy and I had convinced ourselves that he would wake from his coma, but truthfully that was just something that we had to believe in order to stay strong. Now that he is with us, I can touch the absolute terror that I felt. Mandy and I sit by his side, stroking his little head as he drifts in and out of sleep. Each day, he has become a little stronger, and he was just awake for over an hour.

Neither of us can imagine getting back on the road. All that we want is to safely raise our son and we cannot fathom, ever taking any action that might put him at risk. If that means staying here in Groton Long Point indefinitely, so be it.

Counselors typically advise not to make big decisions in times of crisis. And given that Tommy needs to stay here to rehab for at least a month, we don't have to finalize anything. But I would like to look into staying, not only for Tommy but for me. I want nothing more to do with traveling on roads.

I am starting to learn about this place. Located on a finger sticking out into Fishers Island Sound, it is a tight community with only a few hundred people living here. Geraldine gave me the lowdown.

Groton Long Point had been a fishing village until the 1980s, but as climate change made that industry less viable, the community went through a few reinventions, from a working-class enclave for service industry professionals to, eventually, a hoity- toity burg of mostly summer homes. When the stock market crashed, the community went through some hard times. As was the case in many communities, some residents were none too pleased to live among a growing number of non-speakers. Luckily, there were more people committed to keeping Groton Long Point a place that was open to all than those who weren't.

Geraldine tells us that tensions came to a head when a small group of residents appealed to Speaker's First members in Groton. The militant group came armed and tried to intimidate the community into committing to its agenda. At first, community members tried working with them to strike a balance that would ensure the speaker's rights would be protected, and that there would be no preferential treatment of non-speakers. But, of course, that did not satisfy the radicals who, for starters, demanded that non- speakers attend separate schools. One thing led to another until three Speakers First members beat the head of the Groton Long Point Association so badly that he had to be airlifted to Boston. That was a turning point, Geraldine explained.

The community demanded that the families who had invited Speakers First leave. Instead, they had barricaded themselves in their homes and awaited help from outsiders. It didn't take long. A convoy of radicals drove into town with long guns protruding from their truck windows. They, apparently, did not think they would meet much resistance. They were greeted with bullets.

Geraldine looked bereft as she described that day just six months ago when shots rang out from both sides of the street. While most community members hid in their houses, away from the windows, the convoy was hit hard by those who stayed to fight for their community. Bullet holes riddled the trucks, and glass exploded on the street. A few Speaker Firsters fired but to no avail. So, they quickly turned their cars around and headed out of town. No one knew how many invaders were hit or whether any of them had serious injuries or died. It was better that way. The families who had invited in the outsiders left by the end of that week.

Ever since, Groton Long Point has prided itself as a sanctuary of sorts, mainly for the long-term residents but potentially for others who want to live in such a place. That's why Geraldine so easily opened her house to us. Her invitation had seemed strange at the time, but now it makes sense. There's no hidden agenda, at least none that I have identified. Her kindness has allowed Mandy and me to focus exclusively on Tommy fully recovering. We will leave the big decisions for later.

64

Knights in White Satin

Sergeant Kenney

Tommy began rehab yesterday. It's helping relieve our anxiety that he might never fully recover. The rehab professional tells us that as long as Tommy sticks to the program, he will eventually get to one hundred percent, with the possible exception of some functioning of his left arm. But with hard work, he might even fully rehab it.

I know that most of the motivation would come from Tommy. He's a tough little dude. That might not be apparent at first glance, but he has his mother's strong will. Just after we returned from rehab, Mandy and I received a message yesterday from the group that Pia had connected us to. Now that Tommy is no longer in danger, I can appreciate the help that they provided, despite how horribly it turned out. It wasn't their fault and offers to help made us both feel that we hadn't been abandoned.

I asked about the Groton Long Point community, and the woman I'm speaking with says that she doesn't know much about it, but that progressive communities like these have been flying under the radar for years, while new ones pop up each week. She promises to get back to me if she hears more information.

I wonder how many similar communities there are in America—places that are more low-key than the Fizz's and Free Harbors. Life here is far from nirvana, but we feel safe. There will be friends for Tommy as he recovers, and Mandy and I are starting to let down our guard and get to know more and more families. There are maybe a dozen African-American families, which I appreciate.

For now, we have decided to stay put. We just moved out of Geraldine's basement into a rented two-bedroom just a stone's throw from the water. On a clear day, we can even see Bridgeport in the distance. It looks so peaceful down the shoreline, yet my mind's eye brings me back to that eighty-mile drive from hell that brought us here.

I've started running. With summer almost here, I am dreaming about spending time outdoors. Maybe I will even learn how to fish. I will be driving Tommy to rehab three days a week, and Mandy and I will supervise his exercises at home on the other days. Doctors tell us that the last ten percent of his recovery will be the hardest to predict. Despite the assurances of our rehab person, the neurologist said that it is possible that he will not recover full control of his left arm. Mandy chooses not to believe it. I'm with her.

Although things are looking up, I can't shake the feeling that Mandy has been acting strangely, even before we left Bridgeport. She seems preoccupied, a trait that some would assign to me, but few to my wife. With Tommy now in a better place and us apparently safe for the time being, I take the plunge.

"Honey, I know that things have been scary for quite some time, but aside from that is something on your mind? You've seemed preoccupied."

The blank look on her face shakes me. My mind races within the span of seconds. Is Mandy having an affair? Is she dying? What?

"Mandy, say something. You are frightening me."

Mandy looks away, shaking her head sadly. "Geoffrey, I don't know how to bring this up."

"For God's sake, just say it, please."

"Do you remember when we argued about our options back in Bridgeport?"

"Yeah, when you threw out cutting a deal, but so what?" Mandy stares straight into my eyes.

"What are you trying to say? No, no. You didn't." "Honey I was scared. We all were. You were." "What did you do?" I yelled.

"I was walking with Tommy when a friendly-seeming guy said hello. I asked which building he lived in, and he said he was there to talk to me about Tommy. I grabbed Tommy's hand and started walking back to our place. He called after me that it was my decision, but ignoring him would result in you going to jail and Tommy to foster care."

"Jeez." That's the kind of shit that Totali and the others always tried to squeeze me. "So, you rolled on us?"

"Fuck you, Geoffrey. No, I didn't roll on us. I gave him just enough to buy us some time to get out of Bridgeport. All that he wanted was more information about what you had told the *Times*. Given that those assholes didn't stand up for you, I figured that I would throw the G-man a few bones."

"But don't you know that he'll be back?"

"Of course, I do. That's one of the many reasons that I knew it was time to run. I'm so sorry that I didn't tell you, honey. But everything was happening at once and then the accident. I'm sorry, please forgive me."

And so began the next chapter of my relationship with Mandy.

65

Embrace Truth

Pia felt unburdened. Since the family blew up over hiding crucial information like the precariousness of her mother's health, she had freed herself from her role as the family's emotional glue.

Immediately after the fight, Pia was furious with Taylor for unloading on her mother. It was only later that she began to focus on her mom's role. She began to question, not for the first time, her inability or unwillingness to see. Was this the core of what Desiree had called her on?

She no longer felt the same drive to keep her mother and Taylor happy. Both were clearly capable of making their own decisions and living with the consequences. It was time for her to do the same. While Pia didn't know how these revelations translated into action, she felt freer to do what she wanted, once she figured out what that might be, rather than what would keep her family and others happy. It helped that her mother and Taylor seemed fine and had no apparent need to discuss the fight.

Pia's thoughts turned to Charlene. The juxtaposition between Pia's new attitude toward her family and Charlene's trial felt like something more than a coincidence. An opportunity! Not just a chance to help a friend but a moment to funnel her anger to take a stand.

She flipped open her laptop and began tweeting about fighting for Charlene and the other fourteen STAM members on trial. Wanting to demonstrate her bona fides and not get lost in the cyber noise, she emphasized her background as a fellow inmate of Charlene's and a victim of the government's capriciousness. The response was stunning and immediate. Tweeters suggested specific actions that she might take. A few asked her opinions and some suggested that Pia was a natural leader for this moment. It was ridiculous yet energizing, and she felt as if she was riding a wave. But at the core, Pia knew the seriousness of the moment, and she was committed to doing everything possible to save her friend. That didn't end on Twitter.

Later that evening, Pia received a call on her burner phone from her Light Rail transporters. She had forgotten about the phone and had zero communication with any of them since the night of the handoff. When it rang Pia, was surprised but answered it. The person on the other end did not identify herself.

"Listen, Pia," came an unfamiliar voice, "a lot of people went to great lengths to get you home safely. You need to stop drawing attention to yourself. Drop the tweeting. Your safety depends on you flying below the radar screen. Active organizing is dangerous. We can only provide so much security, even within the walls of FiZ. If you become too much of a nuisance, the feds might attempt a raid that would endanger the whole community. If you understand what I am saying, please tap the phone twice."

Pia did so. The voice disconnected.

But Pia felt clearer than she ever had. There might be risk, but so what? Everything was now a gamble. It was time to act. No more deferring to everyone else's opinions. This was her time. She would do something for Charlene.

So, Pia continued to tweet. Within days, she had tens of thousands of followers, all exchanging support and ideas for the next steps. Vague plans began to take shape around holding a rally in the Village. Pia didn't love the idea of holding an in-person demonstration, because it might bring undue risks, and it might not even be as impactful as digital organizing. But she didn't have great alternatives in mind, and there was power in seeing and touching each other. That could not be duplicated online. Maybe a large-scale gathering in full view would galvanize others to act.

Pia had only left her apartment five times in the months that she had been living with Taylor and her mom. She worried that taking on an in-person action might be a breach of trust. Would longtime residents resent her and feel that Pia was being selfish? But those fears were quickly washed away by what Pia read online from her neighbors. With a few exceptions, most were ready to do something. The capital charges were so outrageous that they seemed to explode whatever moderation was left in the hearts of the resistance.

Pia spoke first to her mom and then to Taylor about the developing plans.

"Pia, please don't," said Delores. "You have done enough already. They took away years of your life. Please reconsider."

Taylor asked how he could help.

"Thanks, buddy," Pia signed. But then she hesitated. "Taylor, we need to talk, right?"

But Taylor said nothing. How strange it was, thought Pia, that he was a young adult. Even stranger was that he was the one with a strong presence and opinions. She pressed forward, trying to get him to talk. But soon the conversation plunged back into the mud. She knew that he was angry, but it now struck her that even more, he was hurt. Finally, he spoke.

"Pia, I grew up worshipping you. I still do. But there's so much about our family that you didn't see, or maybe didn't want to. Why?"

"I don't know Ty; I wish that I had a good answer." She started signing, haltingly at first, trying to access her memories and how they felt. "I don't understand all of it myself. And I don't want to make excuses. But growing up an early non-speaker was hard, probably harder than I ever let on. Much of the time, I wished that could have been like the normal kids. Mom and Dad helped me by always fighting for what they thought I needed, and by making me feel not only normal but special. I think that in order to make it all work, I erected a story about them and our family that made me feel safe. I told myself that everything was perfect with us, even if it wasn't. You know how the story went; Mom was the iconic Rock, Dad a highly respected and confident professional, and you, my sweet little brother who looked up to me and whom, somehow, I would protect. I know now that it wasn't real."

Pia choked back tears. She didn't want to cry anymore. She looked at Taylor pleadingly, not to excuse her behavior but to understand it.

"But Pia, you were my big sister and I depended on you for the truth." Tyler started to tear up but then his face flashed anger. "Goddammit, Pia, you should have, you could—"

Pia interrupted him. "I'm sorry for not being there for you and holding so much of myself back. I really am. I know that I can't make it all right. But Ty, please believe me when I say that If I could do it again, I would do many things differently."

Taylor made enough eye contact with Pia for her to feel that at least he was thinking about what she said.

The next morning, Pia left the apartment for the sixth time and walked two blocks for a planning meeting for this hypothetical rally. A date had been set for two weeks away. The meeting was to be held at the Last Loop, a well-known coffee shop. Security was assumed to be better if they met in a very public place. Pia was nervous but not scared as she left the apartment, wearing sunglasses and occasionally looking back to make sure no one was following her. The streets were busy and full of life.

Two blocks from her place, Pia found the Last Loop, peeked inside, and kept walking. She returned a minute later satisfied that her extensive security experience gleaned from novels had paid off, it was safe. About twenty folks were gathered around three tables that they had pushed together. Pia shyly edged her way into the phalanx of bodies. But to her relief, once she introduced herself, most treated her like a long-lost friend. Participants were evenly divided between non-speakers and speakers. The facilitator was Nancy, a non-speaker with blue hair and a flair for signing with great emotion. She asked whether the group should get started or wait a bit longer for late arrivals. They decided to jump in.

Nancy began by asking the group whether the potential action should be centered on the fight to free the STAM-15 or something even bigger. The group quickly coalesced around the goal of applying maximum pressure on the government to drop all charges.

“Great” she signed, “but how?”

A lively debate ensued about scenarios with skepticism that one rally would make any difference. Justine, the person to Pia’s right signed they needed to make the event dramatic in order to attract maximum attention and support.

“I don’t want to just hit the bell,” she signed. “This has got to be more than making ourselves feel better.”

Pia raised her hand. "Jump in Pia."

She started signing and integrating LOTs. "Charlene is my friend. I know what she believes in and might communicate if she were here. It would be to go big. Exactly what that looks like, I do not know, but I agree with Justine that we need to do something dramatic. Perhaps it involves bringing the protest beyond the protected walls of FiZ. That might be risky, given how out of control the streets have grown, but let's be assertive in whatever we do. We need to inspire others to act, so let's be creative."

Pia noticed Justine elbowing the man next to her so strongly that he jumped. Pia later learned that he was Ared, her speaking boyfriend. He was a computer geek with a long proud history of hacking into well-protected communications systems. Justine's elbow motivated Ared to speak.

"Well, we might be able to simulcast whatever we do by hacking into some streaming platforms and even networks he said. But to make it worthwhile, we would need to be sharing something dramatic. Otherwise, no one will watch. If you are all in favor, me and my geek friends will begin to plan."

All that remained, said Ared, with no obvious sarcasm, was to figure out the action.

Pia had an idea. It flooded her brain. If the key was communicating a compelling message who better to deliver it than she? It made her feel slightly sick to her stomach at the thought of suggesting such a role for herself, but she knew this was the type of risk Desiree and Charlene always wanted her to take.

"I think that we need to think about something other than a rally," she communicated quickly, almost frantically. "We have held hundreds, probably thousands of mass events over the past years, and to what effect? If Ared and his friends can, in fact, hack into various media outlets, why not use the opportunity for me to make a personal statement about Charlene? And by extension, the others on trial? I know that it might sound crazy but…"

Pia did not finish the sentence because Justine signed that of course this made the most sense. The others snapped their fingers to second the idea, and so Pia's public speaking debut was confirmed.

When she walked home, Pia did not notice the ambulance until she was less than a half block away. Startled, she began to jog before she recognized Taylor and raced to his side. He was looking down at a gurney. It was their mother.

"One second she was sitting on the couch," he said, "and all of a sudden, she crumpled over. I think it's bad."

Pia bent over and pressed her face within a few inches of her mother's.

"Mom don't worry Taylor and I are here. It is okay. We will take care of you."

The EMTs pushed Pia brusquely to the side as they raised Delores into the ambulance. Taylor went with her but insisted that it wasn't safe for Pia to come. So, all she could do was wait. And then the phone call came. Now Pia had even less to lose and even more to fight for.

66

Where's the Beef?

Chief Totali squirmed in his seat. Facing him was the staffer assigned to him from the undersecretary of Homeland Security.

"Chief, please tell me what resources you need that we haven't provided?"

"Well, nothing. For now, you've given me what I need to get the job done."

"Okay, then what's the problem? It's been two months, and frankly, we were expecting more results. None of our problems have been eliminated. You don't get any points for near misses. Perhaps we were wrong about you."

"No, the undersecretary was right about me. I'll deliver. But I would like to talk to him again. I've got some big bold plans and I want to make sure it's not going too far."

"Fuck, Chief, are you kidding me? The undersecretary is not involved in any of this? Do your goddamn job if you want to keep it, or we will find someone else. The prisons certainly have openings if you want to go back to play warden."

"Fine, but I don't appreciate you speaking to me like that. I've done more in my lifetime to protect America than most people, I am sure more than you, so please show me some damn respect."

"Whatever, Chief. I'm sorry if I hurt your feelings. But I have bosses too, and as you know, the shit rolls downhill."

67

My Name is Pia

"My name is Pia. I am very nervous yet excited to be speaking with you today. I will sign, and there will also be a closed caption so that everyone can follow.

"My understanding is that my words are being streamed over many news and social media platforms, so hopefully millions of people will hear my plea. I am not a political person; I want to talk with you in very personal terms. Our country has been ripped apart for many years, and people have been hurt. My family, too, has suffered. My father committed suicide, partially due to the pain of seeing me, a non-speaker, hurting. Some of you may have heard about my mother, Delores Johnston, who was shot two years ago while holding a vigil asking for my release. My brother, Taylor, and I are now mourning her as she passed away just four days ago, indirectly from the wounds suffered that horrible day.

"Whether you are a speaker or a non-speaker, a mixed family or a homogenous one, I am guessing that you, too, have felt the sadness of our times. I believe that most, if not all, of you long for peace, regardless of the anger that you might feel. At the end of the day, what mattered most to me once I left exile was seeing my brother, hugging my mom, and living as a free person. Yes, I was angry over all that had happened to us. A part of me wanted to hold onto the anger for being sent to a camp for no other reason than because I was born unable to speak. But the anger eventually leaves you empty and alone, and that was not how I wanted to be.

"My hope is to spend the rest of my days living, not fighting. I believe that it is what all of you want as well. To see your children grow up safely and happily, to start a new family, to fall in love, to spend time with your friends, to try something new and succeed. I share these words knowing that you may experience them as hopelessly naïve. But I can assure you, that they come from extreme hurt and loss. Still, I hold onto hope. My family has been through hell, and I don't want anyone else to suffer like we already have.

"I could have written very different words today. I have well-documented facts to make the case that my friend Charlene Vicnacious is innocent of the charges the government has made against her. But I realized that what can free Charlene and the other STAM political prisoners is our collective empathy for each other, not legal arguments and facts. I knew Charlene as a friend in the camp and bunk that we shared. In many ways, she saved my life. I love Charlene, and I'm asking you, begging you, to help save her and the other's lives.

"She does not deserve to die. Charlene does not in fact deserve to spend one more day in prison. She wants what you want, to live her life as a free person. Charlene is very much like all of you. If you spent time with her, I think you would like her. You would appreciate the sensitivity and warmth that comes out. She would make you laugh, and sure, she might also make you angry. But once you got to know her and learned about her life, I am convinced that you would demand her freedom.

"So, here we are. Might this be a turning point? I do not know, as I have looked for one so many times over the past many years. But I can say with some assurance that if we continue down the present road, no good will come of it. Stopping this trial, not only of Charlene, but the other fourteen would be a gift to all of us. We would be investing in better days for our families, for all we love, and for ourselves.

"So, I humbly ask you, beg you, to step forward and demand an end to all of this. At the very least, think about what I have said. Please do not go out and fight one another. Sit back and think about all that is dear to you—your dreams for the future. They may be possible but only in a sane and loving America. Thank you."

Once Pia signed those final words, time seemed to stand still. It was over, and she had said what she felt needed to be said. Immediately, she felt her usual fear of being the center of attention but then pride rushed in. She had risen to the occasion. As the cameras shut down, she tried not to look at the faces for reactions, but it was hard. She heard applause from the small crew and planning committee. She found Taylor, and the pair made a beeline for their apartment.

As soon as they walked in, Pia collapsed on the couch experiencing a post-adrenaline crash. Taylor flipped open his laptop. Pia had fallen asleep for a while as the sun had fully retreated from her window. She heard Taylor say, "Pia, this is crazy. Come look."

Taylor didn't wait for her to respond. He just sat next to her on the couch and started showing her the headlines.

PROTESTERS AND COUNTER-PROTESTERS CLASH IN DOZENS OF CITIES
SPEECH HITS A NERVE ADMINISTRATION OFFICIALS CALL FOR CALM
SPEECH DENOUNCED BY SOME ACTIVISTS AS SELLOUT

The last one got Pia's attention. She took the laptop from Taylor and started to read the article from News Slam, an activist publication. One person she had never heard of denounced Pia as either a government agent or a fool. She handed the device back to Taylor who continued to search for articles and reaction.

"Pia, here's another whacked-out article," shouted Taylor.

But she just smiled and waved him off. She felt good. Pia had said what was in her heart and believed that it was the right message. She did not care if some people hated it. She was trying to free her friend. Pia was convinced that this was the best way to do so.

68

All Things Must Pass

In the midst of mourning her comrades, Pia went with Taylor to scatter their mother's ashes in the morning at a small park four blocks from their apartment. Taylor carried the urn and the two walked hand in hand to the park. The sky was overcast as they set out, but the sun peeked through the clouds as they entered the park. Birds sang, and children played, unaware that the siblings were saying goodbye to their flawed hero.

Their mom had been a force of nature. Many children, as they grow into teenagers, slowly realize that their mothers are far from perfect. That was true for Taylor, but not Pia. She imagined that she would mourn differently than her brother. Pia struggled to process that her mother was gone and that she and her brother were orphans. It had a surreal feeling.

After the two returned from the park, they sat on the couch, shoulder to shoulder, Taylor staring straight ahead and she glancing at his profile. What a handsome young man he had become, she thought. Pia tried imagining him with a girlfriend or boyfriend, and eventually a family. He would be a good father. The scars from a family such as ours can turn some people bitter, but Pia was hopeful that Taylor would be a warm and centered dad.

But first, there was a new world to be built and Pia prayed that there would be room for good-speaking people like her brother. Otherwise, the non-speakers would simply be re-creating what they were trying to overthrow.

Later the two went for a rare walk. Their tiny apartment felt large and lonely. They headed away from the park in which they had scattered ashes in the morning and toward the bustle of Eighth Avenue. It felt good to mingle with people.

Did people know that they had just lost their mom? They tumbled upon a tee-shirt store and decided to check it out. The merchandise was lightly pornographic while attempting to be funny. Pia turned to walk out hoping that Taylor would follow. But he grabbed her hand, "Pia, you know that I love you, right?"

So, there in the middle of this weird little store, the two held each other tightly and sobbed. They didn't notice whether anyone was looking at them. Outside of the store they wiped their eyes and started to laugh.

69

Step Lightly

Make the Change was buzzing from the overall positive buzz from Pia's speech. The group which now formally called itself Make the Change met once again at the Last Loop. Everyone agreed to double down on their recent successes in support of the STAM- 15 prisoners. Despite Pia's grief over the loss of her mom, hope was in the air. Pia could feel a perceptible gain in momentum and a simultaneous weakening of the authorities' ability to crack down.

"Pia, I need a few minutes with you," signed Nancy.

It snapped Pia out of her dreaminess about the future, and into a curious and worried state. Pia followed Nancy into a back room.

"I've gotten several heads up from our perimeter guards that unknown people have been asking about you. No one that we know of has said anything or would even necessarily have information about your whereabouts, but we need to be very careful. As your profile increases, so does your personal risk."

Pia didn't show any reaction or sign for nearly one uncomfortable minute. "Thanks for telling me, Nancy. I have started to think more and more about the risk and my options. But I won't stop at least until Charlene is safe. And even then, what am I going to do? Sit on the sidelines and hope that we win. And that Taylor and others can inherit something better?"

"Yeah, Pia, that's all well and good, but the last thing that we need is to lose you. All that I am saying is to be careful. Pay close attention to your surroundings at all times. You need to be present at all times and not escape into your head. Okay?"

Pia walked home after that very much in her head. Was she afraid to be imprisoned, hurt, or even killed? Absolutely! But she wasn't going to let up.

70

Here Comes the Judge

"This is Vicki Hightower with CNN's breaking news team. I am standing outside of the federal courthouse in Washington D.C., where the presiding judge in the trial of the STAM-15, Lamar Jackson, just announced that he had dismissed the most serious charges of sedition and conspiracy. The defendants could still face up to ten years in federal prison if found guilty of the remaining offenses.

"Judge Jackson stated that the prosecutors had failed to provide sufficient evidence to support the other charges. This development raises as many questions as it answers, including whether the government might drop the other charges. And even if it did, how would it change the status of the STAM-15 who have been incarcerated for over four years now?

"We will go shortly to our correspondents around the country to dig deeper into this developing story. But now, I would like to bring in Julie Justine, our legal analyst who has been covering this story for the past several months. So, Julie, please tell our viewers what you are hearing."

"Thanks, Vicki. While Judge Jackson's announcement is a surprise, we are hearing some interesting speculation that extends well beyond the courtroom. As the overall security situation in the country has continued to deteriorate in the past few months, partly sparked by the charges against the STAM-15, rumors have been circulating about dissatisfaction within the intelligence community about the administration's policies toward the non-speaker crisis. That is not to say that Judge Jackson's decision to drop most charges is an outgrowth of that, but still, it is worth mentioning."

"Julie, just to be clear, are you inferring that there may be political forces at work in this decision?"

"Well, Vicki, I don't want to accuse the judge of tilting toward the shifting political winds, but he may be part of a changing tide. While some conservative outlets have continued to push a hard line toward non-speakers, there has been a notable modification of tone and message from many, especially within the intelligence community. Again, this may have nothing to do with Judge Jackson's decision, but I am sure we will be hearing more about this in the coming weeks."

"Okay, thanks, Julie. Let's go to John McNamara in Denver, where he is with Joanie Shoshanie, a speaking leader of Americans for a Free & Just Society, a group that takes a hard line in defense of non-speakers. Joanie, thanks for coming on with such short notice. Let's get right to it. What is your reaction to the breaking news?

"My reaction is that these charges were obviously fabricated from the start and given that the government is losing control, they were forced to back down."

"But Joanie, to be fair, the judge is not the government, right?"

"Excuse me for laughing, John, but I would say that for the purposes of this discussion, they are one and the same. But let me speak to the more important issue which is our demand that Judge Jackson drop all charges and the government release every non- speaker still being held in the camps or western territories."

"Okay, Vicki, sending it back over to you"

"Thanks, John. I have an interesting guest with me, one whom I am guessing our viewers have heard little about in the past. But I think that's about to change. Thanks for coming on with such short notice. Please introduce yourself to our viewers and tell them the context for what you are about to share."

"My name is Joseph Nightingale, and I was until one month ago a leading attorney for the *New York Times*. Per my position at that time, I was involved in the earliest discussions with Geoffrey Kenney, a former correctional officer. The information that he provided to the *New York Times* became the cornerstone for the series about abuses toward non-speakers in the correctional system. I resigned my position one month ago in protest of the *Times'* decision not to run key portions of Sergeant Kenney's story. I have agreed to come on the air today to share what the *Times* refused to."

"So just to be clear Mr. Nightingale, you are telling our viewers that there is even more information that you have access to that has previously not been released?"

"That is correct."

"And is any of this new information relevant to the case of the STAM-15, or the explosive speech from Pia Johnston?"

"Yes, Vicki.".

"Excellent, please proceed Mr. Nightingale."

71

Drinks with Friends

As another meeting of Make the Change was wrapping up Pia sidled up to Justine and signed whether she wanted to grab lunch somewhere. Justine smiled and motioned for Pia to follow her to her apartment half a block away.

Justine and Ared lived in a basement apartment, which was cuter than it looked from the outside. It had three little windows that faced the streets so that you could literally see foot traffic and not the bodies above the feet.

"Ared and I sometimes play a game in which we make up stories to fit peoples' feet and legs," Justine said.

"How does it work?"

"Well, I'll see a pair of legs and say, "Hey Ared this guy is a businessman off to see his mistress during his lunch break. He lives in Lawrence on Long Island but has a secret life including a daughter with his girlfriend. His wife knows nothing of this.'"

Just then, Ared walked through the door and looked surprised to see Pia. Justine gave him a funny expression that was intended to say just chill. He laughed and went into the kitchen. Justine waved Pia in and the two sat down and devoured a salad with sardines on top. Ared later joined in and joked that the sardines made him salty. He broke out a bottle of red wine. The three sat drinking glass after glass. Pia felt happy and relaxed.

Later, the three moved to the living room couch where Ared sparked up a joint.

"You two want a toke?" Justine shook her head no while Pia also passed but tipped her glass toward him for another splash of wine. The smoke curled through the air and turned the room pungent. Justine and Pia looked at each other. They didn't sign a word but Pia interpreted the expression to mean that she might have found a long-term friend.

Ared looked pretty stoned and headed to his room. Justine followed to make sure he was okay and quickly returned. She told Pia about how Ared and she had met at LaGuardia Community College five years ago before things turned really ugly.

"At first, we were just friends and attended some of the same resistance meetings. I thought that he was a nice slightly nerdy guy until the incident. We were at a rally in Queens, near the college campus, when cops swinging huge batons attacked us. People were being badly beaten and I tried to run but a cop grabbed me by the hair and started to drag me to a bus while beating me. Ared came from nowhere and launched himself into the air, landing on top of the cop and almost knocking him unconscious. He was arrested and charged with assault on a police officer. He spent a few months at Riker's Island before being released on parole. We've been together ever since."

“Are you two in love?” signed Pia. She immediately wished that she hadn’t as Justine hesitated.

“I don’t know, Pia. I find it hard these days to feel a lot of things, but we are definitely happy and we depend on each other. That is enough for now.”

It was getting dark already, with winter fast approaching. Pia always found this time of year in New York bittersweet. She remembered the days when her parents, Taylor, and she would go out to see the Christmas lights. They more than made up for the lack of natural light. Pia was lost in this image when Justine came up close to her face and signed for her to return to earth. They both laughed. Pia gave Justine a big hug and was sure that they would hang out again.

72

About a Girl

Dear Pia,

Sorry to be writing you a letter but it's easier for me. I know that I've been a little hard to talk to this past week. I met a girl eight days ago. Her name is Toni.

I was feeling sad about Mom, and I remembered what fun we used to have going ice skating at Wollman Rink and eating jelly apples. So, just went. It was dumpier than it used to be, but there were still people skating and having fun, and it still seemed like a happy, family place.

Then I saw Toni. She was skating with two friends and I was nervous as hell to approach them. But I couldn't take my eyes off her.

I ended up joining her group, and then she realized I was a speaker. At first, I was too shy to even remember sign language but I got over it. We ended up ditching the skates to get hot chocolate and wander over to Central Park.

We talked for what felt like hours, but it was only thirty minutes. She goes to the High School for Music and Art and lives on the Westside with her father. Her mom had died of breast cancer years ago, and she's an only child. She wants to go to college in California and become a dancer.

I know I shouldn't feel this happy and excited about a girl so soon after Mom died, but I really like her, Pia, and I'm excited to see her again.

73

Please Stand

Charlene

"Charlene Vionacious, do you have anything to say before I pronounce a sentence?" the judge bellows.

I hear those words and think that there are so many things to say, and yet nothing. Even though the judge dropped the most serious charges before the trial began, I knew in my heart that there was no way they were going to let us go. Still, the last few months have felt lighter, almost happy. I wish that I could explain why but I do not have a simple answer. Growing up with my parents I was terrified that they would withdraw whatever modicum of love that they showed me. Later, when I started having relationships with other women, I could not understand why they would be with me, so I lived in a state of flux waiting for each to say goodbye.

When I was first sent to Tranquility, I was anointed a leader, but I felt like a fraud. Who was I to lead others, to fight for a cause? I was nothing but an insecure little girl looking for approval. Not that I would ever show it because the fear of being found out was stronger than the stress of playing along. When I met Pia, something inside of me began to change. I think that it was her guileless belief in right and wrong and in me. For the first time, I began to see myself in a positive light through the reflection in someone else's eyes.

In the years since, living in various camps and prisons, meeting other inmates and jailers, some cruel, I've come to accept who I am. I am not a movement hero as the press would like to conveniently label me. But neither am I a bad person undeserving of love. I am me, and that is okay.

I got the sweetest letter two days ago from Pia. She apologized for supposedly having failed me. *I am free and you are not.* I laughed at what I imagined would have been Pia's earnest expression as she was writing those words. I wrote back just this morning and hope that the prison authorities will let it be delivered. I told Pia that I was doing fine and that I had gradually let the psychological boulders slip off my back. I'm feeling freer than ever and her respect and loyalty are part of the reason why.

I also expressed my admiration for the work that she has been doing, not that I ever doubted that she would try everything to help me. I praised Pia for her extreme courage and humanity. She likely won't believe me. But I want Pia to at least read those words. I am convinced that our future lies in building relationships, and community. We humans are still a relatively primitive species but there is lots of hope. We need time. I hope that we have it.

"Ms. Vicnacious, are you here with us?" "I am sorry, what, your honor?"

"I had asked if you have anything to say before I pronounce the sentence."

"No, judge, I have nothing at all to add."

74

It's Independence Day

Since Pia's speech, reports from across the country continued to describe nascent efforts to build from within.

But it was far from clear what would survive and spread. Still, compared to the dark days of Tranquility, Pia was excited for the future. The group that Pia had been working with changed its name to Rev9. It had become increasingly proactive with the message that non-speakers and allies needed to work to transform themselves while thinking about effectively taking over the country—preferably through elections. Whatever the time horizon for non-speakers becoming the majority, thirty to fifty years, there was so much to do to figure out how they wanted to live and govern. By the last count, there were more than one-hundred-fifty similarly minded chapters around the country and surely others that weren't being counted.

On the home front, Taylor left for his graduation wearing a funky tie that Pia had bought for him. It broke her heart not to attend, but she didn't want to be a distraction or worse, a danger. She kissed Taylor and made him promise to tell her everything.

"Everything, what?" he said. "I don't even want to go. It will be a bore."

"Yes, you do. And even if you don't, be there for me. I wish that I could go to see you graduate but I can't. So yeah, you're going and will tell me *everything*!"

Pia wondered how it was possible that Taylor, her baby brother, was graduating. She imagined the warmth of the ceremony, all of those kids and families celebrating, washing over her. And then she imagined her handsome brother in his cap and gown, with his arms around Toni and her mind did a double take.

Since Taylor met Toni, Pia had seen him less and less and assumed that Taylor was spending most of his time with his new girlfriend. It was good, Pia reassured herself. She knew how smitten he was but hoped that he wasn't getting ahead of himself. Toni was his first girlfriend.

Later that evening, Pia held a small party for Taylor at their place. Six attended: Taylor, Toni, Justine, Pia, and two of Taylor's closest friends, Max and Sammy. They celebrated with Red Hook IPA for those of legal age. Pia toasted Taylor by signing how much he meant to her when they were kids, while she was away, and now that she could witness him successfully navigating this crazy world. Toni hung on him for much of the night, and Pia again saw how sweet they were together.

"Look at those two love birds, Justine," Pia signed. Justine laughed at Pia's pretend frown. The two friends loved ribbing each other. An hour later, the party broke up. Pia let Taylor share the final beer. He was already an adult in so many ways.

They clinked glasses and Taylor put his arm around Pia's shoulder.

"I love you, Pia, so much. But even more, I respect you and feel proud when I tell others that you are my sister."

Pia, feeling embarrassed, started to play it off but Taylor looked directly into her eyes and slowly said, "No, Pia, I so love and respect you. You have always been my hero."

Pia started to cry. Then he told her that it was time for him to leave. Pia held her breath.

"Toni is going to Berkley, and I am going with her. Not to live together but to be near her. I have never been outside of New York. I don't want to leave you, but I need to explore. You have developed a life here with your friends and community. I need to find my world. I don't know whether Toni and I will stay together. But I need to get out there. I know that you will be fine. But please tell me that it is okay."

Pia smiled at him and told him what he needed to hear. And it was okay despite the lump in her throat and the acid feeling rising from deeper down. She would see him again. This wasn't forever.

"Go Taylor. Go and do great. You are my hero!"

75

Doves Cry

Pia was feeling as good as she had in months if not ever. Charlene was safe, Taylor was off on his next life adventure, and she felt fulfilled in a way that perhaps she never had before. While she may not have conquered all of her demons, they were in abeyance.

It was a beautiful morning as she opened her apartment door and looked around for anything suspicious. Seeing nothing, Pia walked to the street and began her trek to Justine's apartment.

She crossed the avenue and entered the alley that led to Justine's. Just then she looked up to see dozens of pigeons take flight from a nearby perch. Pia stood there wondering where they were going when a loud voice rang out.

"Pia Johnston, this is Homeland Security. You are under arrest. Put your hands on your head and lie down on the ground. We won't give you another warning."

Several feds in body armor and with automatic weapons started to close in on her. Pia stood transfixed.

"Get your hands on your head and lay down. This is your last warning."

Pia raised her hands up in the air while continuing to look around.

Suddenly she heard a voice she recognized but could not place.

"She's got a gun: she's got a gun."

Shots rang out, and Pia was knocked backward, stumbled for a few seconds, and then collapsed in a pool of blood.

After pausing to see if there were any signs of movement, the feds rushed in and surrounded Pia's limp and bloody body. At the very front, wearing body armor but unarmed was Joseph Totali. He kicked Pia several times and then bent down to check for a pulse.

"She's dead."

"Chief, where's the gun?

Totali smirked and mockingly looked around. "Son of a gun, I could have sworn that I saw one."

Epilogue: 2071

Charlene was finally starting to settle into her life. It had been over two years since she had been released from federal prison. Her physical health was okay but her slight facial tic was now a full-blown involuntary response. And she looked as if she had aged twenty years, even though she had been locked up for half that time.

But she was free and alive. With the fall of the speaker- dominated government, there was little risk of her being returned to jail. Nearly everyone in America knew the name Charlene Vicnacious, and many viewed her as an iconic figure. But the years had taken an emotional toll on Charlene, and she now desired as much solitude as possible.

One year ago, Charlene met a woman, and two months ago, they moved in together. Her partner was a self-described "apolitical" non-speaker, which was fine with Charlene. Young progressives often texted her with various requests for advice, direct involvement, or just to converse. Charlene mostly responded with a friendly but firm no thank you.

One exception was anything to do with Pia Johnston. Upon hearing of Pia's assassination, Charlene was devastated. It would not be an exaggeration that it exceeded any pain that she had previously felt, including her betrayal by LJ. For nearly one week she refused to eat and barely spoke. But over the next few weeks, she refocused on doing what she could to ensure that the name Pia

Johnston would forever be remembered. To this day when the media asks her to comment she does so enthusiastically. Her words always contain the same basic message: her friend is a hero, not just to non-speakers but to America as a whole. Pia overcame her personal demons to stand up for what was right. And she helped save my life.

Sergeant Kenney and Mandy still lived in Groton Long Point, but they separated several years ago. They remain friends, but the strain of the many years of national chaos and personal trauma proved too much. While he eventually forgave Mandy for talking to the government, they slowly grew apart. But they remain united in their love and support for their son, now a bright teenager interested in studying electrical engineering at New York University.

Taylor Johnston became a writer and blogger. He is part of a united front of speaking progressives who are working with non- speakers to build a new America. Taylor often writes about Pia, not to glorify her, but to show that someone who struggled so much with her own frailties could make such a huge impact.

Finally, Joseph Totali exchanged seats with Charlene Vicnacious. He and dozens of former police, intelligence, and government officials have been convicted and imprisoned on a variety of counts including murder and seditious conspiracy. On the day that he was sentenced to twenty years in federal prison, he yelled at the judge and then leaped at him before several court guards dragged him away.

Acknowledgments

I have always daydreamed about stories. Some of these I told my daughters, Jessie and Lauren, and much more recently my grandchildren, Michael and Ruby. About seven years ago two stories entered my head. The first became the starting point for "Replay Earth" which my good friend Mark Schlack deepened and authored.

I put the second, "Silent Thunder" on the back burner but began writing it two years ago with the encouragement of Julie Wittes Schlack. Julie provided constant feedback and editing suggestions throughout. It is not an exaggeration to say that without her support I never would have finished the book.

As with most of my stories, Silent Thunder began with a big idea. How would those in the majority and with power deal with a minority that would eventually grow into the entire population? In the case of this book, the minority is non-speakers. My next step was to invent the characters that would help spotlight the conflicts rippling through society. As I wrote the book, I felt these characters come to life, and with it, I imagined a world in which the "good guys" might win despite facing unspeakable terror.

In addition to Julie's unwavering help, I want to acknowledge the tremendous role that my childhood friend Stanley Weiser played. If the name sounds familiar it is because he is an accomplished Hollywood screenwriter best known for the screenplay of "Wall Street." As kids Stanley and I would watch the Twilight Zone and then call each other during commercials to talk about who was most scared. Stanley helped give the book a thorough line that I believe keeps the reader's interest through the end.

Finally, a few more shout-outs. Dash Finley, who I believe is a rising Hollywood writing talent was extremely generous with his time providing extensive feedback for several drafts. The cover was designed by Adam Mendola; my son-in-law who as you can see is an imaginative artist.

Made in United States
North Haven, CT
29 December 2023

46771685R00202